Maelstrom of Fate

Maelstrom of Fate

Waves of Darkness Book 7

Tamara A. Lowery

Steele Rose Publishing

Maelstrom of Fate

By

Tamara A. Lowery

ISBN eBook 978-1-956849-13-4

ISBN print 978-1-956849-14-1

Table of Contents

Dedication

This book was originally dedicated to Michelle Oesterling and William Forth, two true fans and diligent/avid readers. It is their enthusiasm over this series and their willingness and eagerness to conscript others to Viktor's crew which has kept my faith in my writing alive.

In Memoriam

We sadly lost William Forth to COVID in 2020.

We also lost Red Shirt winner Brandon Garrison to an automobile accident not too long after this book was originally published. He fell asleep behind the wheel on his way home after an overtime shift.

Tamara A. Lowery

Acknowledgements, Foreword, and Warnings

I wish to acknowledge all my Red Shirt contest winners and volunteers for this book: Michelle Oesterling, Brandon Garrison, Aaron Plotkin, Doug Crowe, and James McGowan. Your sacrifice has been noted.

For those wondering what a Red Shirt is, outside of sports references, on *Star Trek: The Original Series,* members of the away team who wore red shirted uniforms were usually throw-away characters who didn't survive to return to the ship.

There is an honorable mention for Johnathan Morris, who initially won a Red Shirt spot during the drawing I held at Con Nooga 2017 and was later disqualified for being entirely too annoying at work (yes, he's a coworker). I later relented and granted him a noble but gruesome death in season two of my Steampunk serial, *The Adventures of Pigg & Woolfe.* This serial is currently in it's fourth season and is available on Amazon. In August 2024 I will be taking it wide through Draft2Digital.

Back to THIS book, my pirates are not nice people. For the most part, my characters are true to the norms and gender roles and behaviors of their time, the late 1700s. This means you will read some serious misogyny. I do not support such behavior, but I want the characters to be believable and to give readers valid reasons to really dislike certain characters.

Writing this book put me in a bit of a dark place while getting into Viktor's headspace. I had to imagine how he, who rarely let anyone get close to him, reacted to the loss of Hezekiah Grimm. I hope I represented his mental and emotional distress accurately.

Maelstrom of Fate concludes the Sisters of Power story arc. It also sets up a new series of adventures for our piratical crew. *Hunting the Dragon: Waves of Darkness Book 8* is slated for release in 2025, the exact date yet to be determined, and starts the Daughters of the Dragon story arc. I plan for 7 books in the new arc.

Once Upon a Tide...

Shouting roused Viktor from his light slumber. He picked out male and female voices; the male sounded like his second mate, Hezekiah Grimm. The man didn't sound happy.

He pulled his arm from beneath the whore he'd shared a bed with, pulled on his trousers, and went to investigate. The wench never stirred, although she let out a soft snore.

Vik stepped into the hallway of the brothel just in time to see a half-naked woman stumble out of the room his mate had rented as if she'd been pushed. Not long after, Grimm appeared in the doorway naked. He shoved a wadded garment at the woman.

"Get out, you worthless bitch!"

"No! Not until you pay me!"

"You haven't earned it." Grimm turned and slammed the door in her face.

Still oblivious to Viktor's presence, the woman began to pound on the door. "You owe me a guinea! I did what you asked, you old bastard! I can't help it if you can't get it up!"

Viktor turned, went back to his room and finished dressing. The sound of the woman's tantrum drifted in through the open door. The whore in his bed finally stirred.

"What is going on? Are you leaving?"

He tossed her a gold piece. "I just need some fresh air. I'll be back before morning."

He stepped out and closed the door behind him. He turned to see Grimm emerge again, still naked, and point a blunderbuss at the wench's nose.

"Scat."

The woman clutched her clothes to her chest and fled for the stairs, only stopping to shout something in Spanish over her shoulder at the landing.

The weapon discharged and took out a chunk of the ceiling above her. She screamed and fled down the stairs.

Viktor smirked and headed for the stairs. As he passed Grimm, he said, "For God's sake, man; put some clothes on or go back to bed."

Grimm muttered something unintelligible. Vik peered at him and noticed a look about him of a sleepwalker. "Get some rest, Mr. Grimm," he said, his voice a little more gentle. Something was wrong with his second mate. He determined to find out what it was. He owed the man his life, after all.

Grimm went back in his room and shut the door. Viktor headed downstairs in search of the girl. He wanted to get to her before she could complain to the pimp who ran this brothel. He'd already heard a few doors crack open behind him. Luckily, all the rooms were taken by members of his crew.

He reached the foot of the stairs just in time to see the girl tuck her blouse into her skirt. She wore a scowl and a touch of fear in her eyes when she looked up and saw him. He gave her his most roguishly charming smile. He pulled out a gold coin and twirled it in his fingers. It glittered in the dim lamplight.

"Care to spend some time with me?"

She put on her professional smile and stepped forward. She reached for the coin and said, "You speak my language, *señor*."

She started to climb the stairs. He grasped her wrist and shook his head. "Mr. Grimm is still in a foul temper, and Daria is asleep in my bed. Right now, I'd like to find a bottle and someplace dark and out of the way."

She visibly relaxed, and her smile grew more genuine. "What kind of bottle do you prefer?"

"Brandy, but rum will do."

"I know just the place."

After procuring some decent brandy, he led the girl through the dark streets in search of a secluded spot. They shared the bottle as they walked along and spoke in low tones.

"Why was Mr. Grimm so angry, pet? I don't think I've ever seen him like that."

She took a drink from the bottle and grimaced at the burn. "I think it is the opium. He sprinkled some in his pipe tobacco, and he had a few drops of laudanum, as well," she said and handed the bottle back. "If I'd known he was an opium eater, I would have demanded payment up front."

"Why's that?"

"Every one of them I've encountered can't get it up. They act like it's my fault, but I know it's the opium."

He stopped and looked around. He saw no one else about. "This looks like a good spot."

"What? Here in the street?"

"Hardly, pet." He pulled out a thin dagger and went to work on the lock of the door they'd stopped by. It didn't take him long to get it open with a soft click. He motioned for her to be quiet and eased the door open.

"Doesn't seem to be anyone about. Come on." He pulled her through the door and shut it behind them. A scrape and click followed by a spark broke the darkness. Viktor dialed down the wick of the oil lamp mounted next to the door and lowered the glass chimney. The illumination revealed a trade goods warehouse.

He grinned. "This is prefect. I think we can find someplace comfortable in here, pet."

It didn't take him long to locate a suitable spot. He moved behind her, lifted her skirts, and bent her over a stack of grain bags. She didn't object and seemed enthusiastic about his staying power.

He finished and withdrew. She didn't get up right away while he tucked himself back in. He smiled grimly at her back as she worked to regain her breath.

He leaned over her and whispered, "That was sweet, pet; the best I've had in a while. Unfortunately, I can't have you going about revealing the Reaper's weaknesses."

She didn't even have time to squeak. With well-practiced movements, he snapped her neck then stepped back as her bladder and bowels released in death.

He retrieved the gold coin he'd given her as well as a few other valuables. Before he left, he pulled a chock from beneath a nearby stack of casks. The iron-banded wooden containers rolled free and tumbled all over the body. When it was discovered, people would think the whore had been killed in a burglary gone bad.

Satisfied with his handiwork, Viktor returned to the brothel.

Over the next few weeks, Viktor kept a close eye on his second mate. Hezekiah had grown to be more than a valuable crew member over the years they'd sailed together. He was one of the few men Viktor trusted with his life. The only one aboard closer to him was his first mate, Jim Rigger.

It troubled him to see the Grimm Reaper deteriorate. He'd known that the man dabbled with opium but had given it no more thought than the tobacco or gin his second mate was so fond of. Grimm had never imbibed to the point of impairment.

This opium proved different. Now it had been brought to his attention, Viktor saw an increasingly adverse effect on his friend. Grimm grew lethargic, irritable, and mentally unfocused.

Had it been anyone else, Vik knew he'd kill him before he endangered the crew. He owed Grimm a life debt, though. He decided to put him off the crew, preferably in a way which would let the man save face.

☠

"You wanted to see me, Captain?"

"Yes, Mr. Grimm. Shut the door behind you, please."

Grimm must have sensed something. He became apprehensive. Most wouldn't spot it; Viktor knew his second mate's body language far too well.

"We need to acquire another ship."

Grimm blinked. Obviously, that was not the statement he'd expected. "Something wrong with this one?"

"No; it will be for you to captain. I'd like to take some prizes in tandem." He watched for a reaction.

Grimm crossed his arms and arched an eyebrow. "Bilge, begging your pardon, Captain; might I ask what I've done to make you angry?"

Vik smiled inwardly. The man could still read him and seemed fairly lucid — for the moment. Perhaps there was hope; but he couldn't afford that gamble with the ship or the lives of the crew.

"How much opium have you had today, Hezekiah?"

Grimm frowned. His stance became defensive. "Who told you I used opium?"

"I've known for some time that you dabbled. Granted, I don't know when you started; but things came to a head back in port."

"That little whore; I should have slit her throat instead of chasing her off."

"She is no longer something to worry about. I made sure she won't tell anyone about your problem." He sat back and looked at his second mate. He never thought he'd have to remove Grimm from the crew. "I've been watching you since then, and I've seen changes which shake my faith in you." He held up a hand to stop any protest and continued, "I don't doubt your loyalty, man. I have merely seen how badly the opium has impaired you."

"Vik, I can stop using, if it's that important to you."

"For your sake, I hope so, Hezekiah. Still, I can't let you put the ship or crew in danger." He sighed, got up, and retrieved a bottle of rum from the cabinet. "Hezekiah, you are one of the best pirates it has been my pleasure to sail with. Hell, you deserve your own captaincy. I think perhaps you need the challenge. You already know you won't get it here."

Grimm took the offered bottle. He took a swig, handed it back, and walked over to the window casement. He looked out it in silence for some time. Vik let him. Finally, he turned back to face his captain.

"I appreciate what you're offering me, Vik. Been with you long enough to realize you'd have killed any other man for this, except Mr. Rigger, possibly. What was his view on this, by the way?"

"He does not know. I have not discussed this with anyone other than you, nor do I intend to."

Vik saw the flash of relief in his mate's eyes and continued, "You know as well as I do that it's not good to let a crew see any perceived weakness, or they'll turn on you. I need the lads to respect you. I also don't want them to think I've grown soft."

"If they knew you knew about this problem and let me live —," Grimm trailed off and shook his head. Viktor noticed he'd broken out in a sweat and nearly soaked his shirt through.

"Are you well, Hezekiah?"

"No, Vik, I'm not. I'd not realized how enslaved I've grown to the poppy until just this moment. I want some very badly right now." The second mate began to shake. "If I've any hope to be free of it I would strongly suggest you have all the laudanum stores locked away."

"I already took that precaution. Durham was puzzled by the order, so I told him I suspected someone had been stealing it. The stuff needs to be reserved for when we have wounded."

"Thank you, Captain. I'm going to miss you."

Vik shot him a sardonic grin. "Keep in mind I was serious about taking some prizes in tandem, Mr. Grimm. With both of us captaining, the bastards won't know what hit them."

Grimm shared his grin.

Never in his life had he feared a woman, at least not a human one. Even the Sisters, as powerful as they were, did not frighten him. He respected them or at least their power; but he did not fear them.

He stopped and corrected himself. Loathe as he was to admit it, he did have some dread or apprehension where *Mamaan* Juma was concerned. He wondered if it had to do with his curse; perhaps something she'd woven into the spell. It seemed like a plausible explanation to him, anyway.

The reason for his dread of facing Brianna Grimm with bad news escaped him. Granted, she was a formidable woman; but she was merely human. Ordinarily, meaning for any other member of his crew, he would have felt no compulsion to even pass along the news. With Brianna, it was different. She'd borne Grimm twins, a boy and a girl; and Hezekiah had passed on some of the Elder's magic to them. The Grimm family was currently in the care of Mother Celie, Viktor's foster mother and the eighth Sister of Power.

He could let Celie give them the news; surely, she'd seen it happen in her ever-present fire. The very moment the thought struck him, a wave of guilt and self-disgust washed over him.

"Stop being such a coward, Vik. You owe it to Hezekiah to hand deliver the news to Brianna," he grumped to himself.

A knock at the cabin door drew his attention. He scented the air and realized it was Belladonna.

"Enter."

The siren closed the door behind her. She raised an eyebrow at him. "You aren't shielding as well as you think you are. Shall I sing up the wind to speed the crossing? We're nearly to Gibraltar."

"No."

"No?"

"I see no reason to speed to Savannah. Why bring bad news so rapidly? Let Madam Grimm enjoy her children and her happiness while she may."

"You really are afraid to tell her." Incredulity colored her voice. "That's not like you, Viktor. Why does this bother you so much?"

He gave her a sour look. "Be glad no one other than Lazarus was here to hear you."

"I tremble with fear." She gave him a *blasé* look. "Honestly, Viktor, do you think I would undermine you like that in front of the crew?"

"No." He sighed. "I don't really fear her; I just dread the pain I know this is going to bring her."

Belle furrowed her brow as she peered at him. "I still find this unlike you, Viktor. You're just as much of a predator as I am. Why waste such emotion on potential prey?"

In a flash, he had her across the cabin, his hand nearly crushing her throat, and held her pinned to the wall. His voice came out in a deadly growl. "Let me make one thing perfectly clear. Brianna Grimm is not potential prey — ever."

She showed no emotion at his outburst, nor did she try to speak aloud. Instead, he heard her through the mental bond they shared.

"Put. Me. Down."

He could sense she would use her talons to free herself if she had to. He squeezed a little tighter, but she didn't even kick.

"Do we understand each other?"

"Yes."

He released her. Rather than collapse to the deck, she landed on the balls of her feet in a crouch. She removed a small flask from the waistband of her breeches and took a drink from it. He knew she kept sea water in it.

He saw she had to struggle to swallow the salt water. As a sea creature, she needed it to heal the damage he'd done. After a few minutes, she straightened and faced him.

"I worded that poorly; you overreacted," she said without rancor. Her reaction reminded him she was not human.

He sighed. "You are right, pet; this is not my usual behavior. I think it has to do with the fact Hezekiah truly loved her. I've seen him with countless women in the past; it was always different with Brianna. Truth be told, I think that theirs is the only real love I've witnessed. Something in me just can't bear to be the one to cause her that kind of pain."

Understanding shone in her eyes. "You are more human than you think, Viktor. I have observed the species for a very long time. Yes, the love you witnessed between Hezekiah and Brianna seems to be rare. It is also strange to me. Each would put the needs of the other above their own. I would think that would make them weak; but it seemed to make them strong instead."

"Aye, pet; it did."

She regarded him silently for a time. He gazed back at her and wondered what she felt about the situation and about him. He'd walled off his emotions from her to hide any perceived weakness; or had she walled off from him? Perhaps some alcohol had made it past his body's enhanced metabolism.

Belle spoke and broke his unexpected reverie. "I won't speed the voyage unless you request it. I know you need time. I would advise against delaying too much, though. You still have the final Sister to deal with."

"Thank you, pet."

He offered her a sad smile as she walked past him to the door. She paused next to him for a moment and caressed his neck. Her skin felt cool to the touch; but his skin grew feverish hot where her fingers had trailed.

"Get some sleep, Viktor. It will do you good."

He began to feel swimmy headed. He heard the door click behind her. His neck began to go numb, and his sight grew dim.

Viktor woke in his bed. He felt refreshed but unclear of how he'd gotten there or what had happened.

"About time you woke up." Jim Rigger sat at the table looking over a logbook. "You've been out for two days."

Unlike Jim, Viktor found this alarming. "What?"

He rose quickly, and a wave of vertigo greeted him. Jim stood and handed him a bottle of blood/liquor blend which was mostly blood. He pulled the stopper and downed half the contents before he came up for air.

"Thanks; that helped."

"She must've dosed you stronger than she thought," his first mate observed.

Vik caught the implication quickly. "Where is our lovely Belladonna?" His voice sounded his most calm and reasonable, a sure sign of his ire.

Jim smirked. "Hunting; imagine she anticipated your reaction. Relax, Vik. It's been smooth sailing; well, really, it's been full stop. We're well provisioned, so we set the sea anchors. Haven't spotted any prizes; but that should change at the Straits."

Viktor finally relaxed. "Good; I'd hate to miss the fun. I do feel better for the sleep."

"Well that worked out, at least."

Both men turned to see the siren enter the cabin. Viktor hadn't sensed her approach.

"Just what did you do to me, Belle? I feel almost human."

She shot him a worried look. "How long have you been up? Have you fed yet?"

"Not half an hour and yes." He held up the half-empty bottle.

"Good; the effects should wear off very soon."

"The. Effects. Of. What?"

"My venom, or one of them; I used a tranquilizing variation. It renders a victim unconscious but doesn't cause paralysis or tissue damage."

"Hmph; I thought I was immune to your venom."

"Only partially; had you been human, the dose I gave you would have been fatal. It was the only way I could be sure it would work on you."

He stared at her for a few moments. She stared back.

"Thank you for the rest. It was refreshing. Don't ever do that again."

"I won't. I don't like how long it took you to recover."

Jim broke the tension. "Belle, you said this worked out in a way which implied something else didn't."

She grimaced. "The delay cost us. There is a British patrol near Gibraltar."

Chapter 2

"Of course."

Viktor took another pull on the bottle and pinched the bridge of his nose. His shoulders shook with low, wry laughter. The siren and the vampire watched and waited in silence.

He finally sobered and looked up with alertness and a touch of gratitude in his eyes. "Jim, I need Lazarus to scout out these Navy ships and try to find out what they're protecting. Belle, sing us up a nice thick fog."

Jim grinned wide enough to show fangs. "Aye, Cap'n!" He quickly grew amorphous, condensed, and solidified as a large black tomcat, leaving his clothing in an empty pile on the chair. The cat bounded over to the window casement, pushed one of the panels partway open, and leapt out. Mid-air, he changed from cat to raven and flew off headed west.

Belladonna didn't move. "You want a wind to get us there first. The fog should wait until we're closer. What is your plan once we get there?"

"We hunt. If they're guarding a prize, I intend to take it from under their noses. If they're just patrolling for corsairs, I'll take them. This crossing won't be fast. I want to make sure we have plenty of blood stock aboard."

"I won't complain about the extra meat." She strode to the window and scented the breeze. She sang a single note and turned back to face him. "There; we should make the Straits in about ten hours rather than a day and a half. Now, how would you like to spend that time?"

The smile she gave him let him know exactly how *she* would prefer to spend it. He took one last pull on the bottle, corked it, and began to disrobe.

Belladonna managed to keep him distracted for a few hours. Eventually, other thoughts began to seep through the fog of physical pleasure.

Lazarus reached Gibraltar and found the patrol ships the siren warned them about. Three medium-sized warships sailed from one side of the strait to the other, stopping and checking nearly every craft passing that way.

The visuals Viktor got from the raven let him know the patrol wasn't looking for him or his ship. Nor were they guarding a specific prize. It looked more like they were looking for smugglers and putting on a show of force to scare off corsairs.

It didn't really matter. They presented an obstacle he would just have to remove.

He sat up and reached for his pants. "Time to sing up that fog, pet; I want all three ships. Their crews will give the cadre a fresh feed and restock our larder."

She propped on one elbow and raised an eyebrow at him. "All three? You're feeling bloody."

"I am. I want that fog thick enough to get them to drop sea anchors. With your help, navigation will not be a problem for us."

The siren stretched and got up. She didn't bother with any clothing. Over the years, Viktor had grown used to her preference for nudity. He watched her walk to the window and fought the temptation to take her back to bed.

She opened one of the panels and stepped onto the sill. "I'll be back shortly." She turned and dove into the sea.

By the time Vik reached the helm, the ship faced a wall of white to the west. It grew to stretch across the horizon as he watched. He smiled grimly and reached out through the blood bond he maintained with the crew to draw their attention. He knew he could just direct them by his will alone, but he still preferred to prepare them for battle face to face.

"Listen up, lads!" Every man turned to face him. He could sense the attention of the riggers who were still aloft on him, as well. "We've three prizes to take today."

The announcement met unanimous enthusiasm. None of the men questioned how they would accomplish the feat. They had every confidence in their captain and any plan he devised. He felt gratitude that they genuinely felt like that and not because of any mental control on his part.

"Now, here's how we're going to do it—."

Viktor's first thought had been to row to the northernmost ship in the long boats with muffled oars. Instead, he'd gone with Belladonna's suggestion to tie the boats together. She towed them to their first victim in silence.

While the boarding party he'd brought silently climbed the sides of the ship, Viktor flew to the rigging. Quietly and methodically, he found and neutralized every sailor still aloft. He wasn't ready to slaughter yet. He wanted these men alive for the moment.

The sound of a shout and a body hitting the deck drifted up through the fog. He knew it would be unavoidable at some point. The Navy men would realize they were under attack sooner or later. His pirates knew to keep the kills to a minimum, though.

More shouting marked the arrival on deck of some Navy men from below. A quick check through the blood bond he imposed on his crew let him know they were ambushing men in the fog as they emerged.

He secured his victims to one of the masts and dropped down to the deck. Once there, he went in search of the Navy captain.

The pirates used the same tactic to take the second ship. Belladonna towed each ship by its anchor chain to the *Incubus*. The crew not part of the boarding party set to transferring the prisoners to the larder hold. Once this was done, they systematically stripped the Navy vessels.

The crew of the third Navy warship met a much more violent fate.

By the time the pirates finished with the first two ships, night had fallen. Viktor instructed Belladonna to allow her fog to dissipate. They set the stripped ships adrift and set sails at half-reefed. It didn't take long to reach the last ship.

The patrol ship hailed them. "Ahoy vessel, state your name, port of origin, destination, cargo, and captain!"

"Ahoy Navy vessel, our captain wishes to come aboard to speak with your captain. He has news about some pirates," Jon-Jon called back at Viktor's instruction.

Some murmuring was heard before they called back, "Permission granted; your captain only."

A few moments later, Viktor climbed down the side of his ship on one of the catch-all nets. He leapt with cat-like grace over to the quarterdeck of the smaller ship. The Navy captain strode down from the aft castle to meet him, flanked by two marines.

Viktor gave a slight bow and waited for the man to reach him. Other than the ever-present dagger sheathed at the nape of his neck and hidden by his hair, he bore no weapons.

"Greetings, sir; I am Captain Vernon Kendridge. Welcome aboard the *HMS Trent*. You claim to have information about pirates, in these waters I presume. May I ask your name and that of your vessel? She is quite an impressive craft, I must say."

Viktor hid his smirk. The man obviously loved the sound of his own voice. Still, Kendridge's tone and stance let him know the man had earned his rank. "Thank you, Captain Kendridge. I am rather pleased with her. You may have heard of her before; she's the *Incubus*, formerly known as the *HMS War God*."

Kendridge paled visibly in the lantern light. "Then that would make you—."

"Viktor Brandewyne, at your service, sir." He smiled tightly, careful not to reveal his fangs, yet. "It seems I've grown tired of piracy. In exchange for pardons for myself and my crew, I will lend my aide and my ship to the effort to quell the Colonials' rebellion."

Kendridge gaped for a moment but recovered quickly. "Forgive me if I find that hard to belie—," he trailed off and stared past Viktor. "Who the blazes is she?"

"Ah, that would be the lovely but deadly Belladonna, a siren." He put an arm around Belle's waist and pulled her nude form to his side in a show of possessiveness.

Kendridge scowled. "Mr. Ferguson, take this pirate and his whore into custody. Send word to his crew to stand down, or I'll have him hung in front of them."

"We outgun you, sir; and I'll wager my lads have seen more combat than these pups under your command." Viktor kept his tone congenial.

"Tell your men to stand down, Brandee."

Vik grinned and laughed. "I think not. Have at, lads! No quarter!"

Six abnormally pale pirates leapt from the much higher deck of the *Incubus* to the quarterdeck of the *Trent*. The Navy sailors, quick as their reactions were, still could not match the speed of the attacking vampires.

The siren stepped away from Viktor's side, extended her talons, and entered the fray. She sliced and stabbed with deadly accuracy.

Men's screams filled the air and faded to gurgles. Blood and internal organs made footing treacherous. Through it all, Viktor calmly faced Kendridge, who held a pistol aimed at him.

"Monster! Call them off!"

"No."

He watched the horror grow on his victim's face as the *Trent*'s crew was horrendously slaughtered. Out of the corner of his eye, he saw Belladonna bite off the front of a man's skull. He knew Kendridge saw it, as well.

The Navy captain turned his gun toward his own head. Bleak despair filled his eyes. "Anything is better than that." His finger started to tighten on the trigger.

The gun discharged.

The mini-ball arced harmlessly through the rigging and out into the water. Viktor stood behind Kendridge and held the man's gun arm by the wrist. He'd moved faster than the man could see.

He leaned over and whispered in the man's ear, "Oh, you don't escape me so easily, Vernon. I'll not be cheated out of my meal."

Without further warning, he bit deep into Kendridge's throat and gorged on blood.

Kendridge rose the following night to an empty ship. The scent of old blood on the decks sent him into convulsions of Hunger. Faster than he could've imagined, he searched the entire vessel. No living soul could be found.

He did find some food in the galley. The moment he put it in his mouth he spat it back out again. It held no flavor whatsoever.

What had Brandee done to him?

The last thing he remembered was the slaughter of his crew by those monsters. Brandee had stopped him from committing suicide; but what then?

The memories of the bloody violence surprisingly redoubled his Hunger rather than quelled it. He tried again to eat. Again, he spit the food out. In the process, he cut his lip on inexplicably long, sharp canine teeth.

Flavors exploded on his tongue as the minute amount of blood washed over it.

Why was there so little blood?

Finally, he remembered. Brandee had drained him. He was dead.

With a sigh of resignation, he gazed up at the night sky. The stars told him he was no longer where he'd been. He didn't know how the ship had gotten so close to the equator in one night; it didn't really matter.

He ran up a distress signal and hoped for a ship to see it in the morning. Some instinct told him he'd need a dark place to hide come sunrise.

Chapter 3

Viktor's impatience eventually got the better of him. He'd grown too used to the enhanced speed in crossing the Atlantic which Belle's weather magic afforded him.

A growing sense of urgency he barely admitted to himself prompted him to have the siren sing them up a wind. As a result, it cut their sailing time to Savannah in half.

When they made port, he went to Celie's alone. This was solely his task.

Something about Celie's tabby hut seemed different. He peered at the small structure he grew up in and at the surrounding live oak grove. Spanish moss draped to the ground on some of the lower of the ancient branches. Mother Celie's ever-present fire crackled merrily in its pit outside the front door, a pot of boiling water on an iron hook suspended above it.

The place appeared just as he'd remembered it from boyhood; but it was different from how it'd looked the last time he'd visited scant months ago.

The extra tabby hut which had housed Brianna Grimm and her twin children was noticeably missing.

"Mother?" he called out.

The old woman poked her head out from behind the hut. "Oh, there you are, boy. Fetch this tub around to the pot." When he didn't react right away, she added, "Hop to it, boy. These crabs ain't goin' t'cook themselves."

His mouth watered at the thought of fresh blue crab. Celie always knew how to season them just right. He smiled and nodded. In seconds, the tub full of live blue crabs sat next to the fire.

Celie looked at the pot. "That looks to be a good boil." She tossed in a bundle of herbs and spices tied in a piece of cheesecloth. The boiling water soon turned orangish red. Once satisfied with the color and the pungency of the aroma, she said, "Put them in now; careful not to splash."

He gently tipped the tub up and sent the crabs to their doom.

"Shame you didn't get in earlier. You could've netted some shrimp to go with this," she said and added some maize and potatoes. "Prob'ly could've 'found' some good smoked sausage to add, as well."

Vik chuckled. "Sounds like you plan to feed my whole crew, Mother." His expression sobered. "Where have Brianna and her brood gotten off to? I have bad news for her."

"Who?"

He blinked at her, taken aback by the question. Could the old witch be going senile? She'd been old all his life, but her mind had always been sharp.

"Brianna Grimm; Hezekiah's wife."

Celie frowned at him. "The Reaper? Didn't know he was married; never figured him for the type, truth be told. Why in the world would you think his wife would be here?"

He reached out and felt her forehead, an action she'd performed on him often enough in his youth. "Are you feeling well?"

She swatted his hand away irritably. "Stop that, boy. I'm not sick or fevered. Now explain what you're going on about."

"You don't remember." He made it a statement rather than a question. Something was very wrong; he just wasn't sure exactly what, yet.

Celie scowled at him. "Viktor Brandewyne, I never forget anything, and you know it. Now explain yourself and don't dawdle."

He leaned back. Crossed his arms and raised an eyebrow at her. "Very well, here is what you *have* forgotten, old woman. Hezekiah Grimm, my first mate, came here with Brianna Belmont, who was pregnant with twins. He married her in Savannah and left her with you to have her children."

She gave him an equally incredulous look. "I'd wonder if you are the one who's been fevered, but I doubt your curse would permit that possibility. You haven't sailed with the Reaper for years. You parted company over his fondness for opium, and he was never your first mate. Jim was until he became Lazarus. Willoby Jon has held that title since," she paused for a moment. "Well, I imagine Jim has the job again. I admit, I hadn't foreseen him getting a good dose of that moly."

"He does, but not because of the moly. He stepped in when Hezekiah died. I don't know why you don't remember. Jon-Jon was only first mate until I saved Hezekiah from a pirate hunter a few years ago, not long after I was cursed." He didn't bother trying to hide his hurt, confusion, and sorrow. Celie had always been able to see through his facades.

She looked at him with concern. With a sigh, she said, "These are done. Scoop 'em up and bring them inside. Let's get a good meal in your belly and see if we can't figure this conundrum out."

She patted his arm and hobbled into the hut.

Viktor sat and stared at the food in front of him. For one of the few times in his life, he had no appetite. How could years of a man's life be so easily erased? He clearly remembered everything he and Hezekiah had been through together since rejoining forces. Some strange magic must be at work.

The thought gave him brief hope; a hope quickly dashed when he drew out the Elder's Stone on its silver chain. The milky crystal didn't react to anything.

Neither Celie nor any of the other Sisters had any spell in place there.

"Well, I'm glad to see you still have the key I gave you. Won't be long until you need it again," she said.

"I'm starting to wonder if it still works," he grumbled.

Celie held her hand out, a silent command. He slipped the chain over his head and handed the crystal to her. The moment it touched her hand it flared briefly but brightly.

She jerked her hand back. Only Viktor's reflexes and superhuman speed allowed him to catch it before it could hit the table.

Celie rubbed her hand as if it had been burned. "Works just fine, boy. Bonded itself to you, too. No one else will ever be able to use it. Why did you think it wasn't working?"

"It didn't react when I pulled it out. I suspected some powerful magic was at work to make you forget about Hezekiah and his role in my quest the past few years."

She gave him a shrewd look. Obviously, something he'd said or the way he'd said it peaked her interest. He knew her body language well enough to expect an interrogation.

"What have you thought of Mother?"

"You say he played a part in your quest, not just that he sailed with you as first mate."

He saw what she was driving at. "Aye, Zeke didn't fully trust Belladonna at first. He forced a portion of his power onto Hezekiah and set him to watch my back and keep me on course."

Viktor watched the color drain from her face. Although he'd seen similar reactions in others, he'd never seen it happen to Mother Celie. The fact she was a Sister of Power made it even more disconcerting.

"Zeke shared power?" Her voice came out shaky.

He nodded. "I take it that has some bearing on the situation."

"I need to get to my fire." She stood and headed out the door faster than he'd give her old bones credit for. He followed and found her stirring the fire. She tossed a handful of some fragrant herbal mix into the flames, turning them green.

Celie peered at the eldritch blaze until it faded to its normal reddish gold.

"That's odd," she mumbled with a frown.

"What?"

"Zeke isn't answering me. I caught a brief glimpse of him by his fire; but he waved his hand over it and broke the spell."

Viktor snorted. "Seems like neither he nor that damned island wants to cooperate."

Celie shook her head. "At least he doesn't seem diminished. Let's go back inside, and you can tell me what you claim I've forgotten. Try not to leave anything out. Even the smallest detail may prove valuable in figuring this out."

By the time he finished, most of the night had passed. Crab shells lay scattered on the table. Celie had insisted on eating, since they wouldn't keep overnight. He barely remembered how they'd tasted, and he felt the most tired he had been since before the curse.

The old woman stood and used a hand broom to sweep the detritus into the wooden tub. "I don't know what to tell you, boy. If Zeke really shared power with the Reaper, and he passed it on to his children by this Brianna, I should've seen them in my fire. The spell was set to seek out the Elder's magic specifically."

"I know I didn't imagine all that."

"I do believe you, Viktor," she said gently. "I think you're right about powerful magic being involved. Zeke is unlike any other being in this world. Even I or Gloribeau aren't powerful enough to comprehend his magic fully, and we are the oldest of the Sisters."

She sighed and sat down. "It is possible time and the world reset themselves when the sea dragon struck Hezekiah down."

He tilted his head. "Reset in what way, Mother?"

"To lose even a small portion of the Elder's power could prove apocalyptic. It would upset the balance too much. To preserve the balance, I think events in the past may have been altered."

He frowned and shook his head. "Why would I remember, then; or the rest of the crew, for that matter?"

She shrugged. "I'm not sure. It may have to do with how close you were, or with the fact your magic is wild and has increased greatly over the past few years. It probably granted you immunity to the change. As for your crew, they are all bound to you in one way or another. Your magic affects them and their perceptions."

He brooded over this theory in silence for some time. Celie sat with her hands folded over her stick and watched him patiently.

"The only way I can know for certain if this is what happened will be to search for news of either Hezekiah or Brianna."

"That will be time consuming. I fear it may be a distraction you can ill afford." In answer to his scowl, she added, "Your quest is drawing to a close, Viktor. Soon, you must face Juma and deal with her. I would not put it off too long."

"I will keep that in mind, Mother."

Chapter 4

Belladonna picked up on Viktor's agitation the moment he left Thunderbolt and returned to Savannah.

She abandoned her hunt and swam back to the ship in the harbor. Once dressed, she went ashore in search of him. She had a general idea of what direction she needed to go but could not discern what he found so upsetting. His emotions were too strong to be contained. His thoughts, however, remained closed off to her gentle probing.

She found him close to the church Grimm and Brianna had been wed in.

"Viktor, what is wrong? Was Brianna very upset?" She could only guess. Mourning a mate was not something she was familiar with.

"She wasn't there." He stopped and glared at nothing.

"Any idea where she went? Didn't Celie tell you?"

The gaze he turned on her held sorrow, horror, and worry; three emotions she rarely saw from him. "Mother Celie has no memory of her, nor of Hezekiah sailing as my first mate. She insists Jon-Jon held that position until Jim gained the ability to regain human form at will."

Belle knew her expression mirrored his.

"Do you think the fact Zeke shared power with Grimm has something to do with this?" she asked.

"Oh, that is a distinct possibility. Celie said his death may have altered the past to keep that small portion from being lost." He paused in thought for a moment. "I remember her warning about what could happen if even the portion carried by the twins was lost. She said it could end the world."

"Did she have any explanation of why we remember?" Belle did not like the theory. There was some small detail which escaped her at the moment; but she felt it was wrong, as magically plausible as it seemed on the surface.

"She could only guess my wild magic interacted and gave some immunity to me and everyone magically-bound to me." He shrugged and looked the most miserable she'd ever seen him. It worried her that he let his emotions show so much.

"Why were you storming toward the church?"

Both anger and faint hope drowned out the misery in his eyes. "I want to see if the priest remembers."

She nodded. "A good idea; human priests, regardless of what deity they serve, have long been the keepers of records and accounts; probably because they were usually the only ones literate enough to do so."

"Welcome, my son, daughter. How may I be of service?" the unfamiliar clergyman greeted them. To his credit, he managed to quickly hide his look of disdain for the siren's mode of dress.

"We are looking for Father William. He oversaw the marriage of a friend of mine," Viktor told him.

"Oh, I am so sorry. Father William died about two months ago. There was a fire in the rectory."

"That is sad news. Perhaps you can still help us, father—?" Viktor adjusted his course.

"Barnabas," the man supplied his name. "How so?"

Viktor gave him a serious and sorrowful look. "The friend I spoke of died at sea not that long ago. I am trying to ensure his widow and children are properly cared for."

The priest looked at the vampire and siren, doubt obvious in his demeanor. "Forgive my saying so, but the two of you look more likely to rob the poor woman. What is your name, sir?"

The vampire's eyes blazed with emerald light. He stepped forward to loom menacingly over the priest. "I am Captain Viktor Brandewyne. The friend I spoke of was my first mate, Hezekiah Grimm; his widow, Brianna Belmont Grimm; their twin children, Celeste Nicole and Henry Sebastian Grimm were baptized here, as well. The widow and children have disappeared, and I am trying to find them. I do intend to see they are properly provided for and protected; I owe Hezekiah that much."

The man blanched but held his ground. He would not meet Viktor's gaze. "I have heard of you. That you seek to do this for Madame Grimm gives me some hope. Will you repent of your wicked ways and turn to God?"

Viktor blinked at him. He could smell the man's fear; yet the priest remained bold enough to ask him to repent. He felt his anger evaporate.

"I fear I am beyond repentance, Father Barnabas."

"No man is beyond repentance while he still draws breath, my son." Barnabas did look up at him then.

Viktor smiled sadly. "Perhaps, but I am no longer a man. I have been cursed to be a monster."

Barnabas shook his head and gave him a sorrowful look. "I will pray for you, my son. I can see you believe this; but I have faith you can still be redeemed."

"I appreciate your concern. Can you help me with locating— no, to be perfectly honest, can you help me verify the fact of Mr. Grimm's marriage and family?"

The clergyman scrunched his face in confusion. "I don't understand. You sounded so sure of it a moment ago."

Viktor took a deep breath and let it out with a sigh. "I am sure of it. The problem is something has happened which may have erased the events. The person into whose care Brianna and her children were placed has no memory of them or of Mr. Grimm sailing with me these past few years. The site where their house stood now holds an ancient live oak."

Barnabas grew ashen. "That smacks of witchcraft!"

Viktor nodded. "Aye; but whoever or whatever is responsible, they are more powerful than any witch I've encountered."

"You've encountered many witches?"

"More than I care to. Some were powerful enough to convince some people they were goddesses." He needed to steer the conversation back on course. "Do you have the records of the marriage or the children's baptisms?"

Barnabas gave him a sorrowful look. "I've no doubt Father William presided over those events. However, several years' worth of records were lost in the fire which claimed his life. Almost none of the records were kept here in the church itself. The fire was only two months ago, and I'm still trying to sort things out. The most recent records I've been able to find intact have been from a couple of decades ago."

"Damn. Well, thank you for your time."

"The timing of that fire seems more than coincidental to me," Belladonna commented as they strode away from the church.

"Indeed; it seems I cannot get solid proof of Hezekiah's family." Viktor's voice sounded tired even to his own ears.

"What about the madam at the Black Flag? She knew about Brianna," Belle suggested.

He stopped in his tracks and looked at her. "You're right; she did." Without further warning he clasped an arm around her waist, kissed her soundly, and launched into flight, heedless of who saw.

They landed shortly after in the alleyway which held the front entrance of the tavern and brothel in question. The moment her feet touched land and he released her, the siren muttered, "By the Abyss, I hate to fly."

He chuckled at her disgruntlement. "You just don't like being out of your element."

"No, I don't."

They went in and headed straight for the bar. He recognized the bar maid. "Misty, pet, I don't see Maggie about."

He noticed sadness in her eyes as she motioned a rough-looking man over. "She's in a bad way, Cap'n. Cord, show them up to Maggie's room."

Viktor didn't like the sound of this. He and Belle followed Cord McVarish up the back stairs. The sight which greeted them made his heart drop.

Maggie lay on her back, her breathing shallow but steady, unseeing eyes staring at the ceiling. A thin coverlet draped her gaunt frame. A sheen of sweat glistened on her face. Only the now-faded ginger of her hair marked her as the woman Viktor gave his virginity to years ago.

"What happened to her?" His voice came out as a whisper.

"A couple or so of months ago, some lads decided to race their horses down River Street. Maggie and a few of the girls went out to watch. On the second leg of the race, one of the horses hit some loose cobbles and went down. It crushed the rider and killed him instantly. It also threw a few of the cobblestones during its fall. One of 'em hit Maggie square between the eyes. She's been like this ever since. We can get her to swallow a little bit of broth if we sit her up; but she doesn't see us or hear us, as far as we can tell," Cord explained.

Viktor looked at him. "Did anyone fetch a doctor for her?"

"Aye." Cord nodded. "Doc Strydam said he couldn't do anything for her. Said we'd be doin' her a favor if'n we just smothered her. He didn't think she could get any better."

Without a word, Belladonna stepped to the woman's bedside and brushed hair away from her sweaty face. This allowed Viktor to see the small pock mark on Maggie's forehead.

"Is there anything you can do for her, pet?"

"I can repair her body, but I don't know how much of the damage inside her head I can heal," she replied. "The human mind is a delicate thing."

"If that doc couldn't help her, what makes you think you can?" Cord eyed her with a mix of skepticism and disdain. "You're just a slip of a lass."

Viktor forestalled any tirade the siren might have launched. He turned glowing eyes to the man and took his will. "Belladonna is more than she appears and has performed healing just shy of miraculous. Now, unless you wish to learn how it feels to be eaten alive, you will bring her whatever she asks for."

"Y-yes sir."

"How hard would it be to get salt water here?" Belle asked.

Cord shrugged. "Wouldn't be that hard, but it would take a bit of time. I'd say about a half hour or so to get out past the salt marshes and the same time to get back. How much do you need?" He didn't question why she would need it.

She frowned and shook her head. "Ideally enough to fill a bathing tub. An hour or more is too long to wait, though. I have enough in my flask to suffice."

She removed a good-sized flask from the leather carry strap attached to her belt. "I need a clean cloth."

Cord immediately left the room; he returned a few minutes later with the requested item. Belle took it from him, uncorked the flask, and saturated the cloth with salt water. Gently, she washed Maggie's forehead.

Viktor could just detect a low thrum of sound. He felt sure Cord could not. Before his eyes, the dent in Maggie's forehead filled in, and the flesh on her skull filled out to its former robustness. Even her hair grew to a brighter red.

Belladonna rewet the cloth and methodically bathed the woman's body. She continued with the ultrasonic thrum, as well. When she stepped back, Maggie's breathing had deepened to a normal slumber. Her eyes closed, as well.

"Call her back, Captain."

He sat on the edge of the bed, lifted her hand, and patted it gently. "Maggie, pet; it's time to wake up."

She didn't respond.

He lacerated his tongue on one of his fangs and kissed her. As soon as he felt the temporary bond form, he spoke to her again. "Maggie, wake up."

"Mm; hmph?" She opened bleary eyes.

"Welcome back, pet."

"Vik?" Her voice sounded scratchy from disuse. "What are you doing here? If the Captain finds you here, he'll skin you alive. You know he doesn't want you getting any more free rides." She peered hard at him. "When did you grow a beard? It suits you."

He felt torn between relief, confusion, and fading hope. "Maggie, old Billy died years ago. You run the Flag now. Don't you remember?"

She scrunched her face. "No."

"What year is this?" His hope dwindled rapidly.

"Well, that is a silly question."

"Humor me."

"1756—. Vik, what's wrong? You look so lost."

He sighed and caressed her face. "Maggie pet, this is around 1777. You had an accident a few months ago and were hit in the head. You've been asleep since then."

Her face flushed and she glared at him. "That is not funny, Vik."

"No, it isn't. I'm serious." He turned to Cord. "Fetch Misty up here. She's not going to believe it until she sees for herself."

Maggie tried to sit up. "What is wrong with me? It's like I have no energy."

"McVarish said they've only been able to get a little broth into you each day. Belladonna restored your body from the wasted state you'd shriveled to, but you've been starving."

"I don't feel hungry," she protested.

"You will." He'd never gone as long as she had without food, but he'd gone long enough to know the appetite shuts down at some point.

"Miss Maggie?" The barmaid poked her head into the door. When the bedridden madam looked her way, she started crying and ran into the room to embrace her employer. "You're awake! You're really awake! That stupid doctor said you'd never wake up again."

Maggie patted her hair, a confused look on her face. The girl's emotions could not be mistaken or feigned.

When the girl finally broke the embrace, Maggie asked, "Are you new? I don't remember you. Old Billy's always recruiting new girls, it seems."

Misty's expression filled with hurt. "What's wrong, Miss Maggie? Don't you remember; you helped raise me. Da put you in charge of me after Mama died. I'm Barbra Davidson's girl, Misty."

Maggie scowled. "You're a grown woman. Little Misty is barely out of infancy; and I just saw Barbra yesterday."

Viktor stepped in and placed a hand on the girl's shoulder. "I'm sorry, pet. Maggie has forgotten the past two decades. Maggie, this really is Barbra and Billy's daughter. Look closely; you can see them in her face." Silently, he willed her to let go of her stubborn denial.

After a few awkward moments, Maggie spoke. "Dear lord, you really are little Misty all grown up." Tears flowed as the realization of lost time and memories sank in.

The girl smiled sadly and nodded. "Don't worry, Miss Maggie. We'll help you remember."

"Unfortunately, I can't wait around for that," Viktor said. "It wouldn't be safe in these times. I'm sure both the Royal Navy and the Continental Navy have gotten word of my ship's presence in port. I need to leave before one or the other decides to either sink or conscript me. I wish you well, Maggie."

"Vik, wait. What was it you wanted to see me about?"

He sighed. "You've lost the memory I need, pet. I came here hoping you'd remember the Reaper's wife and children. He was my first mate for the past six years and fell in battle a few months ago."

"Never figured him for the marrying kind. Still, if I hear word of his family, I'll pass the message along."

"Thank you, pet."

Chapter 5

Cord McVarish followed Viktor and Belladonna down the stairs. Obviously, weepy women made him uncomfortable.

"Captain Brandee, a word with ye?"

The vampire and the siren turned to see what the man wanted.

Cord gulped; intimidated. "I recall something about the Reaper's family."

Viktor advanced on him eagerly; and he took a step back. "How do you know about them? Did Maggie tell you?"

"No! She never told anyone about them. It was Chad Harris, and he didn't tell me, he told that Navy man who came sniffing around a while back. Harris said you and the Reaper had delivered a pregnant girl to the old witch out at Thunderbolt."

"Has anyone been out there recently other than me?"

"Not that I've heard tell of, Cap'n."

Vik clapped him on the shoulder. "Thank you, Mr. McVarish. See to it that Maggie is well cared for."

"Aye, I will."

The *Incubus* sailed down the Savannah River. The only heading Viktor had given the helmsman was for the open sea.

He sat in his cabin and brooded; a bottle of blood/brandy blend close by. He didn't bother with a cup.

Shortly after sunset, Jim Rigger knocked at the door. He entered at a silent signal from his captain. "What's troubling you, Vik?"

"Powerful witchcraft; grab yourself a bottle, Jim. I know you're Hungry." He took another pull on his own bottle.

Jim pulled the cork on one of the bottles with the least amount of brandy mixed in. "Powerful witchcraft has become an everyday occurrence for you, Vik," he snorted.

"This is powerful enough to nearly erase Hezekiah and his family from my recent past; powerful enough to make Celie forget; powerful enough to leave no trace of them or their tabby hut behind hers."

Jim's eyes bugged a bit, and he downed a large gulp of the blood. "Damn, that is troubling."

They drank in companionable silence for a while. Eventually, Jim asked, "I know we remember; is that why you say nearly erase?"

"Partially; I think the spell, or whatever, is focused primarily on people I know should remember. Celie's memory is completely different, and an ancient oak now stands where Brianna's hut was. The priest who officiated over Hezekiah's wedding and the baptism of his children was killed in a fire which destroyed the records of them, as well. Maggie had a head injury which robbed her of twenty years' worth of memories."

"Oh, is she well, otherwise? I always liked Maggie," Jim commented.

"Aye; Belle healed her body, at least. Hopefully her memories will return." Vik put the cork back in his nearly empty bottle.

Jim corked his bottle, too. "What's the plan now?"

"Tomorrow night is the full moon. I'm going to try to summon Hell's Breath. If anyone, Zeke should know what has happened. I owe it to Hezekiah to see to Brianna's welfare."

The next night proved cloudy. The moon barely presented a watery light in the ominous sky. Viktor ordered the sea anchors set and all the sails furled. For the moment, the sea surrounded the ship like black glass.

He tied a sounding line to the chain from which hung the Elder's Stone. The milky crystal held a pale glow in its depths. It gave him hope that this would work.

Carefully, he lowered it over the side and into the water.

As with the first time he used it to summon Hell's Breath Island, a flash and a shockwave spread out from the crystal in ever-widening circles. There, the similarities ended.

Without warning, a sharp tug came on the rope, followed by the line going taut and moving back and forth in the water. Viktor quickly began to pull the rope back in. The moment he saw a small form clinging to the necklace, he yanked with superhuman strength.

Rather than let go, the creature arced up over the railing, the Elder's Stone still in its clutches, and landed on the deck with a stunning thud. Viktor and those near him watched what appeared to be a miniature dark-haired mermaid as her tail transformed into legs. Several men ran at the sight.

"It's another siren!"

"Run for it, lads!"

"Be still!" Viktor boomed, power riding his voice.

Every man within hearing distance stopped in mid-motion. Even the young mermaid grew still and stared at him with eyes a clear sea green.

"Papa?"

Vik smiled. The child's question confirmed his suspicions; she was one of Robert's get.

"No, pet; I'm your Papa's father, Viktor. What is your name?"

"Naia; I found a pretty, but I can't get it loose. Will you get it loose for me?" She held up the Elder's Stone.

"I will get it loose, but I cannot let you keep it. That pretty is very dangerous."

"But I found it!" She got a stubborn set to her jaw and a possessive gleam in her eyes. Before he could stop her, she stuck the knot securing the chain to the rope in her mouth and began to worry at it with her teeth. If left unchecked, he knew she might manage to get it loose on her own.

He sent a quick mental message to Belladonna. A few minutes later, she arrived on deck with one hand behind her back.

"Stop that," she ordered in a magical language only she, Viktor, and the young mermaid understood.

Naia froze, a look of instinctive terror in her eyes.

"Naia, this is Belladonna. Do you know what she is?"

The child nodded and whispered, "Death."

"Smart girl; she has two things to give you if you let me have that necklace back." He turned to the siren. "Belle."

Belladonna brought her hand from behind her back. In it she held a golden necklace set with three deep red rubies. She twisted her wrist to allow the stones to catch the lamplight. Naia's eyes grew wide, and a half-smile crept onto her face.

"I can have that?" she asked hopefully.

Belle continued to speak in the magical language with the full knowledge she would be bound by her words. *"Give Viktor his necklace, and I will give you this one."*

Naia's next words reminded Viktor how quick mermaids were to catch onto things. "He said you would give me two things."

The siren slowly smiled to reveal her true, needle-like teeth. *"I will also give you my solemn promise not to eat you."*

Naia's eyes grew even wider, if possible. She tossed the Elder's Stone away from herself and scrambled to the railing and over the side.

Belladonna threw the ruby necklace underhand behind the young mer. Viktor reached the side just in time to see Naia catch it.

"Naia don't lose that. As long as you wear it, you are safe from Belladonna."

"I will remember. Thank you for the pretty!" She fastened the ornament about her neck and dove beneath the surface.

"I wouldn't have eaten her, anyway. She's of your line." Belle gave a look of indifference and returned to her cabin.

He wondered if her restraint was more out of respect for him or fear of binding herself closer to him. He decided it didn't really matter. He undid the knot holding the Elder's Stone and slipped the chain of the talisman back around his neck.

Belle found him brooding in his cabin.

"Jim is worried about you."

He glared at her. "He has told you this, I suppose?"

She remained unfazed by his apparent ire. "You know he hasn't. He doesn't have to. His very attitude screams it." She flopped down on the bed and stared up at the ceiling. "I see the breeding out of my favorite food has already begun. In another couple of years that one will be ready to join a pod of juveniles and start spawning. At least she'll have to breed with a merman. Zeke told me your bloodline wouldn't be compatible with humans." She sighed. "It's just a matter of time before there are enough males to present a problem, though."

"Damn; and I thought I was broody," he commented.

She propped up on her elbows and looked at him. "I was just making an observation. I'm not wallowing in my own misery."

Her words stung him, she could tell. His color heightened and his eyes flashed brightly. She smiled. She knew she only needed to give him an outlet for his emotions now.

"Admit it; you're moping because we didn't find Brianna. You're pissy because of a few obstacles."

"I. Am. Not. Pissy."

She laughed. "Oh, no? Just listen to yourself."

"And what would you suggest I do to improve things?" He sneered at her.

"Fuck me."

Clearly, it wasn't the answer he'd expected. He stood and blinked at her for a moment; then he narrowed his eyes and smiled his most predatory smile. In seconds, he crouched over her on the bed.

She felt her pulse quicken, and everything grew brighter as her eyes dilated. Sometimes she forgot just how fast he could move.

He leaned down to put his face barely an inch from hers and whispered, "You'd like that, wouldn't you, pet?"

"Mmhmm."

Just as quickly, he returned to his seat, an arch expression on his face. "No."

It was her turn to blink at him. "No?"

"You think I can be that easily manipulated, Belle? You should know better."

She scowled in frustration. "It was for your own good, Viktor, and the good of the crew." He raised an eyebrow at her proclamation. "Yes, I take an interest in the welfare of your crew, and not just as food. You need them to reach your goals. Admit it; without their skills and unique insights, you wouldn't have been able to meet all the requirements the Sisters have placed on you so far."

"Of course, I admit that, pet. What surprised me was your concern for them. How, exactly, was seducing me to their benefit?"

"Your broodiness has a tendency to explode in violence against whoever is in closest range. I hoped to improve your mood. Usually, Hezekiah helped you maintain balance and a steady course, at least where dealing with the Sisters was concerned. Jim and I are trying to take up that job. The task is not proving easy for us. We are both bound to your will, where Hezekiah wasn't. My lack of humanity makes me ill-suited for it, as well; but I am determined to do my best. You need it."

While he contemplated her words, she opened her end of their mental bond. She could sense his pain over the realization of how much Hezekiah had served as his compass.

On a hunch, she said gently, "You once said you protect what is yours, even from yourself. I am only trying to help you do so."

He walked back over to her with a sad smile and caressed her face. "Thank you, pet. I will take you up on your offer of a most excellent distraction in a little while. I have something else to do first."

She watched him head out of the cabin with a purposeful stride.

Chapter 6

A couple of nights later, Viktor sailed the small ketch up the coast to Charleston. He left Jon-Jon and Zach in charge of the crew and ship after sailing it up the mouth of the Altamaha River.

Lazarus had spotted British patrol ships near Charleston when Viktor sent him to scout the port. All his mates agreed it would be best to hide the *Incubus*. Even though the former warship was more than capable of holding her own against most of the ships the Royal Navy had in these waters, it was deemed an unnecessary risk to the crew.

Viktor took Jim and Belladonna with him. His first mate could prove helpful both as extra muscle and, in his capacity as Lazarus, to scout ahead. Belle, he planned to use as bait and a diversion.

She wore the teal silk dress Brianna had given her. Its existence proved to him his memory of the past was correct. He could only attribute Mother Celie's altered memories to magic.

Once they reached the shore, Jim secured the boat. Viktor picked Belle up and flew the short distance to dry ground. He didn't want to get the dress soiled.

Belle grumbled about the treatment. "This is silly. I'm the last person a little salt water would hurt."

"You know what happens when you're exposed to brackish water, pet. It takes all your concentration to keep from reverting to your true form. That dress is part of the bait for Worthing." He looked over to his first mate. "Dawn is in a couple of hours, Jim. You have the message I prepared?"

"Aye, Cap'n." The vampire grinned as he pulled a sealed missive from inside his shirt.

"Good; Belle and I will head to one of the more reputable inns. You head to Worthing's and deliver that. Wait for an answer. I'll let you know what place to have his representative come meet at. After sunrise, I'll need you to spy things out."

Jim nodded and took to the sky shortly after entering the shadows.

Viktor and Belladonna headed into the port proper. It took some time to reach the better area of the town, but the real fun came with getting admittance to an inn at that time of night. It took a good bit of pounding to get the innkeeper to the door.

A bleary-eyed man in a nightshirt opened the door with a large candle in his hand. "Have ye any idea of the hour?" he demanded irritably.

Viktor sensed Jim had reached his destination and delivered the message. He didn't have time to stand and argue with this man.

"Aye, I do," he replied.

The glow from his eyes cast a slight greenish hue to the innkeeper's face. The man squinted at him, then his face went slack. Viktor smiled as he took the man's will temporarily.

"We are in need of lodgings. I have business here in town and am expecting a messenger early this morning."

"Of course, sir. I have some rooms available," the innkeeper said with a smile. His smile broadened at the small bag of gold coins Viktor handed him. "Whom will your caller be asking for?"

"Thomas Brigham," Vik readily supplied an alias.

"Very good, Master Brigham; right this way, please."

They followed the man to a small but well-appointed suite of rooms. Viktor looked around and nodded his approval. "These rooms will do nicely."

"Begging your pardon, Master Brigham, have ye any baggage? It's no trouble to roust Max and have 'im fetch it up."

"No sir, thank you. Our belongings are still shipboard. I won't be in port that long." Viktor willed the man to leave them and only remember sketchy details; just enough to play his unwitting part in the plan.

Percival Worthing finally deigned to come out to the foyer to speak with Jim. He gave the pirate a peeved look. "This is highly irregular, Mr. Rigger. My procurement practices are well-known among your kind."

"Just doing what the Cap'n told me, Mr. Worthing." Jim played the lackey. He'd never cared for the snobbishness of the pimp and would love nothing better than to give the man a permanent attitude adjustment.

"I will not buy a specimen without inspection." He sneered at the pirate again. "I also will not pay premium for one that is not virgin."

Jim couldn't suppress a snort. "Oh, this one would be worth it, trust me."

"After even a few days among pirates, I doubt it. Probably every man aboard your ship has had her by now."

"Cap'n Brandee doesn't share; and if he says don't touch, you don't if you value your life."

Worthing paused and swallowed. "Captain — Brandee, did you say? Well, that changes things considerably. Very well, I will see what he has to offer. Where shall I send my coach?"

Jim felt grateful for the poor lighting. It hid the fact he grew slightly transparent when he communicated with Viktor vampire-to-vampire. The problem was only a recent discovery since he'd gained the ability to hold his human form scant months ago.

He must've taken longer to reply than was acceptable. Worthing snapped his fingers under Jim's nose. Jim almost bit him out of reflex.

"A moment; I had to remember where the Cap'n said to tell you," he snapped irritably. "He said to ask for Mr. Brigham at the Stratton House."

Worthing blinked. "My! That is one of the finer establishments. I'm impressed he could get rooms there."

"The Cap'n can be very persuasive."

Viktor noted the slightly stunned and very appreciative leer the coachman gave Belladonna that morning. He kept his own expression neutral, in keeping with the persona he portrayed at the inn. He also kept a proprietary hand on the siren's elbow when he helped her into the coach.

Once seated inside, he gave a nod to the coachman. Soon the vehicle rolled through the streets of Charleston towards a grand manse which housed a world of decadence.

"How long do I have to remain silent?" Belle asked through the link they shared.

"I'll let you know, pet. We want our prey to believe you are some high-born girl I stole away. He likes them pretty, young, and spirited but breakable."

A sour tone entered her mental voice. *"I take it he prefers to do the breaking."*

"Sometimes; more often, his clientele do. They pay high prices to basically rape without consequences or risk to their freedom or reputation."

She snorted softly, eliciting a raised eyebrow. He thought he understood her amusement. *"There are men who think bedding a high-born virgin is somehow better than having any common wench."*

Belladonna gave him a raised eyebrow in turn. *"While I'm sure that's part of it, I've a feeling such men are more interested in showing dominance over women. I'd be willing to bet they either aren't married or have wives who dominate them. Rape is rarely about pleasure; it's about power and often vengeance for perceived slights."*

He blinked as he gazed at her. That thought had never consciously occurred to him so clearly. *"That is why you were angry with me about Paella; it wasn't just jealousy."*

She gave him an almost imperceptible nod.

The carriage slowed to a stop. Belle donned a veiled bonnet Viktor had given her for this ruse. He didn't want Worthing to see her face or hair until just the right moment.

The coachman opened the door, and they disembarked.

Worthing kept them waiting nearly half an hour. Viktor had Lazarus hiding in the house keeping an eye on the pimp. This let him know the man was observing them from a secret alcove.

He suppressed the urge to smirk. After dealing with six Sisters of Power, this human had no hope of testing his patience. He did silently urge Belle to fidget. She needed to portray the spirited but innocent victim.

She wandered around the foyer and inspected the décor. Viktor used the excuse of keeping an eye on her to make note of which items held true value and which were just for show but cheap. The habit was an old one and barely registered on his conscious mind.

"Master Worthing will see you now," a house boy announced. "If you and the young lady will follow me to the study?"

"Lead on." Viktor nodded and held his arm out for Belladonna. *"Mademoiselle* Dubois?"

"Coming, Captain Brigham," she replied in flawless French. *"Are we to meet the man you told me of?"*

"Oui, ma chere."

She took his arm, and they followed the servant.

Percival Worthing struck Viktor as a bit of a popinjay; from his powdered wig to his pale blue frock coat with its excessive gold brocade, to his red-heeled, brass-buckled shoes. The man waved a handkerchief in an affected manner, the copious lace at his cuffs fluttering with the movement.

"So, this is the young lady you've brought me, Captain—?"

"Brigham; it is."

Worthing gave her a slight bow, and Belladonna replied with a curtsey. "What is your name, my dear?"

"Quelle?" She stuck to her persona and looked between him and Viktor.

"You will have to excuse the *mademoiselle*, Mr. Worthing. She does not speak the King's English," Viktor supplied as excuse.

"Ah, and I think she does not know the true reason you brought her here."

"No."

Worthing smiled, but it held an air of disbelief.

"Ask her yourself, if you don't believe me," Vik said.

"Pardon moi, ma'm'selle, what is your name?" the pimp asked in French.

"I am Belle Janelle Dubois." She extended her hand.

He bowed over it and laid a kiss on her knuckles. He did not release her hand right away. "*And what brings you to my door?*"

She ducked her head as if embarrassed. The veil hid her expression from him. "*My father and I were on our way to New Orleans. He'd inherited a fertile tract of land and was to take possession of it. He'd hoped to find me a husband. Alas, now I am come seeking charity.*"

"*How so?*"

"*Pirates attacked our ship and,*" she managed a sob, "*they killed my father. Fortunately, Captain Brigham arrived before they could harm or dishonor me.*"

"I must admit, I am intrigued by this tale," Worthing said in English.

"I have been known to prey on other pirates. She killed a couple of them in the fight, too. Put me in mind of your preferences, and we were close to this port. She is untouched."

Worthing turned his attention back to Belladonna. "*May I see your face, mademoiselle?*"

She undid the ribbon which held the bonnet in place and lifted it off her head. Crimson hair cascaded down around her shoulders, the teal silk setting off the color dramatically. She kept her eyes in their human guise of sea grey.

"Magnificent," Worthing managed a breathy, awed whisper. His breeches began to tent outward. "I want to see the rest."

"Thought you might. I took the liberty of giving her something to make her more compliant. That dress is too valuable to damage." Viktor stepped up behind Belle and placed his hands on her shoulders. He switched to French.

"It is time, pet. Do you think you can go through with what we talked about? Monsieur Worthing must be seduced into taking you in. That is how things are done in the New World."

She looked back at him uncertainly then back at the pimp. She blushed and nodded. *"Oui; I will be brave."*

He unlaced the dress and loosened the waistband then slowly slid the garment off her shoulders. She shivered a little as his hands continued down her arms, and she even managed to blush when her breasts were bared.

"All of it, please." Worthing's voice deepened with lust.

Viktor nodded and pushed the skirts down past her hips. He let the dress puddle on the floor and helped her step out of it. He lifted one of her hands above her head and had her turn slowly one rotation.

Worthing couldn't hide his leer as he reached for her. She flinched back from him with a defiant flash in her eyes. He grinned, grabbed her, and kissed her roughly. She made a show of struggling with him.

He released her, stepped back, and clapped his hands twice. A couple of large servants entered. "Shall we begin price negotiations?"

Viktor broke into a slow, evil smile. "I've decided not to sell." He stooped down, gathered up the silk dress, and stuffed it in a corner. "Shall we show him what you are truly capable of, pet?"

"With pleasure," Belle said though multiple rows of needle-sharp teeth. She extended her talons and gutted the two men who'd been summoned to collect her.

Blood spattered the vampire and the pimp. The siren turned, her talons retracting, and sashayed up to Worthing to drape a bloody hand on his shoulder. He looked back at her with an expression of numb terror.

"Where is Brianna Belmont?"

The man just sputtered.

"She isn't here, pet. Lazarus couldn't find her or her scent anywhere in the house. He doesn't have her," Viktor told her.

The statement gave Worthing time to recover. "Belmont? You had something to do with the failure of that one to be delivered to me? I paid good coin for her! You owe me, sir!"

Viktor ran his hand back through his hair. "Never let it be said that Viktor Brandewyne doesn't pay his debts."

His hand flew forward, and his dagger buried itself in Worthing's eye.

He stepped forward and retrieved his dagger from the twitching body. He cleaned it on the man's coat and replaced it in its sheath. "I don't know about you, pet, but I'm Hungry."

Chapter 7

Thanks to Lazarus' reconnoitering during his search of the mansion, Viktor knew the exact location of every soul in it. He methodically went through and gathered the occupants, herding them into the study. Belle and Jim made sure each small group stayed put while Viktor gathered their victims.

The siren made this possible by closing the heavy draperies over the only two windows in the room. This allowed the multi-form vampire to take on his human form. Jim could withstand and function in full daylight only as the cat or raven known as Lazarus.

The presence of three dead bodies in the room, two of them mutilated somewhat, led Jim to borrow one of Viktor's tricks. He cut his hand with a letter opener he found on the desk and mixed the blood into a handy decanter of port. He and Belle made sure every human had a swallow of it.

Within half an hour, Viktor completed his roundup. He stalked around the group of servants, clients, and women. Jim allowed them to "wake up" from the stupor he'd placed them in just enough to be aware of their surroundings and the peril. He did not let them move from where they stood.

"I see you've separated the women from the men," Viktor observed.

"Aye, Cap'n. I know your mind on the men, but I wasn't sure what you plan to do with the wenches."

"I haven't decided yet." He looked over at Belle. "How is your appetite?"

"Voracious," she replied. Mentally, she added, *"If you want to spare the women, I won't object. They aren't as flavorful to me. Fear makes their meat sour. The males taste better."*

"Put the wenches to sleep; we'll transport them to the ship after sunset. Pick out your meals. Belladonna will take care of the bodies."

"Aye, Cap'n!"

The fact Jim sent the women to various chairs in the study before he willed them to sleep elicited a chuckle from Viktor.

Belladonna stripped the three bodies already present before she started to devour them. Vik couldn't think of any better way to describe it. The speed with which body parts disappeared down her gullet was frightening.

The two vampires watched for a moment, then ordered the men who weren't already nude to strip. Viktor figured it was easier than stripping dead bodies.

Without further delay, they began to feed.

"What are you going to do with those women?" Belle asked after they got under way.

Viktor ignored the question for the moment. The only sound in the cabin was the scratch of his quill in the logbook. He finished his entry and sprinkled sand over the page to dry the ink. Once satisfied with that, he brushed it off and closed the book.

"I'll take them to Maggie. She can decide whether to employ them or not."

She drew back and looked at him as if he'd grown a second head.

"What did you think I was going to do with them?"

She crossed her arms. 'I half expected you to give them to the cadre."

He shook his head. "I saved back some of Worthing's household for that purpose. Those wenches have already suffered enough. But for our intervention, that would have been Brianna's fate."

She sat on the edge of the bed and gave him a contemplative gaze. This was a side of him she'd rarely if ever seen. It almost felt alien to her. She began to gently probe his psyche through their blood bond. What she found made her recoil and throw up her strongest mental shields. She knew he was powerful enough to shatter even those; she doubted he would, though.

"You're shielding, pet. What's wrong?"

She debated on whether or not to tell him. She honestly didn't know how he would respond.

"Belle?"

She sighed. "I'm not sure how to respond to what I just saw. I'm not sure how to describe what I just saw."

He gave her a sad, tired look. "You saw remorse, pet, remorse and regret. I regret my reluctance to return sooner. We may have gotten here before whatever spell that took Grimm's family was cast. My remorse is for my inability to save Hezekiah in the first place."

She frowned. "Now it is you who is shielding or lying to yourself. Yes, that was in there, but there was another, deeper reason for the remorse."

"I don't know what you're talking about." He grew slightly sullen.

She narrowed her eyes and leaned forward. "I think you do, Viktor; you just don't want to admit it. You touched on it back there with your comment in the carriage. You feel remorse over things like how you abused Paella. There were others, as well."

His color rose, and his eyes blazed emerald fire. He snarled and sat forward to get right in her face. "Yes!" he snarled. "Are you happy now? I've admitted I've been a bastard."

Belle didn't back off. The predator in her would not allow her to show intimidation. She saw the hurt in his eyes. The admission had cost him. She took a deep breath and kept her voice calm and neutral.

"My happiness has nothing to do with this. I just find your remorse confusing." When he drew back and tilted his head at her in his own confusion, she backed off, as well. "You forget, Viktor; I am not human. While I do recognize most human emotions, I don't always understand them. I have felt regret but not remorse."

"How is that possible? They are the same thing."

"No, they are not." She shook her head. "If my actions have adverse consequences for me, I regret them. I feel no remorse if my actions have adverse consequences for someone else but not me. Empathy with one's food doesn't work out so well for a predator."

He scowled. "Paella was not food."

"Still doesn't mean I understand the emotion." She shrugged. "Seems like a waste of energy to me. You need to concentrate on surviving your curse, not whether you hurt someone in the past. What's done is done."

Viktor sighed. "You are right, pet. I've been mopey and maudlin ever since we lost Hezekiah. After our brief stop in Savannah, I'll have Brumble set a course for Hispañola. It is time to face Juma."

"Good."

Viktor kept his shields up until the siren left. Even though he'd let her help him shed his remorse, his thoughts remained morose. He sent the cabin boy to fetch one of the prisoners and bring them to him.

While he waited, he allowed his thoughts to drift back to the slaughter he, Jim, and Belladonna recently wreaked. The memory turned visceral. The scent of blood filled his nostrils. The coppery sweet taste of it filled his mouth and made it water. The silky warmth of it slid down his throat, and gooseflesh rose all over his body.

The memory felt almost as good as the actual act of feeding. It felt almost orgasmic. An unconscious smile spread across his lips. A knock at the cabin door broke his reverie.

"Enter." A bit of irritation colored his tone.

The cabin boy came in with a shackled man shuffling behind him. "Is this one all right, Cap'n? I know you said you didn't care which one."

Viktor nodded. "Thank you. Now get out."

"Cap'n?"

The vampire snarled and bared his fangs. With superhuman speed he crossed the space from his desk to the door and seized his prey. The boy grew pale at the suddenness of it and stumbled back.

Unable to bring the boy's name to mind, Viktor said, "Run!" in a voice more beast than human.

The lad needed no further prodding and fled for his life.

The terrified screams of the vampire's victim soon faded out, barely registering on his consciousness. Throughout the feeding, Viktor reveled in the sensations. If the memory had been wonderful, the real act felt glorious. The prey's initial struggle spurred savage glee. The slowing pound of the man's heart gradually soothed him. The growing coolness of his prey's skin as his warmth entered Viktor's body left him nearly drunk on power.

Through it all, a small part of him noticed that he felt no pain, sorrow, regret, or remorse while he fed. He only felt good. That part wondered if it would be so bad to just give himself over to his monstrosity and relinquish all humanity.

Chapter 8

Not for the last time, Captain Wormsloe wished the Lady Carpathia had kept her pet vampire with her in New Orleans. For the past few months, the creature became nearly impossible to deal with. He'd seriously considered binding it in the bilge hold with silver.

Thankfully, they would make port before nightfall. She could get the bastard back under control. As it stood, he needed to recruit nearly half a crew to replace the ones Westin had drained; probably more than that if as many deserted as he expected would.

He couldn't figure out why Nolan Westin had gone on a feeding frenzy. Countless times during this hunt for Brandee, the Lady sent Westin with him on errands while She stayed in a port on vampire business. Wormsloe never encountered a problem like this with him before. He didn't know if Carpathia was just too distracted to control her Childe or if She had deliberately instructed him to be a murdering ass. He intended to find out, though.

No envoy met them at the docks. Wormsloe immediately knew something was wrong. He'd worked for vampires long enough to know that they strictly followed protocol where a vampire of Carpathia's standing or one of her minions was involved.

With less than an hour to sunset, he made a quick decision regarding Nolan Westin.

"Mr. Borescue!"

"Aye, Captain?" his quartermaster replied.

"Secure Mr. Westin before he can rise. The Lady has sent no one to meet us, and I need to check on our welcome."

"Aye, sir; hopefully She will let us get him off the boat and keep him off."

"Agreed." As an afterthought, Wormsloe added, "You are in charge until I return, or Jeorge sends word of his decision regarding us."

"Be careful, sir."

"Always."

Wormsloe arrived at Jeorge's door without being intercepted, another anomaly which worried him. He started to wonder if something had happened to her ladyship. Even one as old and powerful as She could fall prey to betrayal. He thought the chances of it very slim but possible. He rang the bell with full knowledge that if the New Orleans kiss had turned on Carpathia, even the protection of Her master might not be enough to keep him safe. After all, *He* was on the other side of an ocean.

After what seemed an eternity, someone came to the door. Before the servant could speak, he told him, "I am here to see your master and Lady Carpathia."

The man's expression never changed. He motioned Wormsloe in. He turned and pulled a bell cord once the door was shut. The sound of a bell in the distance echoed faintly in the foyer.

Within seconds, a male vampire appeared in the doorway. Wormsloe recognized him as Jeorge's lieutenant.

"Ah, Captain Wormsloe, we had not received word of your impending arrival. Have you come to collect Milady's trousseau?"

He blinked in surprise at the vampire. "She is ready to leave?"

Anton showed a flicker of confusion before he schooled his face into an impassive mask. "The foyer is not an appropriate setting for this conversation. I have alerted Jeorge to your presence. He wishes you to await him in his study."

"Very well."

He followed Anton through a maze of passageways until they reached an ornate set of double doors. Anton opened one of the doors and ushered him through. He then shut the door behind him and plunged him into darkness.

"Bloody vampires," Wormsloe muttered barely audibly. "They always forget humans can't see in the dark."

A chuckle from the other side of the room presaged the opening of a door and appearance of a lit candle. Unable to suppress his startled jump, Wormsloe squinted his eyes against the sudden brightness of the flame. More candle flames appeared in its wake as it moved about the room.

Finally, his eyes adjusted to see what appeared to be a teenage boy carrying the first candle to various sconces scattered here and there. He knew the boy to truly be an ancient vampire almost as old as Carpathia.

"I apologize for Anton's thoughtlessness, Captain Wormsloe. I fear the confusion your arrival caused left him a bit rattled."

"I didn't intend to cause any confusion, Jeorge. In fact, I'm puzzled by everyone's reactions. Did her Ladyship not alert you about my return?"

Jeorge shook his head. "No. She has not sent us word. I had hoped She would so we could have her things put in order for you to collect and deliver to a place of her choosing. It is my guess She is too preoccupied."

"Where is She? I've had to bind her pet with silver. His feeding has gotten out of hand, and he's taken nearly half my crew. I imagine a good deal of the ones remaining will abandon ship tonight." He realized his tone sounded more demanding than he intended, but his patience and nerves were worn raw.

"She did not send you?"

"I haven't heard from Her since I left Her here."

Jeorge frowned. "And you say her Childe has grown unmanageable. This is very odd. Could Captain Brandewyne be that distracting?"

Wormsloe felt his color rise. "She hasn't killed him yet?"

Jeorge allowed a worried, almost fearful look to cross his face for a moment. "I am not so sure She is capable of killing him."

He gave the vampire a hard look. "She is the second most powerful vampire in the world."

"I know that well, Captain. I also know that Brandewyne is more powerful than I am. She was angry that I did not send word to Her of my knowledge of the pirate. She made a display of power to him and absorbed the life from two of my Children. She tried to do the same to his Childe, Melanie. He shielded the youngling and took no damage to himself."

Wormsloe felt the blood drain from his face. Abstractly, he wondered if he looked as pale as a vampire.

"I see you understand the significance of this. Lady Carpathia is the eldest Childe of our Lord. Only He should be able to shield another vampire from her powers. I believe I understand all too well why She was sent to hunt Brandewyne."

"Do you think he killed Her?"

Jeorge shook his head. "I do not believe so. Given her age, lineage, and power; her death would be felt by vampire kind throughout the world. It is more likely She left with him. Not long after their quarrel, he sent Her word he wished to make peace between them. She accepted his offer and left to meet him. The next day his ship left port. The Lady's presence has not been felt in my territory since."

"How long ago was this?"

"Several months, I should say. The passage of time has little meaning for me, save for how close sunrise is."

"Damnation!" Wormsloe growled. "Do you think you can get some sense out of Westin; or at least get his Hunger under control?"

"This is the youngling She travelled with?"

"Aye, although I wouldn't call him young."

Jeorge laughed, but it held no mirth. "Many would not call me old. The vampire you want help with is not even half a century old yet. I can influence him."

At Jeorge's instruction, Wormsloe ordered the entire remaining crew off the ship and well away from the dock. He told Mr. Borescue to have a small group return after an hour to resume normal duties. Jeorge even helped by placing compulsions on the crewmen to willingly return to the ship when ordered to do so and to not mention anything about vampires to anyone on shore.

"You didn't have to do that; but I appreciate it," Wormsloe told the ancient vampire.

"You are welcome, Captain. It was in my best interests as well as yours. Wild talk of vampires tends to attract those who hunt my kind."

"I see. Shall we go aboard and tend to this?"

"I must graciously decline your invitation to board your ship. Yes, I know it is yours not Hers; I could sense the barrier. However, She would see it as an invasion of Her territory unbidden." Jeorge looked up at him and smiled serenely. "You carry our Lord's protection, Captain Wormsloe. Westin cannot harm you any more than I can. You must remove the silver before I can do anything with him. Just as it binds him, it also protects him from my influence."

He frowned sourly down at the seeming teenager. "Wonderful."

He turned and trudged up the gangplank wishing he had as much confidence in the protection of a being half a world away as Jeorge did. If Westin was turning revenant, could it really keep the vampire from ripping his throat out?

He made his way below deck to the cabinet Westin used for a daytime resting place.

"Captain Wormsloe! I demand you release me at once!"

"Well, at least he sounds coherent," he thought. "Calm yourself; I had to make sure no one else was aboard first. Your Mistress isn't here."

He stepped back barely in time to keep from colliding with Westin in his haste to exit. The vampire burst from the cabinet the second the fine silver chain which had been placed under the edges of the cabinet door was removed.

The vampire rounded on him and stopped just short of grabbing him. Some invisible barrier held him at bay.

"Where is She?"

"Jeorge thinks She may have left with Brandewyne months ago. He is on the dock and wants to speak with you."

Westin got an unreadable expression and looked toward the hatch to the deck. "Very well."

Jeorge drew power from all the members of his kiss in preparation for facing Carpathia's Childe. He knew he probably didn't need that much power to rein the young vampire in, but it gave him peace of mind. There was always the dim chance that She was shielding him.

Finally, Wormsloe returned to the deck with the agitated vampire not far behind.

"Nolan Westin, Childe of Carpathia, heed my command." He let a wave of magic roll out.

The younger vampire grew instantly motionless. His attention centered on Jeorge as if nothing else existed.

Satisfied control was established, Jeorge said, "Come here to me."

Westin obeyed.

"As Captain Wormsloe has informed you, Lady Carpathia is no longer in my territory. It is assumed She left with Captain Brandewyne some months ago as her departure coincides with his. I have not sensed her presence since then, nor have I felt her death. You are her Childe with a more direct link to Her. What have you sensed?"

"I can't reach Her." Westin's voice held a lost and almost panicked tone. "Probably around the same time you say She left here, I rose to sensing nothing from Her. At first, I thought She was merely keeping her privacy; but when She has done that in the past, I could still feel her presence. Now, other than the basic compulsions She placed on me when She made me, it is as if She doesn't exist. I know She is not dead. From everything I've heard from other vampires, a sense of freedom accompanies the loss of one's dam or sire."

Jeorge nodded. "*Oui*, but it is more than that. You see their death. Some weaker vampires die with their sire, because the sire draws on the life force of their Children in an instinctive effort to save themselves."

Westin caught on quickly. "So, She is still alive, for I have not had such an experience."

"I thought as much. Now, Captain Wormsloe informs me that your feeding habits have been excessive. I took the precaution of preventing the remainder of his crew from discussing it here."

"I don't understand. Why would what a human says matter to us?"

Jeorge blinked. He saw the younger vampire clearly didn't understand. "You have never been part of a kiss, have you?"

"No; I have travelled with the Lady or on her bidding since She made me."

"That would explain it. There are still those who hunt our kind. Such talk can and has drawn their attention. Now, why have you been so indiscriminate?" He had a sinking feeling he already knew the answer.

"She always dictated when I could feed and how much."

Wormsloe interrupted, "Are you saying She deliberately had you decimate my crew?"

"No, I mean no control by Her was placed on me. Not knowing when She might impose a fast on me, I indulged myself."

Once again, Jeorge released a wave of power. "You will not do so again. A ship must have a crew to function, you fool. Your indiscretion could have left you stranded at sea at the mercy of the winds and tides. You will apologize to Captain Wormsloe, and you will restrain yourself to one small feeding per night, no more than one victim at a time, and preferably no more than a cupful of blood at a time while you are at sea."

"I have to take him with me?" Wormsloe protested. "What's to keep him from doing as he pleases once we are well away from here?"

"I will not allow him to remain in my territory, captain. I have no way of knowing when or if She will reassert control over him, and I have done nothing to merit such potential observation. Rest assured; my constraint will stand until She reclaims him."

He could see the human captain was not happy with the situation. He imagined he would feel the same in Wormsloe's place. "Captain, since you are under my Lord's protection, it is in my best interest to make good on that promise. My constraint will stand, because I have enough power to make it so."

"Very well, I accept your word on it."

"How long do you need to recruit a fresh crew?"

Wormsloe appeared to think about it for a while before he answered. "Normally, I would only need a couple of days; given how many men I lost this trip, it will take me at least a week. I intend to over-recruit specifically to keep him fed. I will have Mr. Borescue see to restocking our supplies."

Jeorge nodded. "I understand. If I may suggest, gather your able seamen first. At the end of this week, I will deliver a supply of food for Mr. Westin which should last for some time without taxing your provisions too much."

"I appreciate it."

"Come, Nolan Westin; join me in tonight's hunt. You are my guest for this week. Perhaps I may offer you some socialization skills within the vampire community."

"Milady did not see fit to educate me in that," Westin replied. Jeorge could hear the relief in his voice that it was offered now.

Tamara. A. Lowery

Chapter 9

Jeorge managed to hide his disgust at Nolan Westin's lack of knowledge concerning vampire culture. He wondered why Lady Carpathia had neglected her Childe so badly.

On the third night's hunt he learned the answer.

He and Westin perched on a rooftop watching the foot traffic in a section of the French Quarter.

"Jeorge, I want to thank you for including me in your excursions to that *fete* last night. I never knew there was more to my existence than feeding and doing my Lady's bidding. I did not know that lesser vampires did more than prey on humans."

Jeorge turned his attention from potential prey to the vampire beside him. "Why is that?" He figured She wouldn't punish him for asking. He exhibited only curiosity not censure.

"She made me vampire as punishment, and I deserved it. I killed my wife in a fit of rage and abandoned my youngest son. My jealousy over the lies told me about her led me to think she had been unfaithful. Years later, I learned of vampires and convinced myself those memories were false, that a vampire had murdered my family. A priest set me to hunting vampires. It took some time to convince my oldest son; but encounters with new vampires I captured to study swayed him to my path."

Jeorge peered at him hard, a sudden suspicion coming to mind. "Your murdering of the human's crew wasn't just over-indulgence, was it?"

Westin looked sheepish. "No, I apologize for not taking into consideration the predicament my actions would place your kiss in. I did hope to attract the attention of one hunter in particular who has hunted my Lady since the night She took me. Lack of her constraint afforded me the rare opportunity to do so."

"You put me in a difficult position. You are not mine to punish. If you belonged to anyone other than the Lady, I would." He let the anger show in his voice. "Is this hunter your son? Why are you trying to draw him to you? To turn him?"

"Yes, he is my son, Brit. For some reason, the Lady spared him; I think to cull the weak and stupid. My hope is that he will free me from this misery. She will not."

Jeorge suspected Carpathia's motives might be more personal to exact such punishment. "There must be more to it than that. Although I and any other vampire not directly descended from Her make a point to have as little contact as possible, I am all too familiar with her criteria for punishments."

"You have drawn Her ire?"

"Not I; my sire and one of his other Children."

"Thanks to that ill-met priest, I was convinced She was the one who killed my family and went after Her and any other vampire zealously. I did not know the priest had a vendetta against Her specifically. I just knew I wanted to atone for my past actions." Westin sighed. "She was not happy with the attention I drew to Her."

"I can imagine not."

He went back to scanning the crowd. Eventually, he spotted someone stagger out of one of the taverns to relieve himself in the alley. A street whore approached the man. They spoke for a moment and reached an agreement. The man turned the woman to face the wall and lifted her skirts.

Neither human knew what happened.

The two vampires struck with lightning speed.

On the way back to Jeorge's manse, he asked Westin, "Could you feel my presence while you were bound with silver?"

"No; now that I think about it, the times in the past when She was ill with me and had me bound, I could not sense Her just as I cannot now." Westin blinked in realization. "Is it possible She has been bound?"

"Given what I have observed of Captain Brandewyne, I would not rule that possibility out. He has done things I have witnessed which should only be within our Lord's capability."

Westin shook his head. "How is that possible? He would have had to have been barely into manhood when I was made. She is ancient."

Jeorge shrugged. "He claims he was not made; he was cursed by a witch and never felt the First Death's touch. His Childe seems to have developed normally, but he has always been anomalous."

True to his word, Jeorge delivered a small crowd of men to the dock the night before Wormsloe planned to make sail. He looked them over and deemed them to be fit for little else than vampire food. He certainly wouldn't have picked them for his crew.

"Not that I mind, since I won't be putting them to work, but why such a worthless lot?" he asked the vampire Jeorge sent to deliver the humans.

"They are healthy enough. My master deemed them good enough for food but not potential sailors. He said that would help keep you from getting upset over their inevitable deaths," Charlotte answered.

Wormsloe nodded his understanding. "Shrewd of him; each one dead will be one less mouth to feed." He turned and yelled up the gangplank, "Mr. Moran, fetch a couple of the lads to help these gentlemen aboard. They're to be guests of Mr. Westin."

"Right; aye, Cap'n," Moran called back.

Wormsloe turned his attention to the hapless fodder, still in Charlotte's thrall for the moment. "Your attention please, gentlemen; you've been brought here because Mr. Westin has need of your unique services. In a few moments, Mr. Moran will help you aboard and show you to your accommodations."

To a man, they gave him stupefied grins. It almost turned his stomach.

"I am your Captain, Ethan Wormsloe. Please don't dawdle; we sail with the tide."

"Will there be beer?" one of them asked.

"There will be rum."

The man jerked a thumb at Charlotte. "She said there would be beer. I demand beer. I agreed to come because she said there would be beer."

Wormsloe grimaced at Charlotte then looked back at the man. "What is your name, sir?"

"Bert Robards."

"Oh; oh my, I am so sorry. Mr. Westin did have us lay in a small supply of beer. He said it was to be saved for Mr. Robards' use only. I didn't realize he meant you," Wormsloe lied. "He's waiting for you in his cabin to share it and talk over some business particulars."

Robards puffed up like a turkey cock and sneered at his companions. They didn't seem to notice the attitude, nor did they protest over the implied favoritism.

Moran and five sailors arrived to escort the victims aboard.

"I'm to go have a beer and talk business with Mr. Westin," Robards boasted.

Moran looked over to Wormsloe who nodded. He shrugged and said, "Right you are, sir. Just follow me."

Once the group was safely aboard, Wormsloe turned to Charlotte. "Tell your master I thank him for his help and the provisions."

"Of course, Captain. May I commend you on your wisdom just now?"

"He was stupid but strong-willed enough to be a problem. Best to dispose of him now, before he could infect my crew with insubordination."

"*Oui. Bon voyage.*"

"Thank you."

☠

Wormsloe answered the knock at his cabin door. "Enter."

Westin came in but stayed near the door. "Captain."

He frowned at the vampire. "What is it, Mr. Westin?"

"You have some knowledge of Brandewyne; it is why the Master paired you with Lady Carpathia in this hunt."

"Your point?"

"What port is he most likely to visit?"

Wormsloe barked laughter until he saw the vampire did not join in. "You're serious? You might as well ask in what direction the wind will blow."

Westin's smile belied an intelligence often underestimated. "I may not have been a sailor, but I did a fair amount of travel by sea in my human youth, Captain. I'd wager you were but a very young man when I became a vampire hunter, before my fateful encounter with the Lady. Someone with experience can predict what direction the wind will blow with a fair bit of accuracy. I also know that vampires not under the direct control of a sire or master tend to have a home territory they frequently return to. Even sailors have a home port."

He looked at the vampire in a new light. He wondered if She knew her pet's true potential.

"You are correct; anyone with a good weather eye can predict the wind."

"I sense reluctance on your part, Captain. You do know of a port our prey frequents."

Wormsloe began to wish he'd left Westin bound in that cabinet. "I do."

"Why have you never mentioned it to the Lady?"

"She never asked."

"And you chose not to volunteer the information; why? You serve our Lord and Master; why would you impede a hunt He sanctioned?"

Wormsloe sighed. He'd hoped this subject would never come up, although he'd wondered from time to time why Carpathia had never taken this tack in her search for Brandewyne. He'd a feeling Westin would continue to press the subject until he answered. He could lie; but the vampire would know it for a lie. They had an uncanny ability to discover a lie no matter how well it was told.

"I am trying to protect my family. Brandee's home port is my home port. My brother and I were the first victims of his piracy when we were just boys. He took our crab harvest and our boat, leaving us to swim home from the salt marshes. He didn't care if we made it or drowned."

He looked at Westin, careful to avoid his direct gaze, to see if this was sinking in. Satisfied he had the vampire's full attention, he continued, "Over the years, I saw that it hadn't been personal. He really didn't feel one way or the other about us. There was no personal grudge on his part. I also saw how he treated those he did make it personal with. It is not a position I envy."

Westin nodded. "I understand, and I admire your desire to protect your family. The fact remains we have been sent to hunt this vampire down and destroy him. If we destroy him, he will no longer pose a threat to your family. I suggest you set a course for your home port."

He gave the vampire a steely glare. "I think not. I'm not just protecting my family from Brandee; I'm protecting my home from vampires, in general. There is no kiss there. Brandee is the only vampire to visit, and he doesn't hunt there, or I'd have heard of it since he was turned."

He could not read Westin's expression. The vampire remained quiet and still for so long he started to wonder if dawn had come early, and the creature had died for the day. He barely managed to suppress a startled jump when Westin spoke again.

"Very well; if you can provide me with acceptable victims, I give you my word I will not hunt the citizens of your home port."

The vampire leaned forward with lightning speed and grasped his jaw, forcing eye contact. Wormsloe tried to fight off Westin's will but found it stronger than he expected. He didn't fall completely under; but he realized the protection he enjoyed might not be enough if Westin decided to push things.

"You will take me to your home port, Captain Wormsloe. What port is it, by the way?"

"Savannah."

"Ah, Oglethorpe's Folly; I must say, the Georgia colony has prospered despite the general's high ideals from all I've heard. Never had cause to do business that close to the Spaniards when I was still human."

He felt his body relax as the vampire released him from his thrall. "Don't ever do that again."

"Do not defy my Master's wishes, and I won't have to."

"Fine; we will make for Savannah," he grudgingly conceded. "However, we may have to make a detour along the way. We'll have to take a prize or two to keep you fed."

"Agreed."

"I'm surprised you haven't taken this opportunity to break free of Her. You are powerful enough."

He saw true fear in Westin's eyes. "She may be contained, but She is not gone. I will never be powerful enough to protect myself from her wrath if I were to defy Her."

"True; She would probably kill you."

"No, She would not; and that is the true horror of my position. She will never be merciful enough to kill me."

He regarded the vampire for some time. "Have you told Her how powerful you've grown, or would She automatically know as your dam?"

"No to both."

"Have you not told Her because She would punish you that much more?"

"No."

"Then why not?"

Westin grinned. "She never asked."

Tamara. A. Lowery

Chapter 10

Hunting turned out to be particularly sparse west of the Florida Straits; a fact Wormsloe found extremely frustrating. He needed to find a ship and crew to take before Westin exhausted the victims Jeorge sent with them.

Another thing which frustrated him to no end; even if they found a prize, chances were strong it would be a merchant with a small crew. He doubted one crew would be enough to keep Westin from having to hunt in Savannah.

He thought about putting in at St. Augustine on the way up the east coast. The knowledge that the kiss there would be about as welcoming as the New Orleans kiss had been decided him against that plan.

He hoped some sort of ship would show up soon.

"Sails approaching! Starboard side!"

Wormsloe moved to that side and brought the glass to his eye. What he saw made him smile. "Mr. Borescue, run up the mail signal. Helmsman, turn to intercept."

Borescue set the riggers to trim the sails and slow the ship. Wormsloe nodded his approval. "Good thinking; we don't want to spook them."

"Aye, Captain; we need to capture as many alive as possible," He paused in thought. "I wonder what her cargo is."

Wormsloe chuckled, a disturbingly mirthless sound. "I recognize her trade flag. She's a Faraday ship; a slaver. Judging by how low she rides; I'd say most of her cargo is intact."

Borescue and every sailor within hearing distance visibly relaxed. They knew they would not fall to the vampire's Hunger.

The two ships tied alongside each other shortly before dusk. Wormsloe figured he could keep the captain of the slave ship occupied long enough for Westin to rise. He didn't worry about getting word of his plans to the vampire. Even he could smell the pungent effluvia from the other ship's cargo holds; he imagined Westin would pick up on the scent once he was up for the night.

"Hoy *Lorelei*, what news have ye?"

"Much; what port are you bound for, *Sea Breeze*?"

"Havana then New Orleans."

"Permission to come aboard?" Wormsloe asked the other captain. "I've a bottle of fine cognac we could share while we trade mail."

"Granted." The slave ship captain smiled at the prospect of a good drink, meaning anything besides grog.

"You might want to avoid New Orleans. There've been reports of plague in the northern territories and fear it may reach the city before long." The lie came easily to Wormsloe's lips; he'd used similar falsehoods frequently since he'd entered the vampires' employ. "You'd do well to just sell your whole cargo in Havana; the cane growers always need extra hands."

The other captain gave him an odd look. "I would ask how you knew this was a slave ship; but I imagine you can smell the buggers."

"Aye; I'd wager a good portion of them are young bucks. They tend to be more pungent."

"That they are. They bring a good price, though; young, strong, maybe a good decade or two of work in them. I'm afraid I'll have to risk New Orleans. I am under contract with a procurer there."

Wormsloe frowned as if in thought. "You sail for the Faradays?" The other man nodded. "I've heard their business has fallen off lately."

"Not so as I've noticed. We did lose a couple of ships a while back, though."

"Oh?"

"Aye; they alternated between Faraday and Brumble & Sons. Word has it old Tobias Brumble has been targeted by Bloody Vik Brandee. Bastard damn near ruined the man; took both his sons, takes every B&S ship he comes across, there's even a rumor he took old Brumble's daughter." The slave captain glanced around, leaned in, and in a conspiratorial whisper said, "Faraday broke off business with Brumble over that. Some of the horror stories of what Brandee does to the crews he takes would make your blood run cold."

Fresh information about Brandee had always been hard to come by; a testament to the fear of the pirate. He leaned in and asked, "Which stories are those?"

"Some say he and his crew have turned cannibal; others say he bleeds his prisoners out and uses the blood for demonic purposes."

"What about him drinking the blood; have you heard that one?"

"Aye, but I don't believe it. The ones who say that also say he feeds the bloodless corpses to some she-devil of a sea monster that travels with him." The slaver made a derisive snort. "I've met some monstrous people in my line of work, but I've never seen any monsters or bogeymen. You ask me, it's all scare tactics and a play on the superstitions of fools."

"Just so," Wormsloe said with a sinister smile. "Still, superstitions came to be for good reasons."

"You mean you believe that bilge?"

Wormsloe allowed the smile to spread to a grin. Full dark had arrived while they'd talked. "I work for monsters, real ones. Mr. Westin, will you join us?"

Westin seemed to materialize beside him, he arrived with such speed. The slaver captain was startled by the vampire's sudden appearance.

"You've done well, Captain Wormsloe. The cargo of this vessel should be more than sufficient to keep me from having to hunt in your home port."

"I thought you'd be happy," he replied. "I just ask that you spare the crew for the time being. I've already gotten more information about our prey from this man than in any of the ports She stopped in."

"You hunt Bloody Brandee? You're a madman!" the slaver captain said, obviously not processing the true danger.

Westin grinned toothsomely. "I think I can manage him."

Just as suddenly as he'd appeared he vanished with only wind to mark his passage. Seconds later, screams of the slaves chained below deck filled the air.

"Sails to starboard!" Sniff called from the crow's nest of the *Incubus* shortly after sunset. The sky still held a reddish glow in the west.

"Jim, set course for them. Their sails are reefed, so little chance of them running," Vik ordered.

"Aye, Cap'n; could do with a fresh feed."

"My thoughts exactly."

In truth, Viktor didn't care if he fed or not; but he had Jim's and his cadre's needs to think of. The two ships sighted would provide fresh blood for the vampires.

Soon, screams and the unmistakable scent of fresh blood reached him on the breeze.

"Belle, pet."

The siren strolled over with an anticipatory smile.

"We need to reach those ships quickly."

Without further prompting, she turned and leapt down to the quarterdeck, up to the fo'c's'le, and ran out on the bowsprit. She began to sing softly.

"Why so quiet, pet?" Viktor asked through their mental bond.

"I smell vampire, and I can read the name of the smaller ship from here. It's the Lorelei."

He had to remind himself Carpathia no longer posed an issue for him. He'd forgotten about the lesser vampire who travelled with her; easy to do since he'd never met him.

Belle must have picked up on his mood. *"You contained and neutralized her. Thanks to Gloribeau's magic, she can never be freed."*

"I know, pet. Hezekiah sealed the bottle; only he could've opened it." He felt her chagrin at inadvertently reminding him of the loss of the Reaper. *"Men die in our line of work, pet. I honestly don't understand why his death has cut me so deeply."*

"I think I do. You don't let people get close to you, a good trait for a predator. Hezekiah got past those barriers," she opined.

He thought about it and found no argument against the theory.

With the siren's weather witching, they soon came within range of the two ships. As an added precaution, Viktor ordered all the lamps shuttered. As a result, no lookout spotted the *Incubus* as she glided up to her prey silently.

At a mental command from their captain, the pirates quickly and quietly swarmed first the *Lorelei* then the larger slave ship. Viktor and Jim flew over to the slaver and landed on either side of Wormsloe and the other captain.

"Hello, Wormy," Vik said with a grin.

"Bugger," Wormsloe responded.

"Nice of you to offer, but you're not my type." He looked about and sniffed the air. "Mr. Rigger, please stop Wormy's passenger from eating all the cargo."

He noticed the odd look Wormsloe gave his first mate. "You look like you just saw a ghost, man."

"The resemblance between him and the Lady's lackey is uncanny. He mentioned once, I think, that he had a son who'd hunted vampires with him when he'd been human."

Viktor raised an eyebrow. "What is his name? Thia never saw fit to introduce him."

"Westin."

"Oh, this should prove interesting. The son he mentioned is still alive. Jim is the one he abandoned as a child."

Wormsloe narrowed his eyes. "Speaking of the Lady, Jeorge assumed she left with you. He had to help me get this bastard under control. I lost over half my crew to him because She wasn't keeping him in check."

"She — is contained," he replied with a chilly tone.

"Contained how, silver? You know that anyone within the sound of Her voice could easily be swayed to free Her. I know from past experience."

"Trust me, Wormy, She won't be getting out — ever. Only the Reaper could open her prison, and he is no more. The magic that sealed her in will not release for anyone else, not even me." He surveyed the new situation and saw his men in place. "I think I'll go below and see how Jim is faring. Don't go anywhere while I'm gone."

Jim followed the scent of blood and shit to the other vampire. The man had a young slave clasped to him with his back to the hatchway. Something about his scent struck a familiar chord.

"That's enough, mate. Cap'n said not to let you eat all the cargo."

The vampire turned with a snarl and dropped the nearly drained slave. "Who —?"

The two vampires stood and stared at each other in shock and disbelief. Jim saw an older version of his brother but knew it not to be him. Britt was just as much a part of him as he was of Viktor.

It had to be his erstwhile father; the man he only barely remembered after overhearing his brother's tale of the death of their mother.

"Britt?" The older vampire's face crumpled as he said the name. "Oh God, I never wanted you to suffer this fate."

Jim felt his expression grow stony. Warm rage flooded through him.

"Fuck what you wanted, old man." His voice came out as a growl. "You can't even tell your own damned sons apart."

"What?"

"I'm Jim."

"Jim? That's not possible. Jim died as a child."

He shook his head; one slow turn to the left and another to the right. "I survived; no thanks to you — Father."

Westin just stood there.

"You murdered my mother!" Jim screamed at him. He winced but did not speak. Pain and guilt shone in his eyes. "Say something, damn you!"

"You are right. I listened to another man's lies and believed them. I only intended to abandon the two of you. I did not mean to kill her; but I did, and I abandoned you to starve." He sounded remorseful; but he didn't beg for forgiveness. "The Lady has reminded me nightly of my sins and punished me accordingly. Suffering at Her hand is my lot."

"Not anymore," a voice said from behind them. Jim recognized Viktor's voice and scent immediately.

"Who?" Westin asked, obviously surprised by Viktor's appearance.

"For a vampire, you are not very observant, Mr. Westin," Vik said. "Viktor Brandewyne at your service; I believe you've already met my first mate. As for the Lady, She has been contained — permanently."

"You have my gratitude for that; but I am still bound by Her sire's directive to kill you."

Jim held up a hand. "We aren't done yet, old man; and you'd have to go through me to get to the Cap'n anyway."

Westin sighed. "Then let us do what we must. Either I will free you from this hell, or you will free me, son."

Jim bared his fangs in a feral snarl. "Before we start, tell me one thing."

"What?"

"What was her name?"

Westin blinked. "Whose name?"

"My mother. What. Was. Her. Name?"

"Beaulah."

"Thank you."

The two flew at each other.

Westin's moves revealed he had little combat skill. Jim's disgust grew. It didn't take him long to put his father on the defensive. He wrapped his legs around the man's arms from behind and pinned them to his sides. The two thudded to the deck on top of Westin's victims.

"You deserve to die for what you did," he snarled in his father's ear.

"Do it now." He heard the sincerity in his father's plea.

"Gladly."

He grasped the man's head and wrenched it to the side sharply. Bones crackled. Tissues resisted; then the spine and windpipe gave way. He kept turning until the face looked up at him. Unlife still shone in the eyes.

He spat in the face and wrenched the neck again. He continued to twist until he heard flesh tear. He dug his fingers into the neck and pulled in opposite directions.

Nolan Westin's head ripped from his body, and the light in his eyes died.

Jim stood, his father's head dangling from his grip, and faced his captain. He found understanding rather than condemnation there.

Chapter 11

Viktor and Jim returned to the main deck. The first mate still carried Westin's head by the hair.

Wormsloe's eyes fixed on it right away.

"Mr. Bland!" Viktor called out.

"Aye, Cap'n," the boson replied.

"Take a few lads below and fetch the dead up to toss over the side: the usual protocol. You'll find one without a head and decomposing quickly."

Bland made a face but nodded his understanding. He went off in search of men who could be spared for the duty.

Wormsloe looked a little green around the gills. Windpipe, some spine, and other gobbets stuck out of the torn flesh of Westin's neck. Unlike the body soon brought up on deck for disposal, the head showed no signs of decay. Clothing seemed all that held the putrid corpse in some semblance of human form.

"How are they able to touch that without emptying their stomachs?" he asked Viktor.

"I'm blocking the worst of it from their minds." Vik looked around and came to a decision.

"With your passenger dead, you really have no need for this cargo now. How about I take it off your hands?"

Wormsloe frowned at him. "What else do you plan to relieve me of, Brandee?"

Vik smiled at him. "You don't have anything else I need, Wormy. As I recall, you've always claimed I owe you a boat. You can keep this one." His smile grew wry at the look on the other man's face. "I keep telling you all you and your brother had to do was give me the crabs. If you had, I would've left you your boat."

Wormsloe sputtered, "What in the bloody hell would I want with a slave ship, man?"

Vik raised an eyebrow at him. "How long has it been since you've careened the *Lorelei*?"

That stopped the man mid-sputter. A look of consternation and realization crossed his face.

Vik nodded knowingly. "She may stink, but this ship is a damn sight more seaworthy than yours. She just needs a good mucking out. I'm guessing Thia didn't allow you much time to properly maintain your ship."

Wormsloe sighed. "No, She didn't." He looked around and up at the state of the slave vessel and its rigging. "This is a newer design than the *Lorelei*. I've not enough crew to sail her, though."

Vik clapped the man on the shoulder. "Not to worry, Wormy; I only intend to take the cargo, as I already said. You can have the ship, its supplies and provisions, and even its crew. I've no need of them at the moment."

"A moment, sir! I am commander of this vessel!"

Viktor and Wormsloe turned to the forgotten captain of the slave ship. The man gulped but stood his ground.

"I am under contract with the Faradays to deliver my cargo to Havana and New Orleans. You will not take them!"

"He doesn't know," Vik stated.

"We never got around to introductions," Wormsloe replied.

"Allow me." He turned to the slaver. "The gentleman who stopped you is Ethan Wormsloe, a man I've known since childhood and from whom I took my first prize. I — am Captain Viktor Brandewyne, at your service sir."

The man blanched. I a-am P-p-p-preston F-f-f-...."

Viktor cut him off. "Your name isn't important. You don't need another captain hanging about do you, Wormy?"

"His value to me vanished the moment you arrived."

"Good; I haven't fed tonight, and those below need to be washed."

Without further preamble, Viktor moved behind his victim with lightning speed. He yanked the man's head back and tore into his throat with ravenous ferocity. The man kicked and screamed. This prompted the vampire to snap the man's neck.

He finished feeding in relative peace and dropped the bloodless corpse to the deck.

"Ah, I feel better now." He wiped his mouth with the back of his hand and licked it clean. "Sanctimonious bastard always leaves a nice aftertaste."

Wormsloe looked a little ashen. Viktor noticed. "Don't tell me you have no stomach for that, Wormy. How long have you been ferrying Thia around?"

"Too long," Wormsloe sighed. "She was a little more discreet about feeding habits than that; so, I rarely witnessed it." He gave Vik a questioning look but carefully avoided eye contact. "Is she really contained permanently?"

"She is. I couldn't free Her even if I wanted to. Would you like to see Her prison?"

"Yes, I think I would."

Vik nodded. He moved with inhuman speed to his cabin and fetched the bottle containing the ancient vampires. Just as quickly, he returned to the deck of the *Sea Breeze*.

"She's in this."

Wormsloe eyed the vessel dubiously. "How?"

In answer, Vik summoned Jim. "Mr. Rigger, find me an empty bottle."

"Aye, Cap'n." The first mate left on his quest.

Viktor turned back to Wormsloe. "I'll wager Thia's cabin has a hidden compartment with no door."

"How did you know?"

"I have good sources of information." Belladonna told him about the interior of Carpathia's cabin. When she retrieved Viktor's son, Robert, a few years ago she tried to find the vampire's hidey-hole without success. "I also know that some vampires can change forms and even take on the shape of mist to slip through wall cracks. Ah, thank you Mr. Rigger."

He took the bottle from his first mate and uncorked it. The unmistakable aroma of gin wafted up to him, and he made a face. "Gah! Where did you find this?"

Jim grinned. "Jon-Jon always has empties lying about."

Viktor grimaced. "Nasty shit, gin. Wormy has doubts about Thia's imprisonment; I'd like to give him a demonstration of how we could have her trapped in this bottle." He indicated the clay-covered vessel he'd tied to his belt.

"Just promise to let me back out is all I ask, Cap'n."

Vik laughed. "My word, Jim."

Without further comment, the first mate turned amorphous. The resulting dark mist siphoned into the empty gin bottle, and Viktor popped the cork back in. Jim's face formed in the mist and quickly dissolved again.

"Convinced?"

Wormsloe nodded. "I cede it is possible, and I cannot imagine why you would lie about Her being in that bottle. I don't see how it can contain Her if She doesn't want to be contained, though. How did you keep Her in there once you tricked Her in?"

"The bottle is silver lined; the cork is sheathed in silver. You can see the silver where the writing is scratched through the bayou mud."

"Cap'n." The muffled voice came from the gin bottle followed by a light tapping.

Vik chuckled and a wicked grin crossed his face. He uncorked the gin bottle and released his first mate. The mist soon solidified into a large black cat.

Lazarus shook gin droplets out of his fur, sat down on his clothes, and began to groom himself.

"You are full of surprises, Brandee. How is it I cannot hear Her demands for release? I heard your — man plainly enough."

Viktor shrugged. "I think Gloribeau's spell may have something to do with it. I could hear Her faintly until Glory dipped the bottle in the bayou muck and spoke her words over it. Haven't heard a peep since."

"May I?" Wormsloe held out a hand for Carpathia's prison.

Viktor eyed him with caution. He had a feeling he knew what the man planned to do. Finally, he handed over the clay-encased bottle. Glory's magic made it unbreakable.

Wormsloe turned the bottle over and examined it from every possible angle. Without warning, he shrugged and flung it into the dark seawater. "No offense, Brandee; but I don't want to take the chance of anyone ever freeing that bitch. She would take out Her failure on my crew."

"Her — failure; ah, you must mean Her mission to kill me." Viktor felt his smile turn far from friendly. "Do you intend to attempt to complete that mission, Wormy?"

Wormsloe laughed harshly. "Ha! No, I am but a humble transport, Brandee. At the onset, I told Her she should pray we never found you. Her master would not have tasked me with your death. I am only human."

"And if he had?"

"I would have told him to go fuck himself. It would have been a quicker form of suicide that trying to kill you."

Vik clapped him on the shoulder. "You are a smart man, Ethan. The lads should be done offloading the cargo before dawn. Enjoy your new boat."

Vik raised an eyebrow at the bottle on his desk. He noticed the charts and logbook stacked away from it and the sodden cloth under it. A glance at the deck showed residual prints of feet too small to belong to any of his men.

"Why did you bring it back?" he asked the siren through their bond.

"You may need it as a bargaining chip in the future," she responded in kind. *"If her master cared enough to send a hunter as powerful as her, he'll send more when he realizes he's lost contact with her. He may even come after you personally. Any advantage you can get in that situation is not to be squandered."*

"I see your point, Belle. Thank you."

Tamara. A. Lowery

Chapter 12

Samantha woke in a cold sweat, her heart racing. She looked about the cabin, disoriented and unsure of what woke her.

Beside her, Britt cried out and thrashed in his sleep. His face, neck, and chest glistened in the moonlight from the open porthole. She took a cloth and mopped the sweat from her husband.

He woke with a start and grabbed her wrist. "What are you doing?" Fearful wariness colored his voice. His grip bit into her flesh. She knew it would leave marks.

As sweaty as she felt, she knew she could break the hold easily, but she didn't. He intended no malice; she'd startled him.

She kept her voice low and calm. "Easy, husband; the heat has us pouring water. I woke from a disturbing dream and thought I'd dry you off."

"Sam?" He let go of her wrist and cupped her face. "Oh love, I didn't mean to hurt you. I am so sorry." He pulled his hand back and put the back of it to her forehead. "You're soaked to the skin! Are you ill?"

She laughed at his sudden concern. "It's just the humidity and weird dreams, silly man. I'm no more sweaty than you are. Speaking of dreams, you looked like you were having a nightmare a few moments ago."

"I was." He nodded. "I doubt I'll be able to get back to sleep now. What hour is it?"

She shrugged. "I don't own a time piece, and I don't think it wise to disturb Captain Bainbridge just to ask the time." She began to towel off her own sweat. "As hot as it is, I wouldn't mind asking him to rig a bathing sail in the morning, before the sun gets too high."

"How often have you used one?"

Sam detected a note of jealousy in her husband's voice and knew the cause of it. "A few times; don't worry Britt; the Captain insists the men keep their pants on. I sponged off in the cabin boy's closet when I was still hiding my identity from the crew."

"Still, I don't like the idea of other men seeing you so exposed. Wet clothing is very revealing."

"Which is why I didn't back when the crew thought me male. Trust me, Britt," she felt irritation creep into her voice, "Captain Bainbridge and his mates make sure the crew treats me with all due respect. Any man who doesn't finds himself restricted and put ashore at the next port."

"But you are a married woman now, love. It just wouldn't be seemly," he foolishly argued.

"And being a woman on a quest to rescue my brothers from a notorious pirate who may also be a vampire is?" She glared at him not caring that the pale moonlight muted the effect.

"Well, um —." He trailed off, realizing he'd done the one thing he'd promised he wouldn't. "Oh, Sam, I am so sorry. I must sound like a possessive, controlling brute. Please forgive me."

Sam softened. "At least you realized what you did. I love you, Britt; but I also enjoy my freedom. Please don't ever ask me to give it up."

"I will try my best not to, love. However, I cannot help but feel protective of you."

"And I love you for that; I just ask that you trust me and my judgement. I am not so stubborn as to not ask for help or protection if I need it."

"Agreed." He sat up and pulled a shirt over his head. Sam gave him a puzzled look. "What say we head topside and cool off? It feels too stuffy in here."

"I like the sound of that." She joined him in getting dressed.

Sam found the night sea breeze refreshing. Stars glittered, and a waxing crescent moon shone down. She and Britt traversed the deck carefully to where one of the long boats sat lashed in. Neither had brought a light, and the deck of a ship held dangers even in daylight. A careless step could easily end in broken bones.

They sat on the upturned long boat's hull and enjoyed the night for the moment.

Finally, Britt broke the companionable silence. "You say your dream woke you. Do you remember what it was?"

"Bits and pieces, mostly; I'm not sure if I can make sense of it, but I'll try. It did leave me with the sense I should discuss it with you." She sighed and concentrated on the fleeting but vivid images.

"I was in a dark, smelly place. There seemed to be a lot of people, but I couldn't see them clearly; more like just their eyes with lots of white showing around the pupils. They screamed and cried. I knew they were afraid, but they were prevented from running away. A few dark forms lay on the deck, dead or close to it. In the middle of this, two men were fighting furiously." She stopped and looked at her husband. "Britt, they both looked much like you."

He didn't say anything. She couldn't see his face well enough to read his expression, but something told her this dream troubled him as much as it did her.

"Britt?"

His voice came out as a hoarse, fearful whisper. "I had the same dream."

"What?"

"I had the same dream; two men fighting who looked like me but not like me, surrounded by darkness and eyes." He stopped and gazed at her. "Did you see the end of the fight?"

"No; I woke almost as soon as I got some sense of recognition of the men."

"Good." He clasped her to him and stroked her hair. "It was horrible." She felt his body tremble.

"Do you want to tell me about it?"

"No; it is best you don't know."

Sam went stiff in his arms.

"What is it, love?" he asked.

"More of the dream just came back to me."

"Oh God; you did see the end."

"No; it's strange. I just remembered the younger version of you more clearly. The other was older than you. Everything seemed to stop in time. The younger man turned and looked at me. He said 'I'm sorry Samantha; I didn't mean for you to see this. Look in Tortuga,' and then he shoved me back, and I woke up."

"I don't like this, Sam. It smacks of vampire mind control."

She nodded. "I agree. From all you've told me of the phenomenon, it does; however, when and where would we have encountered the same vampire?"

They sat in silence and pondered the question for a while.

Sam broke the silence first. "Assuming that one of the figures in the dream is a vampire, which one is it? I know your father is one, and the strong resemblance points to the older man being him. The thing is, I've never seen that man before. I did, however, recognize the younger one who spoke to me."

"The older one definitely was my father. I assume the younger one is the nighttime visitor you originally mistook me for; the one who ravished you then vanished from the ship." Britt rubbed the back of his neck. "I admit the resemblance is uncanny; but I have never encountered him before."

Even in the poor light, she saw the anguish on his face. "Some deep part of me wants to say he is my little brother, Jimmy; but that's not possible. He was murdered along with my mother."

"Is it possible he was turned?"

Britt shook his head. "Very doubtful; it is rare for them to turn a child, because they will remain in that child's body until destroyed. The dead do not age, Sam. That couldn't have been Jimmy."

She hugged him from the side. He put an arm around her shoulder and cradled her against him.

"I won't tell you how the fight ended, but I was told to look in Tortuga, as well. I think we ought to discuss this with the captain in the morning."

"I agree."

"Well, you two are up bright and early," George Bainbridge said by way of greeting. "Please, join me for breakfast." He waved the young couple into his cabin. "Hoy, Petey; fetch two more breakfasts for Mr. and Mrs. Westin."

"Aye, Cap'n."

"Thank you, Captain Bainbridge," Britt said for both of them. "We have something we'd like to discuss with you after breakfast."

Bainbridge gave them a calculating look. Concern soon crept into his expression. "Are you sure we shouldn't discuss this now? You both look like you pulled night watch; and given your expressions, I doubt those wee hours were spent in pleasurable activities."

Sam shook her head. "I think we need food first, Captain. It will provide a buffer."

"Very well, Samantha."

Petey brought in a large, covered tray from the galley. The cabin boy lifted the lid to reveal bread, bean porridge, and a jug of cider.

The trio ate in companionable silence.

As Petey cleared away the dishes, Bainbridge put his elbows on the table, folded his hands together, and rested his chin on the prop he'd made. He fixed the young couple with a stern but curious stare.

"Now then, what is the issue which has kept the two of you from sleep? I hope you haven't been quarreling."

Britt grimaced and said, "Well, we did a little; but Sam convinced me of my error."

Bainbridge raised an eyebrow. "What did you quarrel over?"

"Whether or not I should make use of a bathing sail along with the crew; that is not why we were up half the night, though," Sam answered.

The Captain's eyes sparkled with amusement, but he kept his silence on the subject of their contention. Instead, he addressed the issue of their lack of sleep. "May I ask why, then?"

Britt sighed and squared his shoulders. "This will probably sound like we've both gone mad…," he began.

"Mr. Westin, we're all mad here; this was established some time ago," Bainbridge interrupted.

Britt blinked at him then continued, "Sam and I shared a dream, although she woke from it earlier than I did. The upshot of the dream is that we believe we need to sail for Tortuga."

"Tortuga; I have to ask what this dream entailed. You say you both had the same dream?"

"We did," Sam replied. "It was very odd. I was forced out of it by one of the men we dreamed about. We believe the other man may be Britt's father."

"And the one who forced you out?"

"He was the same man I initially mistook Britt for, the one we could never find. Just before I woke, he said to look in Tortuga."

Bainbridge frowned and looked at Britt. "Sam, would you mind if I spoke with your husband alone for a moment?"

Britt added, "Yes please, love. I need to speak with Captain Bainbridge about the rest of it, but I don't want to burden you with it. It is far too disturbing."

She frowned but nodded. "Very well, but I don't like it. I'm your wife. It is my duty to help you bear your burdens."

"Just this once, Love; please."

"All right." She rose and left the cabin.

Once the door shut behind her, Bainbridge spoke in a low tone. "I had hoped she wouldn't have a relapse of this illness."

"Sir?"

"I saw how flushed she was. The first time she dreamed of that man she'd been ill and weak for two days. She has also suffered serious head trauma more than once. Such has been known to cause unpredictable bouts of madness in otherwise healthy individuals." He sighed and looked Britt in the eyes. "I understand and applaud your desire to offer your wife moral support, Mr. Westin, but I question the wisdom of supporting her in this particular delusion."

Britt remained silent for a few moments. Part of him wanted to be angry at the captain's stance; he repressed that. Years of hunting the creatures few people believed in anymore taught him how to deal with this kind of rational doubt.

"I appreciate your concern, Captain Bainbridge. I know you think of Sam as a daughter; I also know about the bouts of fever and the concussions. She has kept nothing from me. The dream is all too real, however."

"You really did have the same dream?"

Britt nodded. "Sam woke me from the nightmare —."

"Nightmare; she said nothing of that."

"She didn't see the end of the dream or the detail I did. I hadn't intended to tell her about the dream. She said she'd woken from a disturbing dream, and I asked her about it. My blood ran cold when she described my own dream perfectly. I'm just grateful she didn't experience the clarity I did."

Bainbridge stood and got a decanter and two glasses out of his liquor cabinet. "I've a feeling we'll need this. As wild and improbable as your account sounds, I have no real reason to doubt it. I must remember some of the impossible and outlandish things we've encountered since Samantha started this quest."

He set the glasses down, pulled the stopper on the decanter, and poured them both heavy shots of scotch, his drink of preference.

"Thank you." Britt took a gulp before he continued. "I saw the vampire which was once my father fighting another man, the man Sam says she dreamed ravished her. The fight was in the hold of a slave ship. I have to assume the other combatant was also a vampire. He literally wrung my father's head off. He held it by the hair and told me to look in Tortuga; then Sam woke me."

Bainbridge picked up his glass, sniffed it, eyed it, extended his arm fully, brought it back, and chugged the entire contents. He held his breath for a moment. When he started to speak, his voice came out strangled, and he started over.

"I do recall Samantha saying this man promised to help her find Brandee. It is said he is a vampire now." He sighed. "Tortuga is as good a place as any to hunt for a pirate. I just hope this isn't a trap."

"As do I," Britt agreed and finished off his scotch.

Chapter 13

Jim rapped at the door of the captain's cabin.

"Enter."

Viktor sat at his desk, a bottle of blood-brandy in front of him and a glass in his hand. "Grab a glass, Jim, and have a seat."

He grabbed a glass from the cupboard and hooked a stool over to the other side of the desk. "I've a favor to ask, Vik."

"Thought you seemed a bit agitated. What is it?"

"Do we have time to stop in Tortuga?"

Vik looked at him over the rim of the glass and quirked up one corner of his mouth. "What is so pressing in Tortuga?"

"I've sent for Samantha and Britt. Her brothers haven't met her husband yet, and I want to tell him in person about our father's fate."

"Didn't you say he hunts vampires?"

"Aye, but I've bitten him. I can keep him in line." He gave his captain his most earnest expression.

Viktor finished his glass and poured a second one. "This really is important to you, isn't it?"

"I hate to admit it, but yes. I've seen how the loss of Grimm has hurt you. Hell, it's hurt me, as well."

"Your point?"

"Vik, you've always been a brother to me; you know that. I grew up as an orphan. Now I know I have blood kin. He grew up believing our father's lies thinking your Carpathia murdered our mother and me. He deserves to know the truth." He sighed and scratched the back of his head with a wry chuckle. "Never would've figured me for such a sentimental fool."

Viktor sat and watched him in silence for quite a while. Because of him being Jim's sire, Jim knew the Captain wasn't angry with him. Had he still been human he would've been worried by this point. Prolonged silence from Viktor normally did not bode well for someone.

"If you think it would take too long to wait for them, we can take care of it after you deal with that bitch who cursed you," he said to break the silence.

"No, this should be done before. We've no idea how things will turn out with Juma, nor how long they will take."

"Do what before?" Belle asked.

"What have I said about knocking?"

"Do I look like I care? What excuse are you employing to delay going to her now?" The siren refused to be distracted.

He glared at her.

Jim fought the urge to ease toward the door. He knew Vik could defend himself; but he owed the man his loyalty.

Finally, Viktor answered. "Jim has summoned his brother and sister-in-law to Tortuga to deal with some family business. We are going to put in there and await their arrival."

"Absolutely not!" Belle protested. "You know as well as I do your time is running short. Viktor, I am well aware of how bad your Hunger has grown."

"I am in full control of my Hunger, Belladonna."

In an effort to ease the sudden tension, Jim interjected, "Mother, Father, please don't fight; it upsets me so."

The vampire and the siren turned their glares toward him, and he began to reconsider his actions.

"Cap'n, I already said it can wait until we're through with Juma."

"And I said it can't."

"Why not?" Belle demanded.

Viktor sighed. "I don't have Hezekiah anymore to help keep me grounded. You and Jim are the only ones left strong enough to defy me and help me keep myself in check, even though you're both bound to my will."

Belle put her hands on her hips. "Yet you refuse to heed our counsel."

He held up a hand to forestall further tirade. "Yes; I need you both focused. As long as this hangs over Jim's head it will be in the back of his mind distracting him."

"Fine." She turned to the first mate. "Do you have any idea where they are right now?"

"Just north of Cartagena."

"Just north — by the Abyss! Do you know how long it will take them to get to Tortuga?" She threw her hands up in exasperation.

"Pet, it won't take so long if you find them and give them favorable winds and currents." Viktor's suggestion was just shy of an order.

She made a grumpy sound but headed up to the deck.

Once they heard her enter the water, Viktor looked at him and said, "She is right about my Hunger; it has gotten much stronger."

"I've noticed, Vik." He held up his glass. Candlelight glinted off the cut crystal but did not penetrate the liquid within. "This batch barely has enough liquor to keep the blood from clotting."

"It keeps the edge off. I know we have a hold full of slaves to keep us supplied, but I will not allow myself to feed directly."

Jim frowned. His Captain's logic escaped him. "Why not?"

"Remember back when Hezekiah had a problem with opium?"

"Aye; if it's been anyone else on the crew, you would've killed him."

"Blood is becoming my opium. The Hunger is like a constant buzz or annoying itch. It is an effort to remain lucid between feedings. The blood-brandy mixture mutes it to bearable levels and allows me to function. Only through direct feeding can I silence it at all." Vik took another sip.

"I'm still not seeing the problem," Jim said.

"If I start, I won't stop until there is no one left to drain, Jim. That is how bad it has gotten — and I want so badly to silence it."

"Damn, Vik; I wish I'd never brought up Tortuga. Call Belle back and let's go on to Juma. My business with Sam and Britt can wait; it isn't worth you risking yourself or the crew."

Viktor shook his head. "No, Jim; I meant what I said about needing you focused when we face her. Remember, she has power over the dead. I don't want to risk her trying to use you against me like Venoma used Belle."

"Oh, I had forgotten about that. She sent zombies after you; nasty buggers."

"Aye."

They drank for a while in silence.

A thought occurred to Jim. "Say Vik, do you still wear the Elder's Stone?"

"I do. I see what you're driving at, old friend. It should be proof against her magic; it has worked against all the other Sisters. You will have to stick close, though."

"Not a problem."

"Still," Vik said after a while, "I'm glad you wanted to stop in Tortuga. It will give me a chance to get news of the Royal Navy's activities in the area; especially around Hispañola."

Jim just looked at him. He detected a faint trace of fear in his Captain's scent; it was so alien it was like a slap in the face. He knew the cause wasn't the bloody Royal Navy.

"You're afraid of her?"

The question caught Viktor off guard. "What?"

"I can smell it on you, Vik. You are afraid of Juma."

The Captain's shoulders slumped. "It's driving me mad, Jim. I just don't understand it. None of the other Sisters have caused me to dread them."

Jim crossed his arms and tilted his head; sudden insight onto his Captain's psyche occurred to him. "I think I know why."

"By all means, enlighten me," Vik grumbled irritably.

"You like being a vampire."

Viktor crossed his arms in turn and leaned back. "What does that have to do with my irrational fear of Juma?"

"Simple; you're a vampire because of her curse. When you finish with her, everything will change. She may remove the curse just to weaken you and try to kill you. She may just use her zombies to overpower you and kill you. Or you will defeat her, take the Sisters' magic and Juma's ashes back to Celie and have the curse lifted. Regardless of how it plays out, you will either be dead or no longer a vampire once it's over."

"Hmph; to be honest, I hadn't thought of that, although I've known it in the back of my mind for quite a while." Vik seemed genuinely surprised by his assessment. "Of course, it begs the question of what will become of you and the cadre once I become human again. Will you continue on as vampires? Will you die and instantly rot without my vampiric powers in place? I hate the thought of losing you too, Jim."

"I don't particularly fancy it myself." He gave Vik his best disarming grin, but he had not considered that possibility. "The sacrifice will be worth it for you to be free, brother. If by some chance we continue as vampires, I give you my word the cadre will stay loyal to you. Any sign of disobedience and I'll kill the man myself."

Vik rewarded him with a warm smile. "Let's hope it doesn't come to that."

"Agreed."

Tamara. A. Lowery

Chapter 14

Just one day after setting course for Tortuga, the lookout aboard the *Shining Star* spotted sails on the horizon. Bainbridge didn't feel too worried about it until the lookout reported the other ship had changed course to intercept them. He called for a glass and peered through it. What he saw made his blood run cold.

"Bugger me," he muttered under his breath. "Mr. Warding, have the riggers reef the sails. She's on an intercept course, and we haven't a prayer of outrunning her. Might as well get this over with."

"Aye, sir; should we prepare for boarders?"

"No, I don't want to give them any reason to attack." He turned to the young lad serving as messenger. "Tommy, go let Sam and Britt know I want to see them in my cabin."

"Aye, Cap'n."

Bainbridge handed the glass to his first mate and turned for the stairs. "You have the helm, Mr. Warding. We've a couple hours before she reaches us. If I haven't returned to the helm within the hour, drop sea anchors and signal for parley."

"You know the ship, Captain?"

"Aye; with those lines there are only two she could possibly be. Either one is a dangerous encounter."

☠

"Tommy said you wanted to see us, Captain," Britt said as he entered with Samantha.

"Aye, Mr. Westin; you and Sam have a seat."

"We noticed the ship slow down," Sam said.

Once they took their seats, Bainbridge gave them a solemn look. "We'll have company in a couple of hours. Sails were spotted and they have changed course to intercept us." He sighed and rubbed the bridge of his nose. "I don't want either of you to show yourselves on deck until I give the go-ahead."

"Why not?" Sam asked.

"I recognize the lines of the ship, even through the glass. There are only two I know of which have those lines; neither one a pleasant prospect as far as I am concerned. I won't know until she gets closer which one she is."

Britt blinked in confusion and glanced at his wife. She wore a look of apprehension. "Clearly you know what he's on about, love. Please enlighten me."

"Vik Brandee's ship is identical to Commodore Critchfield's flagship."

"Ooooh; yes, I can see how either one would be unpleasant."

Bainbridge nodded. "Aye, at least if it's Brandee, there is a hope of resolving some things. Critchfield would prove much more dangerous. He has warned us not to cross his path again. Sam gave him a nasty cut on the cheek last time we encountered him. Knowing your history with the man, you are no safer from his ire than she."

"We need a plan for if it is Navy rather than pirate," Sam stated.

"Simple enough," Bainbridge said with a shrug. "The two of you will hide in the hold, and we'll pray the bastard doesn't decide to search the ship."

Sam opened her mouth as if to protest, closed it again, frowned, and opened and closed her mouth again. Britt stifled a chuckle, and she turned to glare at him.

He laughed outright. Even Bainbridge snorted a bit.

Sam's face grew dark, and Britt relented. "I'm sorry, Love; but your expression was just so comical."

"This is not a laughing matter," she growled.

"I know; I know. I don't like that plan either, but I just don't see a better alternative."

She sighed and allowed her shoulders to slump. "You're right. I can't think of anything better. What does it say about us that we'd rather face a vampire pirate than a British Navy commodore?"

"That we're all mad," Bainbridge supplied.

Within the hour, the interloping ship drew close enough to positively identify through the spyglass: the *HMS Quicksilver*.

Bainbridge returned to the helm and ordered Samantha and Britt to the hold. The two spent a good half hour figuring out the best hiding places.

"I don't like this," Britt complained. "These are too easily discovered."

"Agreed, but they're what we have to work with," Sam replied.

"Thought you said this ship was used to smuggle goods."

"It was, but emeralds don't take much space. There was no need to build a hidden compartment. They just put them in a specially marked powder keg in the powder magazine," she told him.

"Clever, I must admit."

Sam nodded. "Besides, Critchfield was father's partner in the venture. He knows this is one of the ships used and would know to look for any smugglers' holds in case we ran any other contraband."

"You have a point. Let's hope the man doesn't decide to search the ship."

They crawled into their hiding place and tried to camouflage it as best they could.

Bainbridge welcomed the boarding party from the *Quicksilver* personally. To his chagrin but not his surprise, Commodore Critchfield led the party.

"Commodore, this is an unexpected honor."

"Captain — Bainbridge, was it?"

"Aye, sir."

"I rarely forget a name. Good of you to await our arrival. Might not have gone well for you had you tried to flee."

"As I am aware, sir. What brings you to these waters?"

"My primary mission is to squelch any piracy, man. I also have standing orders to search and conscript any colonial vessel I encounter. This pesky rebellion has gotten entirely out of hand." Critchfield gave him an assessing look. "I've not heard of Brumble throwing in with the rebels; in fact, I've not heard much of him at all."

"I'm afraid I have no news for you of him. Haven't been in the man's employ for a few years now," Bainbridge told him. "Haven't been anywhere up the coast in a few years, either, for that matter. I prefer the warmer clime of the Caribbean and the Gulf."

"I see. You own this ship, then?"

He nodded. "I do, sir. Originally contracted with B&S to train the old man's sons for their captaincies. Liked the lads enough to stay on afterward." Bainbridge told the half-truth without a thought. Technically he still worked for a Brumble; and the ship belonged to her family, not him. "Considering Bloody Brandee has targeted Tobias and his family; I eventually decided it was safer to leave his employ."

"And what of that little hellcat daughter of his?" Critchfield wore a lustful expression Bainbridge did not care for in the least. "You seemed rather loyal to her when we last met."

"Miss Brumble is married now." He fought the urge to grit his teeth. His dislike for the Commodore multiplied by the minute. He knew he couldn't afford to lose his temper, though.

Critchfield looked genuinely surprised. "Is she now? Her husband has his work cut out for him; I'd wager. Glad to know she came to her senses and abandoned that foolish quest to ransom her brothers."

Bainbridge couldn't resist baiting the man. "How do you know we didn't find Brandee?"

The Navy man gave him a droll stare. "You are still alive, sir. That I all the evidence I need of that."

He shrugged. "You have a point."

Critchfield shifted his attention to business. "Normally, I would assign one of my officers to inspect a vessel; but given that I am acquainted with you and your vessel; I felt it best to conduct the inspection myself."

Bainbridge's heart sank. Had it been one of the lesser officers, there would have been a chance of only a cursory inspection. The fact the commodore wanted to take a personal interest meant the inspection would be much more thorough.

"I believe I will start with the holds and work my way up," Critchfield announced. "You have a key for your cabin, sir?"

"I do; why?" The question puzzled him.

"Lock it. I don't want anyone tampering with the logs or other contents before I can inspect them. You will then accompany me on my tour, Captain Bainbridge; after all, this is your ship; who knows her better?"

"Right then." He gave a resigned sigh. "Let's get on with it."

"Hmph." Critchfield snorted and looked around in the cargo hold. "Not seeing much cargo beyond ship's provision."

"We're in between runs. I was thinking about heading up to Havana to pick up some tobacco and sugar, maybe a few passengers, as well. Most of what's down here now are spare timbers and rope, oh, and ballast."

Critchfield said nothing but shot him a skeptical look. He gazed around the hold once again and looked at a group of large casks near the bulkhead. "Those look like they've been moved recently, and they aren't secured properly. Surely you know the perils of loose cargo in high seas, Captain Bainbridge."

"Aye sir, I do; probably the work of a few of the younger lads looking for apples or some such." He hoped in vain the man accepted the excuse. "Looks like I'll have to have a word with them about it."

"All the same, I would like to have a look at what's in them myself." Critchfield moved toward them and startled a rat in the process. The creature scurried in among the casks.

Shortly after, an angry female voice yelped in pain and exclaimed, "You little bastard!"

This outburst ended with the dying squeal of the rat.

Critchfield smirked. "Hello Miss Brumble, or should I say Madame —."

Sam stood from behind one of the barrels with the dead rat in her hand. She removed her knife from the creature and wiped the blood off on its fur. She only spared Critchfield an unfriendly glower.

The glower turned into a smirking sneer at the commodore's look of stunned surprise when Britt rose to stand beside her.

"It is Madame Westin, sir," he said. "I had hoped our paths would never cross again, Commodore Critchfield."

"Yes, I am surprised to find you here, Mr. Westin." Critchfield turned to his men. "Continue a sweep of the ship. I shall retire to Captain Bainbridge's quarters along with the captain and Mr. and Madame Westin."

"Aye sir," the accompanying officer replied.

All four kept their silence until safely behind the closed door of the captain's cabin.

Britt spoke first. "Tell me, sir; did Commander Turlington ever seek absolution and cleansing?"

Critchfield frowned at him. "Not to my knowledge. His headless body was found washed up near Tybee Island. His head was found a few leagues from the body."

The three looked at him with varying expressions of disgust and horror.

"You are certain it was him?" Britt asked.

Critchfield nodded. "Crabs had been at the head, but the body bore the same scars as the commander. Captain Bainbridge, I wish to see your logbooks now."

"Very well." Bainbridge knew he had nothing to hide. Although Samantha had offered to finance the years-long search for her brothers, he'd convinced her to employ the ship in honest trade to keep them afloat. His reasoning to her had been she couldn't ransom her brothers with her dower if she spent it all looking for them.

Critchfield laid the books out on the table and sorted them by date. Occasionally, he had Bainbridge clarify some notation or other.

During this time, Samantha tended to the rat bite on her arm. Throughout, she maintained a sullen silence. Britt attempted to help her. She pointed him to the liquor cabinet. It took him a few tries to find the bottle she wanted, since she stubbornly remained silent.

Finally, his frustration boiled over. "Sam, why are you angry with me? I'm only trying to help."

Critchfield and Bainbridge looked up in surprise. Sam sighed, and her shoulders sagged. "I'm not angry with you, Love." She glanced over at the commodore, and her expression hardened. "I'm just afraid I'll let my anger rule my tongue, and I'll say something to this odious man which may cause difficulties for the Captain."

"Odious." Critchfield gave a mirthless bark of laughter. "Aye, I guess I've earned that appellation from you."

He stood and looked around him. "Well, Captain; your logs show you have not been in colonial waters since our last encounter. Therefore, it is safe to assume you have not taken part in any collusion with the rebels. You also were nowhere near Savannah during the timeframe of Commander Turlington's death. That clears Mr. Westin of any possible connection to it."

Sam sputtered indignantly, but he held up a hand to forestall her tirade. "In truth, I never really suspected your husband in that. Although I know he wouldn't hesitate to behead the man if he were killed to prevent him from rising as a vampire, he could not have done what was done to the commander."

"Why? What was done to him?" Britt asked suspiciously. "I thought you said he was beheaded."

"Aye, but not with a blade; granted, the crabs did some damage, but my source informed me his head looked like it was ripped from his body with brute force. No man could do that." He paused and gave Sam a grim look. "My source also informed me Viktor Brandewyne was in port around the same time. I take it by your presence here you still hunt him."

"I do." Sam looked shaken by the gruesome fate of Turlington, but her voice held firm.

"You know, I had thought to leave a contingent aboard this vessel and use it as bait for the bastard, but I don't think I will."

Bainbridge raised an eyebrow. While glad he wouldn't be saddled with any military, he wondered what changed the commodore's mind. "If I may ask; why not?"

"I just told you what happened to Commander Turlington. I'd set him to commandeer and sail the *Georgia Belle* as bait; its captain was one of Brandee's favorite targets. It was well-known in Savannah that Brandee would harry Chadwick Harris often, conscript his men, but always leave him alive and just enough crew to limp home with. Unfortunately, someone spirited Mr. Harris away in the night. Turlington sailed the *Georgia Belle* out under my orders. We thought the ship would be enough" He sighed and shook his head. "Oh, it was enough to draw Brandee's attention; it just wasn't enough to keep my men alive."

"I still don't understand why that changed your mind about using this ship, not that I'm complaining," Bainbridge replied.

"Even though I can be a bastard, I am still civilized enough not to put a woman in direct danger of death, mad though she be. Besides, I don't think the bait would be sufficient. I'm sure Brandee knows you're hunting for him by this point. Either he doesn't care or doesn't consider you even a nuisance, let alone a threat. There is nothing to lead me to believe he would pursue you."

"I see your point." Bainbridge purposely neglected to tell the commodore they were headed to Tortuga to hopefully meet up with Brandee, or that the plan was based on a shared dream the young couple had a few nights back. It looked as if Critchfield wouldn't detain them; why give him reason to change his mind?

"Well, everything looks to be in order. I will leave you to your business. Thank you for your cooperation, Captain Bainbridge."

Bainbridge inclined his head.

Critchfield turned to Sam and Britt. "Mr. Westin, Madame, I wish you well in your marriage."

"Thank you, sir," Britt replied cautiously.

"A word of advice, if I may?"

Britt frowned but nodded.

"Get her pregnant and settled somewhere. Live your lives instead of chasing your deaths." With that parting shot, Critchfield turned and left the cabin.

Back aboard the *Quicksilver*, Nathan Critchfield met with the commanders under him.

"Mr. McGowan."

"Aye sir?"

"Take one of the small ketches and follow that ship. I saw in their log they had made course for Tortuga.

Confirm and observe who they meet with there," the commodore instructed.

"Very well, sir," McGowan replied. "I take it you do not want them to know they're being followed."

"I do not. I suggest you sail west after sunset; give them time to lose sight of us. Fly no flags. In the morning, turn back northeast and reacquire sight. Do not intercept. Once you've confirmed they are making for Tortuga continue past them. The smaller vessel should be faster than the *Shining Star*. Wait for them in port.

"Aye sir; I'll take Wilkins with me. More than two men in a ketch would draw suspicion."

Critchfield nodded his approval. "Inform Mr. Wilkins and make ready to depart at nightfall."

Chapter 15

"I don't like this, Captain," Sam said. She and Britt stood with Bainbridge on the aft castle and watched the sails of the *HMS Quicksilver* vanish below the horizon. "It feels too easy."

The older man grunted and gave a curt nod. "Aye, it does. I'm grateful he didn't leave a contingent aboard or commandeer the ship; but I don't trust him."

"You both know where my opinion of the man lies," Brit grumbled. Sam rubbed his shoulder soothingly.

Bainbridge stood gazing at the young couple for a few moments. "What say we retire to my cabin? I've some mellow scotch in the cabinet. I believe we could all do with a bracer."

Britt frowned as they followed the captain down the ladder to the quarter deck. "Don't you think that's a bit strong for my wife?"

Sam let out a harsh bark of laughter. Bainbridge looked at the young man with a wry smile and opened the cabin door, waving them in. "She can handle it; trust me. Maybe one day I'll tell you about an incident in New Orleans."

"Captain!" Sam blushed brightly and shot him a look.

Britt raised an eyebrow at her reaction, a half-smile on his face. "Oh, I think you'll have to now."

"Don't, please!" Her blush grew even redder.

Bainbridge retrieved glasses and the bottle of scotch from the liquor cabinet. He set them on the table and poured each glass half full. "It wasn't that bad, Sam. I admit, I was worried about you at the time, but you were impressive."

She deflated, took the glass, and took a small sip from it. "Fine; tell him."

Britt waited with an eager expression.

"This one," Bainbridge pointed at Sam with the hand he held his glass in, "was still passing as my cabin boy in public. We were making the rounds of taverns asking for news of Brandee and not having much luck. We finally found a place where someone was willing to tell us something, provided the 'boy' could down a mug of rum."

"Oh my, and keep it down, too, I suppose?" Britt interjected.

"Aye, that too," Bainbridge continued. "Unbeknownst to me, this imp had been learning how to drink and gamble from the riggers. She grabbed the bottle from the barkeep, poured the mug to the brim, downed it without taking a breath, and repeated her actions."

"I kept it down, too, at least until that unpleasantness with the *gendarmes* outside the tavern," Sam piped up.

"What's this?" Britt grasped her arm gently, concern in his eyes.

"Remember, I was passing as male," she qualified. "Someone overheard the name Brumble. Brandewyne had assumed one of my brothers' names to gain entry to the Lord Mayor's house. He kidnapped the mayor's daughter. The *gendarmes* were, shall we say, less than gentle. Luckily, the Lord Mayor immediately recognized my true gender, and I was able to reveal the real culprit to him."

"Brandewyne has wronged your family greatly, my love. I pledge to do my best to make him pay for it."

Sam shook her head. "I don't want to lose you to him, too. I just want my brothers back."

Bainbridge cleared his throat to draw their attention. "We are getting off course. There is still the Commodore to deal with. I think we are in agreement he let us go too easily."

They nodded.

"Good; I do not expect him to follow us in his flagship. He strikes me as more subtle than that.

"You think he'll send a smaller ship to trail us?" Sam asked.

He nodded. "I do; I'd even wager he'd order it to pass us and wait for us to arrive in Tortuga. He saw the logs. He knows that's where we're headed."

"Should we go elsewhere?" Britt asked.

"No; let him think he's outsmarted us. If by some weird chance Brandee is in Tortuga, we'll be done with our business with him by the time the Navy arrives in force. Critchfield's spy will have to report back to him. He wouldn't dare take on the pirate alone unless he's a fool. Remember, Brandee's ship is the sister to the *Quicksilver*."

"We're on a suicide mission, aren't we," the young man sighed.

"Quite possibly."

The lookout reported sails late the next morning. A small, single-mast ketch approached from the southwest.

Bainbridge suspected them immediately. Had they been closer to land or in heavily travelled sea lanes, he wouldn't have questioned it; but a lone ketch this soon after parting ways with Critchfield just felt wrong.

Even though the smaller boat came from a different quadrant than the *Quicksilver*, he knew it could travel fast enough to sail perpendicular to their course for several hours and still catch up or even pass them later.

The ketch flew no identifying flags, and no excess crew or activity could be detected.

As the day wore on, the smaller boat shifted course to nearly parallel theirs, but made no effort to intercept or even get near enough to hail them. Eventually it pulled ahead of them going in the same general direction.

Just before it vanished beyond the horizon, near dusk, Bainbridge caught the unmistakable glint of sunlight on the lens of a spyglass. That alone was enough to confirm his theory that the ketch was a spy boat.

"Mr. Warding, did you get a good look at that ketch today?"

"I did, Captain. I particularly noticed a few old patches on apparently new sails. Thought that a bit odd. You think she's a pirate?"

"No, I think she's a Royal Navy spy. That ruse might fool some green sea captain or an unobservant one; but we've been sailing treacherous waters for years. That commodore knows we're headed to Tortuga, a known pirate haven. He's hunting Brandee, too."

"Should we try to throw them off course?"

"No, I care not if he wants to take the bastard on. He's certainly the best equipped to do it with that dreadnaught of his. I just want to get our business with the pirate done and get out of there before he shows up. I've no desire to get caught in the crossfire."

McGowan and Wilkins passed up the *Shining Star* without incident. The merchant ship barely acknowledged the small *Hermes*. The two Navy men took that as a sign their mark didn't suspect they were being watched.

Their observations confirmed the ship was making for Tortuga. That night they took shifts sailing the *Hermes*. The lightness of the smaller craft would allow them to reach the port several hours before their mark, provided they didn't set anchor overnight.

They reached Tortuga late the next morning. Once they secured lodgings and had a meal, they scouted the harbor for the best observation point to watch for the *Shining Star*'s arrival.

While they scanned the harbor, McGowan saw something which drew his attention.

"How the blazes —?"

"What is it?" Wilkins asked.

"Here," he said and handed his partner the spyglass. "Look due east and tell me what you see."

After a few moments Wilkins exclaimed, "But that's impossible; there's no way the Commodore could've gotten here before us!"

McGowan thought about it a while before he said, "He didn't. That is Bloody Brandee's ship. You hadn't come aboard yet, but a couple or so years ago we gave chase to him. No one knows how he managed to steal the *War God* or keep her hidden for three years before renaming her *Incubus*; but he has the sister ship to the *Quicksilver*."

"What happened?"

"Freak fog sprang up, and he escaped. We wasted a couple of cannon rounds on our reflection in the fog before we realized it wasn't him turned to attack." McGowan took his coat off and laid it aside. "Too bloody hot for this thing. Stay here and keep an eye for the *Shining Star* to make port. If I'm not back by then, look for me at our lodgings."

"Where are you going?"

"To listen for gossip of Brandee. If we can learn where he's headed next, we can best judge where the *Quicksilver* can intercept him."

"Good idea, James. Doubt he'd stay here long enough for the fleet to arrive," Wilkins agreed.

"My thoughts exactly, Fred. Don't forget to bring my coat."

A watchful raven circled high overhead.

Sam and Britt stood by Captain Bainbridge as the *Shining Star* entered Tortuga's harbor. Sam spotted the *Incubus* first.

"Look! He's here! I can't believe it!"

"What are our plans, Captain?" Britt asked.

Bainbridge remained silent for a while. Finally, he spoke. "Mr. Varner, maneuver us facing out of the harbor. I want to set anchor aft of that dreadnaught but not in direct line of her guns. Get us close enough to row over in the long boat."

"Aye, Captain," the helmsman replied.

"Why there, sir?" Britt asked.

Sam answered for him. "It will give us the advantage on escape, should we need to. In this crowded harbor it will take some time to swing that monster of a ship around to give chase."

"Ah, well that makes sense." He remained silent for a time, looking over at the ship the pirate occupied. "Captain, Samantha, I need to ask you something rather personal."

Bainbridge nodded, and the three of them stepped to the aft rail, away from the helmsman. "What is it, Mr. Westin?" he asked.

"How strong is your faith in God?"

He blinked at the younger man. "I was raised in church, although I've not darkened the door of one in years. Life at sea isn't conducive to piety."

Britt shook his head. "Piety isn't my concern. Do you believe, and if so, how much? How sure are you of God's grace and providence?"

"Hmph." He thought about it for a while before answering. Obviously, the answer held great importance to Britt. "I've been through too many seas and perils to think only luck brought me through. I believe the good Lord has had His protective hand over me throughout my life."

Britt nodded. "Good; Sam, you still haven't said anything."

"I've never really given it much thought before. Father saw to it I had governesses to see to my spiritual upbringing, but I spent a good deal of my childhood driving them to distraction with my boyish ways. I've been called a little heathen on more than one occasion and told I would burn in Hell if I didn't behave like a young lady. Fear of my father's wrath more than fear of hellfire played a part in my civilizing." She paused and tilted her head to the side. "I do believe there is a God; but I don't know how much He controls things in our lives. I've seen some strange things that have to do with powerful magic; but they don't have much to do with God, going by everything I was taught."

Britt looked a bit perplexed, but he seemed to accept it. "There is a reason I asked. Since Brandee is rumored to be a vampire, I think it best we all wear crucifixes, preferably where they're visible. The thing is, they won't protect you if your faith is weak or corrupted. A vampire's power will not work in the presence of holy objects if they are visible and backed by faith. Doubt can get you killed."

"I see." She looked down in thought. "I do not doubt your words, my love; but I do not think my faith is strong enough."

"Then we shall do our best to shield you with ours, Sam," Bainbridge said. Britt nodded his agreement.

She sighed and gave them both a sad smile. "I ask only one thing, and it may prove a hard thing."

Both men looked at her expectantly.

"Regardless of what happens to me, I don't want either of you to put yourself in harm's way on my account. Do. Not. Die for me. Please. I don't think I could bear it."

Both their faces fell.

"I mean it," she said with determination. "If you say you can't promise me this, I will go over there alone."

"No, you will not! I will lock you in our cabin before I'll let you face that monster alone," Britt insisted loudly.

"She'd just pick the lock," a male voice said from below them. "Ahoy *Shining Star*; permission to come aboard."

They peered over the railing to see a longboat alongside the ship. In it sat Zachary Brumble flanked by two gigantic men, one covered in tattoos, the other so dark-skinned he carried a blue sheen in the sunlight.

"Zach? Oh God, is that really you?" Sam's voice shook with disbelief.

"Of course, it's me, you stubborn, silly woman." He shook his head with a rueful smile. "I should have known my note wouldn't reach you or would do no good if it did. You almost never do what you're told."

She narrowed her eyes at him. "That's him."

Bainbridge took control of the situation. "Name your companions, Mr. Brumble. Good to see you alive and well, by the way."

"Hullo Captain Bainbridge! George, these are Mr. Jon, second mate of the *Incubus*, and Anvil, ship's smith."

"If they give their word to behave honorably and bring no violence, I will grant permission."

The tattooed man grinned up at them. "Cap'n gave orders for us to be on our best behavior and not start anything."

"You're pirates. That hardly makes me want to trust you."

The indigo giant spoke up with a voice like contained thunder. "Captain gave orders, like Jon-Jon said. Any man don't obey Captain soon be dead — or worse."

"He's telling the truth, George," Zach said. "I've seen what happens to shirkers or anyone foolish enough to cross Captain Brandewyne. It's not pretty."

Bainbridge saw the horror in his former protégé's face. "I'm convinced. Permission to come aboard granted."

He hoped he wouldn't regret the decision.

Chapter 16

Samantha could barely wait for her brother to make it to the deck. After years of searching, fighting to hold onto hope, she would finally be able to embrace one of her brothers again. Part of her couldn't believe it. She hadn't even met Brandee to bargain with him yet.

The moment Zach's feet touched the deck she nearly knocked him back over the railing in her rush to hug him. She buried her face in his chest and squeezed for all she was worth.

He returned the embrace with a breathless grunt. He patted her on the back and said, "Good to see you too, Sam; can I please breathe now?"

Mr. Jon arrived on deck in time to see Sam release her brother. "Wouldn't mind a greeting like that, meself."

"I'll thank you to keep your hands off my wife."

"Your wi—." Jon-Jon turned to face Britt with a taunt and stopped dead cold. Without a word or breaking eye contact, he fetched out a flask, pulled the cork, and took a long swig. He handed the flask to Anvil, as he came over the rail, and said, "You see what I see, mate?"

The smith, who dwarfed the six-foot-seven Jon-Jon, took a long swig, scrunched his face, and said, "Mr. Rigger?"

"Who?" Britt replied.

Jon-Jon took the flask back, had another drink, replaced the cork, and shook his head. "No; but bugger if he don't favor him strongly."

"Yes, he does," Zach agreed.

Sam noticed his less than friendly expression and stepped back to stand in front of her husband protectively.

"You called my sister your wife. Who are you, sir, and do you have our father's approval?"

"My name is Britt Westin, Mr. Brumble. I have never met your father. Samantha nursed me back to health when she found me cast adrift and left to die by Commodore Critchfield."

Zach's expression did not grow any friendlier. "Exactly why would a Royal Navy commander mete out such a punishment to you? What kind of a rogue are you?"

Sam's temper flared. "He is not a rogue! He's a vampire hunter. That Navy bastard sought him out to learn more about vampires then tried to get rid of him when he learned Critchfield was in league with a vampire called Lady Carpathia," she growled.

Zach exchanged a look with the two pirates. When he turned back to her and Britt, she saw his eyes soften a bit. He gave a formal half bow and said, "Forgive me, Mr. Westin. Sam is my only sister, and I tend to be a bit overprotective of her; much good it does." The last came out as a growling sigh.

"So, I'm beginning to learn," Britt replied. "Ow!" he added when Sam stomped his foot.

"I am standing right here. Do not talk over me as if I wasn't present."

Bainbridge couldn't stifle a chuckle at her outburst. She shot him a peeved look which only made him laugh harder.

Jon-Jon and Anvil stood in bemused silence.

"A word of advice, Mr. Westin; don't ever make her mad enough to fight you. She fights dirty, and she has a mean streak," Zach said. He dodged the slap she aimed at him. "Peace, Sam! I'm just teasing. Thomas will be happy to see you."

She felt a jolt go through her. Tears stung her eyes. "Thomas?" Her voice came out as a strangled sob.

"Sam, what is it?" he asked as she crossed back to him and buried her face in his chest once again. Her shoulders shook in silent sobs. He held her and stroked her back until she could compose herself.

"I must look a fright," she said, trying to laugh it off. She scrubbed the remaining tears from her eyes and saw her brother and husband exchange puzzled looks.

"Samantha," Zach said, "please tell me what upset you so."

"Someone in New Orleans told me Thomas was dead."

"Who?"

"I can't remember. I think it was a woman, but I cannot recall her face or name or even how I encountered her," she replied honestly. The lack of ability to recall the encounter frustrated her. She looked over at Britt and asked, "Do you suppose she was a vampire?"

Even as she asked the question, she felt Zach stiffen a bit. She pulled back and narrowed her gaze at him. "What are you trying to hide form me, Zachary Brumble?"

"I'm not at liberty to discuss it here, Sam. You'll have to take it up with the Captain. He invites you to dine with him."

"She is not going to face him alone," Britt growled.

Zach shook his head. "Of course not; you and Captain Bainbridge are invited as well, Mr. Westin."

Sam placed her hand on her brother's arm. "I intend to bring you back with me, Zach, Thomas, too. I've managed to save a sizable chunk of my dowry to use for your ransom."

He cupped her cheek and gave her a sad smile. "I love you, Sam; but as long as you've been searching for us you should know by now it's not that simple."

"Yes, it is! I know father tried to have you put on the lists, but Commodore Critchfield gave me his word he would not add you. Captain Bainbridge explained to him what really happened."

He shook his head. "Nonetheless, I am on the lists. I have willingly committed acts of piracy, many against Father's fleet. I resigned myself to my lot years ago and threw in with Captain Brandewyne. Sam, I like being a pirate."

Bainbridge sighed and shook his head. "Have to say I'm not surprised, son. Don't know if it would've happened had we not run afoul of this lot." He pointed at the two burly pirates. "But you always had a fascination with the stories and the lifestyle. Old Tobias feared it, and his acts in the past forced you to it. Unbeknownst to Samantha, I've done some digging and learned he came into his fortune and business through less than honest beginnings."

"Father doesn't have an honest bone in his body," Sam grumbled. "I'm well acquainted with his shadier side businesses. It allowed him to prosper despite the ever increasing and arbitrary taxes the Crown kept imposing on colonial trade."

"Aye, I forgot you did much of his bookkeeping," Zach commented. "I don't think he ever realized you'd deciphered the codes and cryptology he used to disguise the illicit businesses."

"He underestimated me because of my gender."

"Very probably." He gave her an intense and stern look. "Captain Brandewyne will not make the same mistake; trust me. Be careful, Sam; you don't know how dangerous he can be."

"Speaking of, Cap'n was clear we shouldn't dawdle," Jon-Jon said.

"Captain, would you please retrieve my dowry?" Sam asked.

Bainbridge nodded. "I'll retrieve those items you mentioned, as well, Mr. Westin."

Jon-Jon raised an eyebrow. "Mr. Brumble, I think you should go with the good Cap'n. Wouldn't want him to bring along any hidden weapons."

Zach shook his head and sighed. "Hope you don't mind, George."

"You? No, I don't mind."

Bainbridge turned to Zach once in the privacy of the captain's cabin. "You look well. I wish we could've gotten to you when it might've been in time to get you out without being on the lists."

"I know. For the first year, I did entertain thoughts of escape. It took me that long to realize those thoughts were futile. Even if I could have gotten away, I would never be able to free Thomas."

"About that; Samantha wasn't the only one who caught your reaction when she said she'd been told he was dead." He fixed his former protégé and captain with a pointed stare.

Zach rubbed the back of his neck and looked sheepish. "Thom is — changed. I'll leave it at that, for now. My reaction was more to Sam wondering if she'd encountered vampires in New Orleans." He gave Bainbridge a worried look. "Chances are she did. The Captain has dealings with a group of them there. George, I won't lie; I wish you'd lock her in her cabin and sail off now."

"I know. I gave up trying to talk sense into her years ago. As she has pointed out to me, I can help her do what she's planned to do, or she'll go try to do it on her own."

"She is just as stubborn as Father; I'll give her that," Zach grumbled. "What about her husband?"

"He's even madder than she is. He's made it his life goal to hunt down and destroy vampires. One in particular, called Lady Carpathia, he holds responsible for the murder of his family."

Zach chuckled mirthlessly. "If he's who I think he is, he's after the wrong one. I still advise against this, but part of me wants to see his reaction to the first mate."

Bainbridge considered for a moment then asked, "Are we dealing with vampires as well as pirates, Zach? I know the question sounds like I've gone mad; but we've encountered some very peculiar things and — beings — in our years of searching."

"Yes, there will be vampires aboard the *Incubus*. The Captain is one of them, but he's not like the others."

"Is Thomas one? Is that why you say he is changed?"

Zach gave him an almost heart-wrenching look of sorrow. Bainbridge didn't need any further answer. He just shook his head and clapped the younger man on the shoulder. Zach nodded in acknowledgement.

Bainbridge released his friend and turned to retrieve the items he'd come for.

Zach questioned him when he saw the crucifixes. "Sam never owned one of those. We weren't raised Catholic. Where did they come from?"

He slipped the chain of one around his neck and replied, "They belong to Mr. Westin. He uses them as protection when he's hunting vampires."

Zach shrugged. "Won't do much good against the Captain, but I don't think he'll be offended by them."

"We'll see."

Jon-Jon chuckled at the sight of the gold crucifix Bainbridge wore out. His smirk grew wide when the captain handed similar adornments to the young couple. Anvil remained silent.

Sam and Britt ignored the two pirates and climbed over the side and down to the waiting boat. Bainbridge followed with a heavy looking sea bag.

Once Zach and the pirates settled in the boat, they rowed over to the *Incubus*.

☠

Samantha ignored the eerily silent throng of pirates they passed on their way to the captain's cabin. All the men stared at them with befuddled expressions.

She jumped when Jon-Jon broke the silence. "Quit yer gawkin' an' get back t'work, the lot of ye!" he barked at the crew.

A few pirates directed obscene gestures at the tall second mate as they returned to their tasks.

"Aye, I know y'want me, Gannt; but I'm more man than you can handle." His retort elicited guffaws from a few of the pirates.

Even Sam chuckled, which drew a shocked look from her husband. "What?" she said unrepentantly. "It was funny."

"Go fuck yerself," Gannt shot back at Jon-Jon.

"Now Gannt, y'know Sniff is the only one with a cock long enough to fuck hisself," another pirate joined in the banter. "Poor Jon-Jon's cock is like a wee babe's."

"Belay that bilge," a commanding voice spoke from near Sam and her companions. "There is a lady present."

The previously raucous pirates quickly found tasks to occupy themselves with. Sam turned to see who held so much sway over such an unruly crew.

A jolt went through her and rooted her to the spot as she found herself face to face with the very pirate she'd hunted for years.

He towered over her as he glared at his men. He wore his long, straight blue-black hair tied back with the tail draped over his left shoulder. A neatly trimmed goatee and mustache left his cheeks clean-shaven and framed one of the most expressive mouths she'd ever seen, the lips not too thick or thin.

For a brief instant, she experienced her pulse flutter as she imagined those lips on hers.

Though weathered by sun and wind, his skin held the suppleness of youth rather than the papery texture of age. His high cheekbones and the reddish gold of his skin beneath the sailor's tan put her in mind of an Indian she'd seen once as a child who'd come to trade furs to her father.

The cheekbones also drew attention to his eyes; strikingly green, they seemed to glow with his irritation at his men.

He turned those eyes down to her, and the corners of his mouth turned up slightly in a smile which carried heat and dark promises.

"Oh, fuck me."

Tamara. A. Lowery

Chapter 17

Sam sincerely hoped she hadn't said that aloud.

The pirate captain's smile quirked up on one corner. He swept his gaze over her and chuckled before he took her hand and raised it to his lips. They proved softer than she'd imagined. Her pulse jumped when he dipped the tip of his tongue between her second and third knuckles.

"A tempting offer, Madame Westin; perhaps another time. I don't think your husband would appreciate me seducing you in front of him."

"I didn't mean it like that," she said.

"I know," he replied. His smile said he thought she really did.

In truth, she wasn't sure if she did or didn't.

A raven fluttered to land on his shoulder and promptly cawed loudly in his ear.

"Ow. Apparently, neither would Lazarus," he added with a laugh and rubbed his ear.

Abruptly, Britt imposed himself between his wife and the pirate, although Brandewyne did not relinquish her hand. Britt held up his crucifix in the pirate's face. "I don't know how it is you can move so freely in daylight, but I demand you release my wife."

The raven hopped over to Britt's shoulder and cheeped.

Brandewyne let go of her hand and grasped her husband's gold crucifix. He scrutinized it intensely then raised his eyebrows and gave an appreciative frown. "That is some of Miguel de la Rosa's work, unless I miss my mark. Rare to see one of his pieces this side of the Atlantic; and yet you present three. It would seem vampire hunting is a profitable business. These must have cost a small fortune."

Britt kept his silence. Sam saw the disconcertion in his eyes.

"For Lazarus' sake, I will overlook your outburst, Mr. Westin. It is understandable you would defend your wife's honor. I would advise you not to take that tone with me again, however; unless you wish to make your wife a widow."

Sam placed her hand on Britt's arm, and he lowered the obviously ineffective piece of jewelry.

"Captain, you've twice mentioned Lazarus," she said. "I assume you mean the bird here and not the man our Lord raised from the dead."

The pirate nodded confirmation. "In this form, he is my eyes. I value his opinion."

"But it's just a bird."

He chuckled. "Is he?"

The raven hopped from Britt's shoulder to the deck. In mid-jump, it transformed into a large black cat with extra toes which gave it the appearance of having thumbs.

Sam felt a chill of recognition. "I know that cat," she murmured more to herself than anyone else present.

"In more ways than one, I'm told," Brandewyne said cryptically.

He bowed slightly and motioned toward the door leading below deck. "We would be honored if you would join us for dinner while we discuss business."

Bainbridge spoke caution. "We will join you to talk in private, sir; but I don't think it wise to partake of the food or drink you offer. As I recall, you put something in the drink when you took Captain Brumble captive."

"I did. I give you my word, Captain Bainbridge, I have not done so to this meal. I hope you reconsider on the food, at least. Mr. Trundle has put much effort into preparing it."

"Trundle?"

Zach spoke up. "Aye, George, the same man who used to run the Dragon & Dodo in Salem. I'd wager we're the best fed pirate crew in the world."

Bainbridge shook his head and chuckled. "I remember the food there. You could eat yourself into a stupor with his egg pies. If you've got him for a cook, you're the best fed crew of any sort. Trundle's cooking is worth the risk of this being a trap."

"Are you mad, Captain?" Britt protested. "He just admitted he drugged you to take Mr. Brumble. How is one man's cooking worth the risk?"

"You've never tasted Trundle's food. Even the King would covet one of those egg pies."

"I still don't like it."

Sam gave him an irritated growl. "I did not come this far in my quest to free my brothers to be waylaid by fears of poison or drugged food. Britt, I love you dearly, but I've understood from the start that this could end badly.

I've never shied away from that. I don't think I could live with myself if I tried to turn back now. It's too late for that anyway."

All of the men stared at her. She did not flinch.

Finally, Brandewyne broke the silence. "I commend you on your choice of wives, Mr. Westin. I hope you appreciate what a magnificent creature she is; and I can see why my first mate is so taken with her."

They followed Viktor to the antechamber originally meant to be the officers' mess by the ship's designer. An impressive feast covered the table, aromas firing everyone's appetites.

As they took their seats around the table, Bainbridge asked, "I assume you remember me from when you took Zachary and that he told you about his sister; but how did you know Mr. Westin, that he is married to Sam, or that he hunts vampires?"

Viktor smirked. "I've always made it my business to know exactly who is hunting me and why. Lazarus has been quite helpful."

"Ah." The merchant captain didn't seem to have any further comment on the shape-shifting creature. "I do have one other question."

Very well," Vik replied.

"Why would the Reaper be interested, or as you put it, taken with Samantha? He can't have possibly seen her."

Viktor looked at him sharply. "You remember Hezekiah as my first mate?"

"I take it by your tone he isn't anymore?" Bainbridge shot him a nervous look.

He wanted to hide the sorrow in his eyes, yet he knew he couldn't. His relief overwhelmed him. "He died in battle some months ago. You are only the second person outside my crew to remember he sailed with me for the past few years. All else who should know it have no memory of it, as if something happened to erase him from existence." He sighed. "Even his wife and children vanished without a trace, remembered by none."

"My condolences, sir; I can see you feel his loss greatly. Who is the first mate you mentioned?"

Viktor's humor returned. The next few moments promised to be entertaining. "Lazarus the raven and Lazarus the cat are not his only forms."

The large black cat stepped forward out of the shadows of one corner of the windowless cabin. He dissolved into a dark mist which grew in volume until he solidified as a nude man.

Jim smiled, close-lipped, then said, "Hullo Samantha."

"Madame Westin, may I present Jim Rigger, my first mate."

Sam stood so abruptly she knocked her chair over. Her husband and Captain Bainbridge both stared at the naked man in stunned disbelief.

In three steps, Sam reached Jim and punched him in the face hard enough to make him lose his footing and sit down on the deck abruptly.

"I see you remember him, even if the two of you were never formally introduced." Vik couldn't keep the mirth out of his tone.

Sam lifted her foot and stomped it down. Only Jim's vampiric speed saved his privates from a crushing.

"Peace!" he cried and quickly morphed back to feline form. The cat leapt to Vik's shoulder in search of sanctuary.

"Pussy." He laughed at his friend's predicament. "Go get some clothes on. She obviously finds your pathetic cock offensive."

Lazarus growled, leapt down, and stalked off through the door which led to the captain's cabin. Vik grinned after him then turned back to face his guests.

"Jim has a wedding present for you; I've advised him to wait until after we've dined. Ah, Belladonna, thank you for joining us." His irritation with the siren's tardiness cooled considerably. She wore the teal silk dress Brianna Grimm had given her. He knew it was difficult to lace up the tight bodice without help.

He leered openly in appreciation of how the garment forced her breasts to mound up, the pale edges of her aureoles visible just above the neckline.

"You should have said something, pet," he spoke to her through their mental link. *"I would've helped you get laced up."*

"Liar," she responded in kind. *"You would've helped me get unlaced and put your guests completely out of mind."*

"Well, you have me there."

"Aren't you going to introduce me to your guests, Viktor?" Belle asked aloud.

"Of course, pet. Belladonna, Captain George Bainbridge of the *Shining Star*, and Madame and Mr. Britt Westin.

Sam and Belle sized each other up. He knew the siren had eavesdropped on his initial encounter with the young woman. Belle could be quite territorial at times.

It amused him when Sam placed herself between the siren and her husband with an almost audible growl. The young man's resemblance to the first mate had drawn Belle's interest, and it seemed Sam was having none of it.

"Belle, pet; I'll thank you not to eat my guests," he warned, but with good nature.

She pouted. "But they look so tasty, especially that one." She pointed at Britt.

"Belle." This time the warning tone was unmistakable.

"Oh, all right; I guess I'll just have to be satisfied with this burnt flesh." She indicated the roast on the table.

Bainbridge leaned over and whispered to Zach, "That roast looks just fine. It's not burnt."

Zach didn't bother to whisper. "Belladonna is a siren. She prefers her meat raw and still screaming."

The siren flashed her true ear-to-ear grin full of needle teeth at them.

Viktor noticed Sam blanched a little; but she held her ground. He liked that. This woman could prove very interesting.

He stood and helped Belle into her seat. Britt did the same for his wife, including setting the chair aright from where it still lay on the deck.

As the vampire hunter resumed his seat, he pinched the bridge of his nose and rubbed it. "I must admit, sir, I am confused," he said.

"What about?" Vik took a bite of food immediately after asking. Trundle had outdone himself on this meal. They'd recently laid in a fresh supply of meats and vegetables.

"Well, you, for one thing; I was told you are a vampire. I've noticed you can tolerate and even touch blessed items; you don't burst into flames in broad daylight; and you are eating solid food. It doesn't make sense. Was it a lie you use as a scare tactic?"

"Would that it was, Mr. Westin. Granted, it has its advantages; but it has its drawbacks, too. I am a vampire; I am not undead. I was cursed to this state by a very powerful witch."

Britt looked at him quizzically. "A curse? So, you are not a true vampire."

"A fine distinction, I assure you," Vik said. "I do require human blood. I can eat regular food, but I must have blood. The longer I go without, the worse the Hunger grows. Loss of self-control is something I must battle daily and can prove much more deadly for those around me than if I were a mortal man."

"I imagine that could prove a great problem at sea," Bainbridge interjected.

"Aye, it would be very bad to eat the crew," Vik said with a sardonic smirk. "Thankfully, I discovered a solution early on in the curse. I cut the blood with liquor. I prefer brandy or rum, but any strong drink will suffice. It preserves the blood and prevents clotting." He made a face. "Don't care much for clots. Of course, fresh, pure blood is much more satisfying."

"Unbelievable."

"What?" Vik suspected he knew what bothered Britt so.

"You sit there talking about murder so matter-of-factly, as if you were discussing the weather."

Viktor grinned tightly. "You hunt and murder suspected vampires, not so different to my point of view. Keep in mind, also, I am a pirate; murder is part of the trade. I've killed men over cargo or even insults; now I get sustenance out of it in addition to satisfaction."

"I protect innocent lives."

"You tell yourself that." He looked at the man with a neutral gaze. "You might be surprised to know I do most of my hunting among the less-than-lawful elements of society. Killing people who wouldn't be missed tends to draw less attention than killing more prominent people would."

Britt frowned at him. "Even they have worth and value. They may be destitute or even depraved, but they deserve a chance to repent and to live."

"Oh, I agree they have value. Their blood is very precious to me and to my cadre. Their bodies help keep Belladonna fed, as well." Vik paused and considered things. "You say you hunt vampires to protect the innocent. I think you truly believe that; but I think your deeper motivation is vengeance and atonement. You could not protect your mother or brother."

"How do you know about that?"

"I just do. Your vengeance is misplaced, you know."

Britt's face went white and then turned livid with rage. "So, you are in league with the bitch who murdered them!"

"I am in league with no one." Viktor maintained his calm, but he felt his Hunger rising and knew the brandy-diluted blood would not be sufficient. "To whom do you refer?"

"Lady Carpathia," Britt growled.

Viktor blinked. He burst into laughter which took a couple of minutes to subside.

Britt frowned in consternation. "She murdered my mother and brother! How dare you mock me! Do you deny being in league with her? You must be. How else could you know about my family?"

Viktor wiped tears from his eyes. "I do deny it. She was sent to kill me by her master. She has been neutralized. As for your family, She only killed your father. By all accounts he killed your mother. I on the other hand, am responsible for the death of your brother."

"What? No, this can't be right."

"Jim, I think it is time to give the young couple their wedding gift."

In response, the first mate returned to the officers' mess, fully dressed and carrying a canvas bag with a largish lump in it.

"He's telling the truth, brother. We only first met that she-vampire a few years ago. Vik turned me shortly after he was cursed," Jim said.

Britt just stood there with his mouth opening and closing.

"You sent the dreams," Sam said. She didn't try to attack him again, but her stare and tone dropped the temperature in the cabin a few degrees.

He nodded. "We'll be facing the witch who started all this soon. I wanted to talk with both of you before that, just in case. I didn't mean for you to see the fight, Sam. I am sorry about that."

"What is in the bag?" Britt asked with resolve. The look in his eyes said he suspected he already knew the answer.

Jim reached in and pulled the severed head of his father out by the hair. Bainbridge raised his napkin to his mouth and looked a little green. No one else at the table flinched.

"Father," Britt said in recognition. "You finally freed him from Her."

"I leave it to you to finish it for him," Jim said. "His body began to decompose almost immediately. As you can see, however, his head remained intact. I can sense a faint presence still there."

Britt stood and walked around the table to him. He took the head and put it back in the sack. He then studied Jim's face carefully, avoiding direct eye contact adroitly.

"He said Carpathia killed you and mother. I never could remember it happening that way, but he convinced me. I guess it was easier than believing my own father could kill my mother in a fit of jealous rage and leave my little brother to starve." He sighed. "How did you survive?"

"Mr. Tucker felt some responsibility for the whole mess, I guess. He took me to Boston and found a family to care for me. When he died a couple of years later, they turned me out. I lived as a street urchin for a few years until Sam's father took me on as cabin boy. He was a brutal bastard. I jumped ship in Savannah where I met Viktor. We've been like brothers ever since."

"But you just admitted he turned you," Britt protested.

Jim smiled. "He had no choice. His Hunger took him, and I was the only one close enough to feed him at the time. We were ashore and far from the crew or anyone else."

Viktor began to lose focus on the conversation. He needed to feed soon.

Britt shook his head. "I know I should kill you and set you free; yet I can't seem to find the will to do so."

"Well, I'm glad of that. I don't particularly feel the need to be freed." Jim laughed.

Belladonna interrupted abruptly. "You humans need to leave now!"

Viktor frowned. Why was she trying to run his prey away?

"Go! Now! Before it's too late!" she yelled at them.

Zach spared a quick glance at Viktor and grabbed Bainbridge by the arm. "We have to get out! Mr. Westin, get my sister out of here now!"

"What?" Samantha asked.

"Vik, no!" Jim cried.

In mere seconds, Viktor sped around the table and snatched the young woman out of her seat. He clasped her to him and buried his fangs into the spot where her neck met her shoulder.

He fed.

Jim looked on in horror. He'd been so wrapped up in the reunion with this brother he'd missed the warning signs from his captain. He knew if he didn't act soon, Sam would die.

With impossible speed, he ran into Viktor's cabin and grabbed a small wooden jewelry casket. He brought it back into the officers' mess and waited until he was right next to his friend to open it.

Viktor remained oblivious to Jim's actions. The first mate could tell only the Hunger mattered to his friend now.

He screamed the moment his hand touched the emerald-encrusted cross. Still, he lifted it from the box and managed to get the chain it hung on looped over Viktor's head before the smoldering flesh of his hand could burst into flame.

Unable to do any more, he collapsed onto the deck clutching the charred appendage to him.

In an instant, the Hunger vanished; no, not really gone but put at bay. He withdrew from Sam's throat and looked about in confusion. He sensed a calming presence, but he also felt his first mate's pain and distress.

He saw Jim on the deck writhing in agony, the open jewelry casket on the table nearby, and the savaged throat of the young woman in his arms.

"Belle, heal her if you can. Her heartbeat is still strong, so she should survive. Mr. Brumble, get them out now. I can already feel the cross' power draining. I'll tend to Jim," he ordered.

The other occupants of the cabin needed no further prompting.

Chapter 18

Belle turned to Zach once they were out on deck in the sunlight. "Seawater; now." He immediately grabbed one of the swab buckets and ran for the side. She held out a napkin she'd snagged on her way out. "Mr. Westin, I need you to hold pressure on the wound to staunch the bleeding."

To his credit, he responded promptly; but his eyes showed borderline panic. "I've got to find a priest. She needs to be purified."

"Good luck with that," Zach grunted as he handed the bucket of seawater to the siren. "The Captain will consider her his, now, and he rarely lets go of anyone or anything he considers his. This is why I tried to warn her off. Sam has always been too stubborn for her own good."

Belle ignored the humans save for the one entrusted to her care. The woman gasped for air, and her body temperature grew lower by the minute. The amount of blood told the siren Viktor had nicked a major artery. If she didn't act fast, her charge would bleed out.

She dipped out some water and poured it over Britt's hands and the blood-soaked napkin. She splashed more water on Sam's face and chest. She held her hands just above her patient's head and heart and began to sing.

Sam's breathing evened out, and she settled into a light sleep. Belle sat back.

"You can remove the compress now. She will need rest, red meat, and dark green plants to replenish. She lost more blood than Viktor realized."

Britt gingerly pulled the napkin away from his wife's throat. Blood-soaked but smooth skin greeted his eyes.

"Even purification doesn't erase the wounds or scars. How were you able to?" Amazement and suspicion colored his tone.

"I am not only a siren; I am a sea witch. Healing is one of my gifts, and salt water is the base of my magic." She took the bloody cloth from his hand and dipped it in the bucket of water. "We need to clean all this blood up. His control is weak right now, and it's almost sunset. Your brother will be able to move freely in his human form; plus, there are other vampires asleep below. If Viktor can't control himself, he definitely won't be able to control them."

"Jim, can you hear me?"

Jim lay very still, his hand clutched to him in the very position he'd landed in when he collapsed. He couldn't move even to speak. It took all his energy just to remain conscious rather than fall into his daylight death. He feared if he gave in to it, he might never rise again.

He couldn't do that to Vik. His friend needed him. As it was, he felt responsible for the attack on Samantha. He'd called her and his brother here. He'd also drawn on Viktor's power to maintain a human form during daylight hours. He suspected that had contributed to the Captain's loss of control.

"Jim don't do this! I forbid you to die!"

He had just enough energy to speak to his friend mentally. *"Then stop yelling at me. I'm fighting it as hard as I can. I don't have enough energy to talk and move right now."*

Vik grasped his shoulder, raw pain etched across his face. "I can't — I won't lose you, too."

Jim's body bucked as his captain forced energy into it.

"Vik, stop," he whispered, trying to use as little as possible of the borrowed power. "This is what started the whole mess to begin with. I was drawing on you to keep my human form." He finished silently, *"I'll be better after sundown. Right now, you need to hunt. I can see the Hunger in you getting stronger by the second. Go now, please; before you kill the whole crew."*

Vik closed his eyes and frowned. "You're right. Thank you for keeping your wits about you, my friend. Come join the hunt as soon as you're able." He stood and left the cabin.

The erstwhile dinner guests felt a rush of wind and caught sight of a blurred shape launch into the late evening sky.

"What was that?" Bainbridge asked.

"The Captain has left to hunt," Belladonna said. "Mr. Rigger must've talked some sense into him."

"How long has he been vampire?" Britt asked.

"Less than a decade."

"He shouldn't be that powerful. In my experience, vampires don't gain the ability to fly until at least after their first score of years if at all."

Belle gave him an indulgent smile. "Viktor does many things he shouldn't be able to. His powers grow at alarming rates. Part of my job is to prevent him from destroying himself with any new and unfamiliar abilities."

He frowned at her. "How can you possibly —?"

"I am ancient, human; in my childhood, the entire world was drowned. My kind fed and fed well on the watery purge of humanity. I am older than all but a select few vampires. I believe I am equal to the task."

"The sun's down," Zach said.

A few moments later, Jim stumbled out on deck. He still clutched his hand to his chest. "Will she be all right?"

"She needs rest and nourishment, but yes," Belladonna answered him.

"Don't suppose you could do anything for my hand, or do I just need to feed?" He gazed at her wistfully.

"Stop with the pitiful act. It doesn't work on me," she said flatly. "As it is, feeding will not heal that burn, and you know it. It came from a blessed object. Vampires can't heal that kind of damage."

"She's right," Britt confirmed. "It's about the only thing they can't heal. I've seen vampires with scars they received centuries ago."

"Damn, this is my sword hand." Jim looked crestfallen. "Still, if Samantha survives, it was worth it. I am glad to see you, brother, more than you'll ever know." He looked back over at the siren. "What about that time in Ireland? Vik's blood healed the burn from that thing."

"His blood was still rich with moly then. I doubt that is so, now. Besides, he is not available currently. I do know what might work, though. I thought about it after that incident," Belle said and brought his attention back to her. "The burn will not heal. If it doesn't go too deep, though, it can be cut away. I realize this one is much worse than the last time you touched that cross; this time you held onto it for a prolonged time."

Jim frowned. "And if that doesn't heal this time?"

"Can you use the hand like it is now?" She crossed her arms and looked at him pointedly.

He looked down at his damaged hand and tried to flex it or move it. He hissed in pain.

"No; I can't even close it."

"Then you have nothing to lose by trying."

"I guess not. Let's do this." He looked at her with determined resignation.

"Over the side away from the humans," she instructed. "You will have to feed after this to speed the healing. I don't think you want to attack the crew or your guests."

"Good point."

"Jim?" Britt placed a tentative hand on his brother's arm. He wore a torn expression. "Thank you for rescuing Samantha. I — I'm not sure what to say. I never thought I'd be grateful to a vampire." He rubbed the back of his neck and looked away. "There is much I'm going to have to rethink."

Jim gave him a lop-sided smile. "It is an adjustment."

Britt released his arm, and he turned to join the siren. She turned her back to him and looked over her shoulder.

"I don't want to damage this dress any more than I already have this evening. Viktor likes it."

Jim chuckled. "Unlacing a bodice is something I can do easily one-handed. Mr. Jon, take this to the Captain's cabin." He deftly loosened the lacing of the dress so the siren could shed it.

Jon-Jon gave her an appreciative leer as he gathered the garment up.

"And don't be trying it on when no one's looking, either," Jim teased.

"Already know it's not big enough for me, mate. You'd look prettier in it anyway."

Belle caught Britt giving her a thunderstruck stare and laughed. "Be glad your wife is unconscious. If she saw the way you look at me now, you'd get the same greeting she gave Mr. Rigger, I'd wager."

Jim grinned. "Aye, I bet she would, too. Don't know if she'd understand Belle has this effect on men." He gave his brother a wink. "You might want to have a peek at her once she hits the water. It may cool you down a bit."

The siren paid them no more mind. She climbed nimbly to the top of the rail and dove over the side. Moments after she entered the water, she felt the sweet release of her legs fusing together and extending to her full shark-like tail. In her true form she measured from head to tailfin nearly three times the height of her human form.

It felt so good to stretch out; she indulged herself with a jump.

To her amusement, Jim had the men lower him in one of the boats. One would think he didn't trust her in the water.

"This seems an unnecessary precaution," she commented as she rested her arms on the side of the small craft.

"I'm not exactly in any shape to swim, and I don't have the energy to fly right now, love. Could I talk you into a tow to the dock?" He gave her a winning smile.

"Probably a good idea. Let me cut the burned tissue away here where the water is less polluted. I'll speed you to good hunting right after."

"I appreciate it, Belle," he said. "With any luck, I can catch up with Vik. There were some Navy spies following the *Shining Star*."

She frowned and tried to reach Viktor through the mental link they shared without luck. "He's shielding from me. You'll have to track him. Give me your hand."

He dutifully held his hand out to her. She took it and extended a talon.

"This is going to hurt. I must cut slowly to make sure all the damage is removed."

He nodded his understanding, and she proceeded. He grunted and moaned during the process, but he never cried out or screamed as he had when he'd grasped the cross. Belle's sonar showed her the burn only went down to the bone in a couple of spots, but they were crucial spots: the webbing between thumb and fingers and the pad of the palm next to the first knuckle of the pinkie finger. No wonder he couldn't flex the hand.

Finally satisfied she'd cut all the damage away; she plunged his hand into the water and began to hum.

"That tickles!" Jim gasped and tried to pull out of her grasp. Only her inhuman strength allowed her to keep a grip on the jumpy vampire.

Flesh reformed over the exposed bones and tendons; the hand maintained a skeletal gauntness, though. A quick glance showed his entire frame had withered and sunken over his bones.

Without warning, she released him and dove beneath the surface. She grasped the boat by the keel and propelled it to the dock, careful not to slam it against the pilings.

As a precaution, she swam to the other side of the pier and only surfaced enough to watch from beyond the lamplight. Jim needed to feed as soon as possible, and she didn't want him to make the fatal mistake of feeding on her toxic blood.

A boy made his way up the dock, a lantern swinging in his hand. He turned to look back at shore when the harbor master called some instructions to him. He turned back to his task of checking moorings and ran into Jim.

The boy didn't even have time to scream.

It took three more kills for Jim to regain a normal appearance. Belladonna disposed of the bodies gladly. She needed to replenish the energy she'd used to heal Sam and Jim.

Jim waited patiently for her to finish consuming the body of the trollop who'd been his last victim.

"I'm good now, love. You can use that dress to keep from drawing attention while we look for Vik."

She made a face and held up the less-than-clean garment. "She had fleas."

"Half the crew has fleas, Belle. You're immune to 'em anyway."

"Doesn't mean I like it."

"Just put the damn dress on. I think I've picked up his scent." A second later, he held his hands over his ears and glared at her. "Damn, what was that for?"

She'd emitted an ultrasonic squeal which nearly burst his eardrums. "The humans didn't hear that, but it got the fleas out of this dress." She slipped the garment over her head and had to tug on it to get the bodice over her breasts.

Jim stepped in close and grinned down at her. "Want me to help you with those?"

She showed her true teeth and replied, "You couldn't handle them, boy."

"Oooh, a challenge!"

She finished adjusting the fit of the dress and shook her head with a smile. "I should know better than to encourage you. Let's find the Captain before he drains half the town."

Jim instantly sobered. "Right." He sniffed the air from several directions before he finally pointed one way. "He went that way."

"Wh-what h-happened?" Sam couldn't figure out why she felt so cold. She squinted at the unfamiliar surroundings trying to figure out where she was. Everything looked dim and blurry.

"Sam?" She recognized her husband's voice.

"Britt, what happened? Where am I? Why is it so c-cold?"

She felt a warm hand on her forehead then cheek. She tried to lean into the warmth, hungry for it, but lacked the energy.

"See if she can drink some of this broth," an unfamiliar male voice said. "It should help build her blood back up. I'm surprised she's even awake."

"Thank you, doctor," Britt said. "Captain, will you hold her up, so she doesn't choke?"

"Of course." Bainbridge's voice that time.

Sam frowned. Her irritation and worry grew. "Stop talking as if I'm not here," she managed to growl out. "Answer my questions!"

"Awake and irritated." Another male voice: her brother Zachary.

"Zach?"

"I'll answer your questions, Sam," he replied. "You're in what used to be Mr. Grimm's cabin aboard the *Incubus*. It's probably too dark for you to see well. Dr. Coffin thought full lamplight might be painful in your condition."

"My condition?"

"Captain Brandewyne attacked you. If Mr. Rigger hadn't intervened, he very likely would've drained you dry. As it is, you've lost a lot of blood. That probably accounts for why you feel cold."

She felt arms lift her to a sitting position. "Please Sam, try to drink some of the broth," Britt implored her. She could hear the worry and distress in his voice, even though he tried to hide it.

"Give," she said. The broth proved to be rich and savory with fine chopped meat in it. She nearly finished the bowl before she felt the need to stop. "That was good! Since I don't feel sleepy, I take it no laudanum was added."

"No, Madam Westin," Dr. Coffin replied. "With the amount of blood loss you've suffered, even the smallest dose of laudanum could prove fatal. Given your husband's chosen trade, I think he'd rather resent me finishing what the Captain started, even unintentionally."

It took a few moments to process what he said. Once she did, she felt her eyes grow wide. "I would have turned."

"But you didn't die, and you haven't turned, love," Britt comforted her. "We just have to find a priest, and have you cleansed so that won't happen."

A blur of movement caught her eye. She turned just in time to see a ginger-haired man slam Captain Bainbridge against the bulkhead.

"You bastard! How dare you bring her here?"

"Thom! Stop it!" Zach reached for their brother. The vampire shrugged him off and drew back as if to lunge for Bainbridge's throat. The action dislodged the gold cross he still wore from behind his cravat.

Bright light flared between the two men. Thomas flew backward and impacted with the opposing bulwark nearly hard enough to splinter the wood. He shielded his eyes and roared with rage.

Before she knew what she was doing, Sam got to her feet, hands on her hips, and faced the ginger vampire.

"Thomas Winfred Brumble! That. Is. Enough!"

Thomas grew instantly quiet and turned to look at her. Zach held up his hands and took a few steps backward.

"Sam," Thomas started to say.

"Don't you 'Sam' me, mister. What do you mean attacking Captain Bainbridge like that? Answer me!"

Britt placed a hand on her shoulder. "Sam, love, that thing is no longer your brother."

She ignored him, but Thomas shot him a murderous glare and a fang-filled snarl.

"Don't you look at him like that; he is my husband. You will show him due respect. Britt, be civil, please."

To her annoyance, her vision grew dim again. "Doctor, please turn up the lamp some. I can barely see."

She heard the man say, "Catch her," in response; but it sounded muffled and remote.

A moment later, she lost consciousness.

Chapter 19

"There you are. We've been looking all over for you, Vik," Jim said when he spotted his Captain.

Viktor turned to face his first mate and the siren. A sense of relief washed over him. His barely admitted fear he would lose Jim as he'd lost Hezekiah had led him to fiercely block out anyone bound to him. He hadn't sensed either of them approach.

"You've fed?"

Jim nodded. "Belle cut the burn away so I could heal properly. I had three or four kills before we started looking for you."

Now that he'd lowered his shields, he sensed the siren's power radiate from her. "Pet, you feel much too potent for eating four corpses."

"I disposed of your leavings as we found them. I feasted tonight. The question is how many more will you take tonight? Even in a port like this, that many disappearances in one night will draw attention." Concern colored her tone.

He gave her a tight smile. "I did take that into consideration, pet. If we sail with the morning tide it will be assumed we took on extra crew. You've already seen to it no bodies will be found to raise the alarm. To complete the deception, I was about to go in and acquire a few fresh hands. I had planned to do a bit of whoring afterwards, but

I think you and I are better suited to fulfill each other's needs right now. I doubt a human would survive me at the moment."

"More for me, then," Jim said with a grin.

"Recruiting first, Mr. Rigger."

"Aye, Cap'n."

Vik shook his head and grinned. "Greedy bastard."

The three entered the nearest tavern.

"Cap'n, the man over at the corner table bears watching," Jim said. "He's one of the two Navy men who followed the *Shining Star* here."

"Pet, why don't you go over and invite him to join us?" Viktor suggested and motioned a barmaid over.

Belladonna stood and made her way to the indicated table. It didn't take her long to convince the spy to follow her back.

"He has no idea who you are, and I didn't feel inclined to educate him. Not much of a spy if you ask me," she told Vik mentally.

"This should be entertaining," he replied in kind.

The barmaid arrived with the bottle and glasses Vik had ordered. She looked at the men, glanced at the siren, and asked, "Will there be anything else, luvs? She raised her skirt hem up to her thigh as she asked.

"Not for me, pet; thank you," Vik replied and tossed her a coin. It quickly vanished into her apron pocket.

Jim hooked an arm around her waist and pulled her into his lap. "I could use some entertainment, my lovely."

"Captain, may I introduce Mr. McGowan?" Belle said.

Vik extended his hand, and the spy took it. "Pleased to meet you, sir; I'm in port looking to take on a few hands. I lost about twenty men to fever off the coast of Columbia about a month ago."

McGowan frowned sympathetically. "I heard it was bad this year. So many men fresh to the tropics fall prey to the local diseases. I'm not personally in the market for a new berth, but I may be able to point you in the right direction."

"Do tell."

"Aye; I've encountered several sailors between ships here. Granted, a good portion of 'em are little more than cannon fodder rather than skilled seamen. I'll be happy to point them out for a price."

Vik smiled tightly. "Ah yes, there is always the matter of price, isn't there. Very well, Mr. McGowan, what do you require in payment?"

The man looked around surreptitiously before he replied. "There's a dreadnaught in harbor named *Incubus*. The man I answer to is very interested in the movements of that ship or any news of its captain."

Viktor's smile never wavered. "You are in luck, sir. I'll wager you've had trouble getting any of the locals to talk to you."

"Aye, I have; been chased out of a few places for asking."

"Understandable; not many are willing to risk Bloody Brandee's wrath."

"He does have a reputation for being ruthless and vindictive. So, you don't share their fears, I take it. What can you tell me about him? Have you heard how long he plans to remain in port or where he might be headed next?"

Jim nuzzled the wench's neck to hide his smirk.

"Tell me, Mr. McGowan, did Nathan Critchfield say why he wants this information?" Viktor watched the man startle.

"Who?"

Vik gave him a pitying smile. "You aren't fooling anyone, sir. I begin to wonder why you were picked for this duty. You're not very good at it."

McGowan narrowed his eyes at the vampire. "Who are you?"

"Where are my manners? I completely forgot to introduce myself; Viktor Brandewyne, at your service."

The man stiffened suddenly, a look of shock on his face. He opened his mouth, but no sound came out. Instead, his body twitched a little, and foaming drool trickled from the corner of his mouth. His eyes bulged then glazed over in death, and his form slumped forward slightly.

Belladonna retracted a talon from the base of the man's skull. The poisonous stinger cells in her fingertip oozed a clear fluid before taking on the appearance of normal skin.

"Thank you, pet. We'll leave him here for now. Jim, meet us back at the ship when you finish. I've changed my mind about recruiting. I want to be away to Hispañola as soon as possible. Chances are the *Quicksilver* is already *en route* here," Vik instructed.

"Aye, Cap'n."

Viktor heard the woman ask his first mate, "Was that really Vik Brandee?"

"Aye, my lovely, it was."

Vik flew back to the ship carrying Belladonna with him. Once they touched down on deck, she stepped away from him and shook herself.

"I will never get used to that. I'll wait for you in your cabin," she said.

"As you wish, pet; I have some unfinished business with Mr. and Madam Westin." He headed for Grimm's former cabin.

He knocked at the door once he got there. Captain Bainbridge answered it, his cross clearly visible.

"May I come in?"

Britt Westin glared toward him from Samantha's bedside. "Do not invite him in here."

Before Bainbridge could respond, Viktor smirked. "I only asked as a courtesy, Mr. Westin. This is my ship. I don't need permission to go anywhere."

Britt paled a bit but held his ground. "I need to find a priest and have her purified. You cannot have her."

Viktor sighed and pinched the bridge of his nose. "In truth, I never meant to harm her. I release her from my thrall. Whether your brother will release the two of you is something you'll have to take up with him when he returns."

The man frowned, plainly confused. "Tonight was the first time I've seen him since we were boys."

"Perhaps, but he has seen you before tonight. I'm sure your wife told you about his first visit to her a few years ago. He also visited on your wedding night. Didn't you ever wonder about that cat bite you woke up with?"

Britt opened and closed his mouth a couple of times. "How did you —?"

"I know everything any of my Children do. I turned Jim, remember." He waited for the concept to sink in.

"Could that be why our crosses didn't work on you?"

Vik laughed and shook his head. He pulled the gold and emerald cross out of his shirt. "I seriously doubt it. I have never taken injury from a blessed object. This trinket only served to rein in my Hunger and stop it from claiming my mind completely. As you can see, it did not burn my flesh like it did Jim. I need to return it to its case soon, so it may replenish. I fear I drained its power for the moment."

"You are unlike any vampire I have ever encountered before."

"So, I have been told. I know a few who are several centuries old who fear me because of my uniqueness. Carpathia was sent to kill me."

At mention of the ancient vampire's name, Britt's face grew dark. "I remember you said she has been neutralized. What did you mean by that?"

"She is contained. If you will come with me, I will show you." He waited patiently for the man's response. He saw Britt struggle with his need to know and his distrust of vampires in general and Viktor in particular.

Curiosity finally won out.

On the way to his cabin, he sent a mental request to Belle. *"Mr. Westin is coming to my cabin, pet. If you would put something on, please; I would rather he not be unduly distracted."*

Her mental snort of amusement was the only response he got.

Belladonna sat on the edge of the bed clad only in one of his shirts. Of course, it hung nearly to her knees; it also gapped open at the neck enough to reveal most of her breasts.

Viktor enjoyed the view. It also drew Britt's undivided attention. Vik casually leaned down and whispered in his ear, "If you are this distracted by female flesh, you wouldn't have stood a chance against Thia."

The man jumped and shied away from him in alarm. "How did you get so close without my notice?"

"At a normal, easy pace, sir; you were too fascinated with my siren to pay attention to me." He looked over at Belle. "Pet, would you step outside for a moment?"

She rose gracefully and sashayed to the cabin door. "Don't keep me waiting too long, or I'll feel compelled to find satisfaction elsewhere," she said over her shoulder and slipped out of the cabin.

"Imp," he said once she was gone.

Britt made an appreciative groan. "You're right; without the proper precautions I would be no match for

Lady Carpathia. I will have to be on guard when I encounter her."

"Not as much as you'd think, now," Vik countered. "As I said, she has been contained." He opened the liquor cabinet and retrieved Carpathia's prison: it appeared to be a bottle shape made with some matte black ceramic with strange emblems etched into its surface. The etchings revealed a silvery substance beneath the ceramic. He handed it to Britt.

"What is this?"

"A silver-lined glass bottle with a silver clad cork stopper encased in bayou mud and magically sealed by the most powerful witch I've ever met. Inside it resides the Lady Carpathia."

Britt shot him a dubious look. "You expect me to believe this bottle holds a full-sized woman."

"No; she is trapped as an amorphous smoky fog. I'm sure you noticed that phase of transformation when your brother first revealed himself. I understand it is a very rare talent among vampires."

The vampire hunter turned the container over and examined it from several angles. "How did you manage to get her to go into a silver-lined bottle?"

Viktor grinned. "I didn't give her any other escape. The salt air has tarnished it black, but every crack and crevice of this cabin is overlaid with silver-- except for this one small hole." He indicated a corked hole in the wall shared with the next cabin. "I invited her in here, closed the door and the trap, and used mirrors to force her to flee through the hole as smoke. My former first mate, Mr. Grimm, held the bottle opening to the hole and sealed it the moment she entered."

"I am impressed, sir. Still, it seems a rather fragile prison."

"It can never be opened or broken. The only one who could open it was Hezekiah Grimm, since he sealed it; that is part of the spell Gloribeau put on it when she encased it." He paused for effect. "I can't even open it; and I have been sorely tempted to, despite the danger to myself. Thia's pull is that strong."

"You were lovers? I thought you said she was sent to kill you."

Vik smirked and nodded. "Aye to both; she had some grand scheme to use my wild magic to conceive, kill me as she was ordered, the use the offspring to overthrow her master. Obviously, her plan failed." They stood in silence for a while, and Viktor reached a decision. "Keep her for me. If I'm not in her presence, she can't drive me mad. She had a tendency to bring out the remorseless predator in me; one who cares nothing for who he takes as prey and revels in the kill for sport. I know I cannot afford to give in to that part of me. He takes no heed of the consequences of his actions or preparation for them."

Britt cocked his head and studied him for a while. Finally, he spoke. "You are an anomaly to me, Captain Brandewyne. I will safeguard this. You understand I will have to find some source to verify she really is in there."

"Of course, if you can find such a person."

"You aren't the monster I thought you were."

Vik chuckled and shook his head. "There are those, Mr. Westin, who would say I've been a monster all my life."

To his surprise, the vampire hunter grinned at him. "Oh, you are a monster, just not a reprehensible one. In fact, you are rather likeable. I can see why my brother took up with you. Did you really meet like he said?"

"Aye; we were both lads at the time. Caught him trying to burgle the same house I was. We fought, well, wrestled. I think he would've won if your wife's father hadn't beaten him bloody before he jumped ship. We became fast friends, and he's the most loyal man I've met in my life. He has been a brother to me, and I love him for it." He sighed and looked down. "As valuable to me as he is as Lazarus, his death is the one thing I regret most."

"And I've already forgiven you for that, Vik," Jim said from the doorway.

"That was quick; you're losing your staying power, Jim," Vik said with a laugh. "Usually, you're racing the dawn to get back to the ship."

The first mate made a rude sound. "Haven't had my sport yet. I spotted the other spy before I could make it to a room with a wench."

"I take it you dealt with him accordingly."

"Aye; I sent the lass from our table over to invite him upstairs. Haven't met the Navy man yet who would turn down some sport if his commander wasn't around to stop him."

Britt asked the question. "What about the woman?"

"She has no memory of what happened tonight," Jim answered. "Vik, since you two are getting so chummy, I think I'll take advantage of Belle's mood and see if she'll entertain me."

He gave his first mate a tight smile and shook his head. "You'll escort your brother back to his wife then go find sport elsewhere. She'd just spoil you for mortal women anyway."

Jim shrugged and grinned. "I had to try." He turned to his brother. "C'mon, Britt; you don't want to be in hearing distance of those two once they get going."

Tamara. A. Lowery

Chapter 20

Back in Grimm's old cabin, Samantha regained consciousness unnoticed for the moment. She cautiously opened her eyes and allowed them to adjust to the dim light. Two figures stood in one corner of the cabin: her brothers. Opposite them, Captain Bainbridge occupied the lone chair. His gold cross glittered in the lamplight.

Thomas turned and stared at her unnervingly. She felt swimmy headed; she would almost swear his eyes glowed faintly. She felt an uncomfortably warm itchy spot inside her blouse. She reached up and pulled out her gold cross. It too seemed to glow.

Thomas shielded his eyes and looked away. Zach glanced over at her and back at their brother. "Thom, what were you thinking?" he asked softly.

"I wanted to convince her to go home or at least away. She won't survive another attack," the vampire replied.

"I appreciate you want to protect me, Thom," Sam said. "I came here to ransom you and Zach from Captain Brandewyne."

He gave her a sad smile. "You can't. I belong to him and Mr. Rigger. I am their Childe now."

She felt hot tears prick her eyes. "I don't care. You are my brother first. I want you back."

He gave her a lost look which broke her heart. "Don't you understand, Sam? I'm dead. Even if I come with you, I am no longer safe to be around. The Captain helps me keep my impulses under control. Left to my own devices, my Hunger would rule me. Your crew would be endangered. Worse, you would not be safe if I lost control."

"You would never harm me, Thomas. I know you," Sam argued. "It's not in you."

The look he gave her chilled her to the bone. Finally, she saw the predatory creature he'd become. "Samantha, I would kill you without hesitation. Listen to your husband. I am no longer the brother you've always known. I can pretend to be human; but at heart all I care about is blood and feeding on it."

"Well, now I am conflicted," Britt spoke from the doorway.

She turned to see him standing there with his brother. "About what?" She didn't bother to hide the tears she could not hold back.

"Everything I've ever known about vampires since I started hunting and studying them tells me his words are true," he said gently and moved to her side to comfort her.

She leaned back, wiped at her eyes, and scowled at him speculatively. "I detect a 'but' in that statement."

He nodded. "I've just had a very interesting talk with Captain Brandewyne. I have no choice but to believe he is unlike any other vampire I've ever known about, and that he really is alive rather than undead. He has retained some of his humanity; and I believe it affects the vampires he sired."

He pointed at Thomas and continued, "Your brother still possesses some of his humanity as is evidenced by his words. Were he truly a completely soulless predator, I don't believe he would try so hard to convince you of the danger he presents. He wouldn't care."

"So, he could safely come with us."

He held up his hands and shook his head. "I wouldn't go that far, my love. I've observed enough vampires to know that one as young as Thomas cannot maintain much self-control outside of their sire's dominion. The majority of the ones I've dispatched have been under a score of years dead. I strongly suspect both our brothers cling to their sire's humanity to keep their Hunger and power from driving them mad and seducing them to become little more than animals."

She mulled over the theory and watched the two vampires in the cabin for their reaction. Thomas wore an expression she recognized from his boyhood; the same one he got when he'd finally understood something his tutors had been trying to explain to him for days or even longer. He obviously agreed with Britt on this.

Her husband's brother proved harder to convince, it looked like to her. Jim stood there giving Britt an appraising look with a slightly crooked smile.

"That may well be true for Thomas and the rest of the cadre," he said. "It sounds plausible enough, anyway."

"You don't think you're drawing on your captain's humanity?" Britt asked.

Jim shrugged. "His power, definitely; his humanity, I doubt it. Hell, it's only been a few months since I've been able to take human form at will and maintain it. Different magicks came into play when I was brought over."

Sam had to argue that. "If my memory serves, you didn't have any trouble maintaining human form the night we met."

Every male in the cabin reacted to her icy tone and distanced themselves from the vampire first mate.

Jim remained un-phased. "If you recall, a crewman lost a finger that day. At that time, the only way I could take my human form was to consume human flesh. I was able to hold my form because I fed on your blood after I ate the finger."

Sam felt her face grow hot. She hadn't given the two tiny scars on her inner thigh any thought since she'd first noticed them. She glanced over at her husband and saw the same realization on his face.

Jim apparently noticed it, too. He turned to his brother with an unrepentant but slightly sheepish smile. "I think I just made things awkward for the two of you, my apologies. That one night was my only time with her. She'd found you by the next time I had an opportunity." He sighed, rubbed the back of his neck, and shook his head. "Never thought I'd say anything like this; it was selfish of me to lay my claim to either of you. There's an old priest in this port, Father Cranaugh. He's an Irishman and could drink Jon-Jon under the table; he's always trying to convert me every time I run into him. I release you both. I know the Captain already released you. I strongly suggest you go find this priest as soon as possible, before one of us changes our mind."

Sam sat lost in her thoughts during the short trip to shore. She felt weak and shaken by the night's events and didn't argue letting Britt and Captain Bainbridge do all the rowing. She even let them help her debark; she still felt wobbly from blood loss.

Bainbridge led them to one of the more reputable looking taverns. He sent them in with instructions to get a room for the rest of the night. He would make inquiries about the priest Jim mentioned.

Before long, Britt was tucking her into bed in one of the better rooms.

"He's in love with you," he said, startling her out of her musings.

"Captain Bainbridge?"

"No, love; my brother. I know the looks he gave you. I've seen them in my reflection when I think of you. I don't claim to know Brandewyne's reasons for relinquishing his hold over you. I believe Jim did it because he loves you."

"You aren't angry he took my virginity." She made it a statement rather than a question or an accusation.

He laughed a bit. "I'm sorry, Sam. I'm still in shock that he survived to adulthood. I've lived most of my life with the belief he was murdered as a child. I haven't really had the chance to think about what he did to you." He looked at her. "Are you angry about it?"

She tilted her head to the side and thought about it for a while.

"Not as much as I imagine people think I should be. I would rather it had been you on our wedding night." She looked up at him and saw the love in his smile. It encouraged her to continue. "I remember he was very persuasive and gentle. He knew I was a virgin, and he made my pain as brief as possible and quickly forgotten."

She felt the heat in her face at the memories.

"It's alright, Sam. I don't fault you for enjoying it. In fact, I'm glad you're able to take pleasure that way. I've heard far too many men complain their wives just lay there or act as if the act of making love is just a tedious duty to be endured." He leaned down and kissed her gently and passionately.

She smiled back up at him, full of love for this wonderful man she'd been fortunate enough to find. She saw the love and the heat in his eyes.

He chuckled lustily. "I really love the fact I can make you look at me like that," he said, but stood and stepped back from the bed. "However, you need to recover more. Sleep, Sam; I'll wake you when the Captain returns."

She pouted a little. "Tease." Without warning she yawned and realized she really did feel too sleepy for any sport. The last thing she remembered before sleep took her was Britt's tender smile.

Britt answered the soft knock. He peered blearily at the two men on the walkway. One wore slightly grubby vestments and looked at him with amazement.

"Mr. Rigger! Ye finally decided to change yer ways!"

Britt blinked at him then realized the man's misunderstanding. "Oh, no; I'm his brother, Britt Westin. Unfortunately, Jim is beyond redemption now."

The priest squinted and looked more closely at him. "Now as I c'n see ye in the light, I see ye are a bit older'n I remember the lad. I'm sorry for yer loss, Mr. — Westin, did ye say?"

Britt nodded.

"Can't say as I'm surprised to hear he's passed, though. Pirates have short lives, it seems. Didn't he sail with Bloody Brandee?"

"He still does."

The priest blinked and frowned. "Thought ye said he's beyond redemption. If he still lives, there's still hope for his soul. Ye can't give up on 'im just because of th' company he keeps."

Britt sighed and glanced at Bainbridge. He, in turn, shrugged and said, "I felt it better if you explained in person."

Britt nodded and turned his attention back to the priest. "Jim recommended your services, Father Cranaugh. Have you any training in cleansing someone and releasing them from a vampire's thrall?"

He had to admit the old priest seemed quick-witted for someone who reeked of beer and rum. "So, yer saying young Jim is a cursed bloodsucker now. I'd heard the tales about Brandee; but I never gave 'em much credence before. Never knew Jim t'have a brother; he never spoke of one; but ye look too much like him t'be lyin'."

"I thought he'd died as a child, when my father took me away. He was too young then to remember me, I guess." He shrugged. "And yes, he was turned by Captain Brandewyne."

Father Cranaugh pursed his lips and nodded. "Very well, Mr. Westin. How may I help you?"

"My wife and I need to be purified. I recently learned I've been bitten by my brother. Samantha was bitten by him before I met her. Last night, she was almost killed and turned by Brandee. She is still very weak, and I'd like her cleansed first. I don't want to lose her."

"Right." The priest checked the folds of his robes and retrieved a small silver box. He opened it and pulled out a small vial of holy water and a wafer of the Host. "Good thing for you, the ceremony doesn't require much. Show me the bites."

Lazarus screamed.

Viktor didn't wonder why. He knew.

The physical and psychic pain of the bond with the Brumble girl breaking felt like being gutted. While familiar with the pain of being gutted, something he'd experienced a time or two since becoming a vampire, he'd never felt the severing of the bond between himself and any of his living victims. The loss of a turned Childe, while unpleasant, did not compare.

The fact Lazarus went through the same torment barely soothed his regret of releasing the wench from his thrall. He doubted he'd ever be willing to put himself through this again.

Just as quickly as the pain hit, it stopped. The abruptness in and of itself left him reeling. It took a few moments to regain any sense of balance or stability.

He looked over and saw Lazarus curled in on himself, his tail wrapped tightly about his body. Without warning, the cat screamed again and began to convulse.

Viktor frowned before he realized the bond his first mate shared with his brother had just been severed. He'd suffered that agony twice.

He moved over to the cat and gently stroked his fur. Lazarus trembled beneath his touch; his eyes tightly shut.

"I'm sorry, my friend."

Tamara. A. Lowery

Chapter 21

"Enter."

The young man entered Commodore Critchfield's cabin. He quickly stepped forward, placed a tightly rolled scrap of vellum on the desk, took two steps backward, and saluted.

Critchfield returned the salute. "That will be all."

Once the man — boy, really — exited the cabin, the commodore broke the seal on the tiny scroll and read the terse message.

"*Incubus* in Tortuga."

Critchfield cursed the delay his choice not to follow the *Shining Star* personally had caused. He knew the chances of Brandee remaining in that port until he arrived were slim. Still, he recognized the fact the merchant ship may have avoided the rendezvous with the pirate if the *Quicksilver* had remained a presence.

Briefly, he admitted facing the sister ship to his dreadnaught in Tortuga's harbor could've proven devastating to the port town in collateral damage. Given it was a known den of piracy and smuggling, he wouldn't have lost any sleep over it, though.

He gave the order to make best speed for Tortuga. Even if Brandee left before he got there, he stood a chance of intercepting the pirate somewhere outside of port or finding someone who knew where the bastard was bound for next.

The return to the open sea worked as a balm on Viktor's bruised psyche. He always felt most himself there.

The temptation to remain at sea searching for prizes warred with a growing sense of urgency to complete his quest for the Sisters. Some deep instinct insisted his time was running short.

He resolved to head toward the norther shore of Hispañola and *Mamaan* Juma. Dealing with her would prove unpleasant regardless; he saw no point in delaying it any further.

He hoped it would provide Jim enough distraction to recover from the double blow he'd just suffered, as well.

A couple of days after the *Incubus* left port, the doctor deemed Samantha healthy enough to travel again. In fact, the speed of her recovery astonished him. Britt assured him it was due to being freed of vampiric influences. The doctor remained skeptical of that reasoning but kept it to himself.

The next day, Captain Bainbridge had the crew make ready to set sail. They ended up delaying their departure another two days to coincide with a convoy bound for Havana. He worried about the delay, sure that the *HMS Quicksilver* was bound to show up eventually. The security and anonymity sailing out with the convoy afforded seemed worth the wait. He just hoped the Navy didn't arrive before they left.

When they finally did sail out, he kept an aft lookout toward the harbor entrance. Just as they neared putting Tortuga on the horizon, the lookout reported a ship too large to be any other than the *Quicksilver* or the *Incubus* approaching the harbor.

When no report came of the ship changing course to pursue, Bainbridge breathed a sigh of relief.

After a day with no sign of pursuit, he gave the order to break from the convoy and change course for New Orleans. Last he'd heard, the French weren't too fond of the English currently. Being in French colonial waters might afford them some protection from Critchfield.

Then again, it might not.

The *HMS Quicksilver* did not enter the harbor. Critchfield ordered the ship to blockade it instead. He knew the island had nothing by way of defenses capable of challenging his ship. The one fort had never been rebuilt from when the Spanish had partially dismantled it nearly a century before.

He put out five of the launches to intercept ships coming in or leaving port. He wanted to find information on Brandee; but he used the excuse of searching for smugglers aiding the rebels in the colonies along the eastern seaboard. As long as he produced a smuggler or blockade runner or two every so often, he knew the Admiralty would look the other way on his obsession with Viktor Brandewyne.

Much to his frustration, he learned he'd missed Brandee by just under a week. No ship stopped by his interceptors knew or would admit to knowing the pirate's heading.

Under cover of darkness, Critchfield donned civilian garb and went ashore. He took one of his officers with him. It troubled him McGowan and Wilkins hadn't made contact yet. He wanted to investigate personally.

He made the rounds of the taverns posing as a merchant captain and asked after them. At the fifth stop, he finally had some luck.

Even drinking moderately, Critchfield began to feel the effects. He'd already visited four taverns in a fruitless quest for information about his men. His mind turned more toward finding a wench and having some sport. He could make fresh inquiries tomorrow.

The woman serving him and Commander Peters caught his eye. He gave her a wink and flashed a gold piece. She soon made herself exclusive to his table.

"What can I do for you, luv?" she asked.

"Been at sea a few months, lass; I've a feeling you already know what I want."

She chuckled lustily. "I'm sure I do." Without further preamble, she sat in his lap and wriggled against his crotch. He groaned appreciatively.

"What brings you to Tortuga, luv?"

"Business; there were a couple of men I was to have met with, but no one seems to have seen them. Noticed that behemoth just beyond the reef; I'm starting to wonder if they were — delayed." He deliberately gave her the impression his business was less than legitimate.

She gave him a knowing smile. "What say we take this conversation up to one of the rooms where it's more private?"

He nibbled at her ear and chuckled. I like the way you think, my sweet." He nudged her off his lap, stood, and took hold of her arm. She didn't protest. "I'll see you on the morrow, Mr. Peters. If you've no luck, we can continue our search then."

"Aye, sir; I may find a wench, as well."

"You do that."

Once in the room, he turned to the woman and said, "Strip; I like to see what I'm paying for."

She laughed. "Oh, you're a forceful one. I like that. Why don't you tell me about these men you were supposed to meet up with? If I haven't seen 'em, I can ask around about 'em."

"I dare say you'd have better luck than I."

"Possibly."

"I don't claim to know what their real names were, but they go by McGowan and Wilkins —," he paused when she flinched at the first name. "What?"

"N-nothing; I thought I saw a rat." He felt sure she was lying. "I don't remember hearing anyone use those names."

He shrugged as if he believed her. "I'll give you their descriptions later. Right now, I want some sport."

She seemed to relax a bit and finished undressing. He stalked around her with a leer then removed his own clothes and let her see he was already fully erect.

She grinned.

"Good," he thought, *"let her think she is in control for the moment."*

Aloud, he said, "Lay back on the bed, sweet, and open for me. I'm ready for you; but I want to make sure you're ready for me."

"I have rose oil to make your entry easy, luv."

His smile turned sinister, but she missed the nuance. "Oh, I don't think the oil will be needed. I know a trick or two to prepare you."

She lay back on the bed and spread her legs wide. "I don't often get a man who wants to take his time; especially when he's as ready as you are."

"Then this should be a treat. I know I am going to enjoy it."

He crouched over her and ran his fingers lightly up her sides, raising gooseflesh on her skin. He gently slapped her hands away and waggled a finger at her when she tried to reach for his erection.

"Oh no, sweet; I want to last a long time. You'll be well paid; don't worry."

"I just wanted to touch it," she pouted.

"Can't have that; I'll just have to tie your hands to make sure you behave."

She giggled.

He retrieved his belt and cinched her wrists together. He then secured them to the head rail of the bed.

"Can you pull loose, my sweet?"

She tugged at her bonds and only succeeded in tightening them. She shook her head no and watched him with parted lips and heat in her eyes.

"Good."

Once again, he crouched over her. He leaned down, kissed her, then moved lower and took her nipple into his mouth. She gasped and moaned. He switched to her other breast and suckled at it hard while his fingers parted her folds and explored them. She was already wet.

He switched breasts again, using teeth this time. He dipped two fingers inside her and flicked at her nub with his thumb. She bucked against his hand.

He rose up above her and saw the abandon in her face. "Like that, do ye?"

"Oh yes! More!"

He grinned an evil grin and added a third finger. Her juices flowed around them.

"Now we're getting somewhere." He added a fourth finger and thrust faster. She began to yip with each thrust.

He added his thumb and she screamed. "Too much!" she managed to gasp out.

"Oh no, my sweet; when I've been this long without, I like them loose and wet. I said I want to last as long as possible; and I can't do that if you're tight. You will take all of this."

He thrust his hand into her up to his wrist and wriggled his fingers until he had enough space to curl his fingers to form a fist. She screamed and bucked as he twisted his fist side to side then resumed thrusting.

"Stop; stop; please stop! N-no more, oh God please!" she gasped and cried.

In response, he twisted faster and pushed until he felt the barrier of her cervix. He leered down as he held that position and grasped her chin to force her to look at him.

"Tell me what I want to know, and I'll pull it out. Otherwise, I'll just leave my hand where it is and fuck you in the ass."

Her eyes grew wide in terror. Tears streamed down her face. "What do you want to know?"

"McGowan; I saw you flinch at the name. What do you know?"

"I j-just s-saw a r-ra—." She broke off in a scream as he began thrusting again.

He stopped once more in the deepest position and said, "Lie to me again."

"He's dead," she said with a trembling voice.

"What about Wilkins?"

She shook her head. "I don't know. I only saw the man called McGowan. The people who killed him called him a spy."

"Who killed him?" He didn't budge from his spot.

"A woman; she was with Vik Brandee."

He wondered if Lady Carpathia had crossed him and sided with the pirate. "Was she black-haired with dark eyes?"

"N-no; her hair was blood red, and her eyes were grey. They looked yellow when she killed the man."

Slowly he straightened his fingers and removed his hand from her. He rubbed her juices and blood on his erection before pushing it into her abused opening.

Whispers, cries, and screams came from the room for the next few hours.

Late the next day, Critchfield called his officers into a meeting aboard the *Quicksilver*.

"Gentlemen, it seems plain our quarry is much feared in this port. I propose we give these blighters something to fear even more."

The men greeted the proposal by thumping on the table and cheering.

"While I still wish to continue the monitoring and questioning of all vessels entering or leaving the harbor, I believe I've discovered a more useful source of information. Mr. Peters, Mr. Church, I want you to take a compliment each of marines ashore. Mr. Peters, you will go to Cayona; and Mr. Church, you will take the Basse Terre side of the harbor. I want you officers to round up every whore in this port and bring them here for questioning."

"Whores, sir?" one of the other officers questioned. "They will destroy discipline aboard."

Critchfield gave him a cruel and cold smile. "Only if they are given free reign, Mr. Fuller. I have no intention of doing that. With the right — motivation, these women can give us much more information and more reliable, at that, than we'd ever get out of sailors or merchants."

"Begging your pardon, sir," Fuller said, "but where will we find the funds for that?"

"I never said anything about paying them. This port has a history of harboring pirates and smugglers. That infers these women are in collusion with said criminals by association. They will answer our questions or face the consequences. Have I made myself clear, Mr. Fuller?"

"Aye, sir."

"Peters, Church, you have your orders. Dismissed."

As the days passed the cruelty of his interrogations increased along with his frustrations. Apparently, Brandee had a stronger control over his crew of pirates than any Naval commander had over his men. Not one whore would tell him what the pirate's heading had been when he left port; and several admitted to servicing his crew.

The only pertinent bit of information he'd gleaned was the fact he'd also missed the departure of the *Shining Star* by mere hours. They'd left with a convoy bound for Havana.

He wasted no time in dispatching a small crew to track down the convoy. He had them use the ketch McGowan and Wilkins had sailed and left in the care of the harbor master.

He reasoned that someone aboard the *Shining Star* should have useful information on Brandee. The very fact the ship had sailed out well after the pirate told him they had the bastard's favor.

Chapter 22

The *Incubus* had to anchor almost at the mouth of the harbor at Terra Beau. The ship's draft ran too deep to safely enter the shallow waters.

Viktor and a select group went ashore. He left Jon-Jon in charge of the ship and crew. A fresh dose of the rum tainted with the vampire's blood ensured none of the men grumbled about having to stay aboard.

Before long, he, Jim, and Belladonna arrived at the Dead Wolf Tavern. Jim made a beeline for the brothel entrance. Viktor and Belle found a table.

He waved one of the serving wenches over and ordered some food. He didn't recognize her from his previous visit.

While they waited, he scanned the room. A few people quickly glanced away when his gaze crossed them. Peripherally, he saw one man glance at him then leave the room.

"The smell of fear is thick in here," Belle commented.

"Indeed; will you dine with me, pet?"

She shrugged. Mentally, she asked, *"Am I supposed to pass as human?"*

He replied in kind, *"Aye; we both are: Jim, too."*

"So that's why you opted to come ashore at night."

"Aye; Jim can only hold his human form by night without drawing on my power. He must be Lazarus by day to survive."

"How do you intend to explain his transformation when the sun rises?"

"I don't intend to be here that long. I don't have to appease Juma; I have to kill her."

Belle shot him an alarmed, angry look. He felt her rage, incredulity, and fear. He smiled at her and sat back to let the returning serving wench place their food on the table.

"Smells wonderful, pet," he said and smacked the girl on the rump. "The food smells good, too."

She smiled, but it carried a nervous tic. She held her empty tray up like a shield in front of her and took a step back.

Belladonna snorted when the girl fled back to the kitchen. "Losing your touch?"

He chuckled. "The cook told her about me. I heard them talking."

She frowned and leaned back. "You are trying to distract me from being angry at you."

He took a bite of the food, chewed deliberately, and swallowed. "Is it working?"

"No."

He shrugged and continued to eat. He also continued their mental conversation. *"This would go so much easier without you angry at me, pet."*

"Have you lost your mind? You plan to kill a Sister of Power?"

"I am required to, Belle."

She opened and closed her mouth a few times, clearly at a loss for how to respond to that statement.

"Eat your food, pet. It's actually quite good."

Once she complied, he resumed silently, *"Juma stole her power. Celie warned me against facing her before I'd dealt with the other Sisters. I've done that now."*

"What about the power balance? Killing a Sister of Power, regardless of how she got her power, is just as dangerous as sharing power with one."

He sighed and looked at her. *"I've finally figured out why they keep calling me the One."*

"Wait; what?"

"All the Sisters acknowledge me as the One Who Will Bring Change. Celie told me the final ingredient she needs to free me of my curse is Juma's ashes. Think about it, Belle; Juma was never supposed to be a Sister. Her removal is the change I'm supposed to bring."

Belle broke off the contact and buried her thoughts deep. She knew he was right, but she knew he'd only scratched the surface. In all her visions she'd caught the sense of what Viktor Brandewyne was truly meant for.

It frightened her.

"Why did we come here? We should have gone straight to her and gotten this over with," the siren spoke low.

"I'm hungry. She knows I'm here. I want her to think she has the upper hand," he replied.

"Doesn't she?"

"No," he said with a sinister smile.

"What do you mean? What possible advantage do we have if she already knows you're here?"

"All in due time, pet."

The siren picked at her food for a while in sullen silence. Viktor savored his meal but found her mood distracting. With everything he had at stake, he knew he couldn't afford distraction.

"Belle, I need you alert; and I need you not to be sullen."

She growled softly. "It seems one of us needs to be angry."

"No, pet; we need to not be angry." He paused and looked at her. "Do you think I'm being too cavalier about this? Is that what has you so irritated?"

"Yes!"

He reached out and caressed her cheek. With a gentle smile, he said, "I appreciate your concern, Belle; and I'm grateful for it. It is misplaced, however. I assure you I do not take my situation lightly. I cannot afford to let my emotions come into play. She will try to use my anger or fear against me. My gambit will be to maintain my calm and use it to irritate her. I will use her irritation against her. I also have the Elder's Stone; something I did not possess when I first encountered her."

Belle shook her head and smiled. "I have been among the humans too long. I've started to think like them instead of the predator I am. Your plan is good."

They'd barely finished their meal when Juma's message arrived.

Patrons near the door of the tavern began a mad scramble for the back. A zombie nearly as large as Jon-Jon or Anvil entered and advanced on Viktor's table.

He sent a silent summons to Jim, and the first mate joined him and Belladonna moments later. He noted with amusement Jim still struggled to secure his breeches properly.

"These buggers again?"

"Just the one; I don't smell any others nearby," Vik replied as the walking dead man moved closer. "I wanted you close enough to me to escape Juma's influence. I don't want a repeat with you of what Venoma did with Belle."

"Aye, that would not be good."

The zombie reached the table, but a barrier prevented it from getting close enough to grab any of them. It flailed its arms at them in vain for several minutes.

Finally, Viktor grew bored with the diversion. "As entertaining as this is, we need to get it over with."

He stood and approached the zombie. It moved back, but not of its own volition. The invisible barrier pushed it back.

"Interesting." He looked the zombie in the eye but saw nothing there he could recognize as consciousness. "I don't know if you can use this creature to hear me or not, *Mamaan* Juma. The time has come to face you again and call you to account. Use this thing to lead me to you or not. Either way, I will find you."

The zombie stopped flailing, turned around, and walked away from them. They followed.

The creature led them out of the town and into the jungle. They occasionally passed through small fields.

Viktor's sense of direction told him they were headed roughly southeast. The land rose gradually the further inland they got. He felt Belladonna drawing on his sense of calm and self-control to combat her growing unease. He knew she didn't like to get too far from the sea.

From Jim he sensed determination. Both of the vampires had a score to settle with Juma.

They came to a clearing on a hilltop. Vik couldn't tell if it was the same one in which he'd been cursed or not. Too much time had passed, and his faculties had been muddled then.

"Be ready," he told his companions silently. *"She's going to do something here. It reeks of her magic; and it just got stronger."*

The Elder's stone grew warm against his skin.

Dozens of hands erupted from the earth, grasping fingers reaching for them. The sound of bones snapping when the magic barrier crushed the sprouting hands before it reminded Vik of walking on dry twigs.

The stone grew warmer, almost hot. He pulled the milky crystal out of his shirt to reveal its glow and widen the bubble of protection from the Sister's magic.

The damaged hands melted back into the ground. The trio remained on guard.

Their guide zombie turned to face them and raised one arm to point. It didn't indicate a direction for them to follow. It marked them as targets.

Fully formed zombies rose from the ground, crawling out like maggots. The creatures surrounded them and began to close ranks.

At first, the Elder's Stone's protective barrier pushed them out of the way. Juma's power rippled over the dead, and more zombies rose. Every time Viktor's group pushed forward, the number of dead grew and pushed back. Eventually, the press of bodies proved too thick to push through.

Belle grew frustrated first and lashed out with her talons. Although the zombies could not breach the barrier, the siren had no trouble. Body parts fell in all directions as the siren waded into the zombies.

Viktor and Jim watched in alarm as dismembered hands grasped and clung to her. The sheer weight of them began to slow her down. A few zombies got close enough for their appendages to fuse back to their bodies.

Vik knew he needed to act quickly. At best, the creatures would immobilize Belle. At worst, they could rip her to bits. Sirens might be hard to kill, but he was pretty sure one couldn't survive something like that.

Thankfully, the damage she'd done to the wall of reanimated flesh gave him some leverage. He shoved through until he could reach the siren. He grasped her waistband and pulled her back into his sphere of protection. The dismembered hands dropped from her as she crossed the barrier.

"Are you injured?"

"Just some scratches," she replied. "They kept grabbing on, even after I cut them up. They'd just put themselves back together. I'd hoped we could cut our way out."

He shook his head. "I should've warned you about their ability to reassemble. That's how Juma was able to capture me to begin with."

"It doesn't look like she's trying to smother or crush you," Jim observed, "more like she just wants to hold you in place."

"Aye; but for how long? Somehow, I don't see her coming to me; and she damn sure isn't trying to force me in any given direction." He thought about it for a while. "She is hoping we will self-destruct."

They both gave him confused looks. "I don't know how long zombies can function, but they don't have to. She has stacked them so deep around us I cannot push through them. Even if she just leaves them here to rot, I cannot get through them. If either of you leaves my protection you will be vulnerable."

Understanding bloomed in both the vampire and the siren.

"If I leave the bubble, I will be subject to her power over the dead," Jim stated. "If I stay, I'll be caught by the sunrise."

"Aye; if she can't use you, she hopes to destroy you. However, she doesn't know about your ability to become Lazarus, which grants you immunity to sunlight."

"So, she is foiled there, which makes me the greater danger to you," Belle said. "She can't control me, but she has cut me off from the sea. I've already seen what happens if I try to carve my way out. I'm sure she knows I will eventually languish outside my element and hopes I'll turn on you and kill you in exchange for my freedom."

"Exactly," Vik agreed. "We do have a means of escape, however."

He scooped Belladonna up into his arms. "Jim, stick close. We're flying out."

The two vampires launched into the night sky. They stopped and hovered a couple hundred feet above the zombie horde.

The clearing they'd been trapped in thronged with zombies, hundreds of them. As they watched, the dead laid down and just dissolved back into the earth.

Belladonna shuddered in his arms then stiffened. "The cadre! Viktor, the crew is in grave danger."

"Calm yourself, pet. I personally oversaw the sealing of their hold with silver chains. I also hung my emerald cross on the latch. It has had time to recharge. They present no danger to the crew."

He felt her relax. Even though he knew she would claim it was concern for maintaining a larder for her use, he believed she truly cared for the crew and their well-being beyond the possibility of them being potential meals.

"Cap'n," Jim interrupted his thoughts. He looked over at his first mate and raised an eyebrow.

"There's a fire on the next hill; a big one."

He adjusted his hover to look in the direction Jim indicated. The Elder's Stone grew warmer when he faced the fire.

"She's there."

Chapter 23

Viktor and Jim landed well away from the fire. Vik set Belle on her feet, and they waited.

No more zombies appeared. Vik reckoned Juma saw the futility in that ploy as he tucked the Elder's Stone back in his shirt. Still, she did not come into view.

"*Mamaan* Juma, you only delay the inevitable. Are you that afraid of what you have made me?" Vik directed his challenge toward the fire.

Still, he got no response.

"What is that?" Belle asked. "Do you hear it?"

"Hell, I feel it," Jim replied.

A rhythmic beat vibrated up through the soles of their feet. It seemed to come from the earth itself. Slowly, it grew louder until Viktor felt his heartbeat try to match it as it thrummed through his chest. He found it mesmerizing yet unnerving. A sense of anxious agitation threatened to overwhelm him.

He closed his eyes; but it only made the sensation worse. He took a deep breath and forced himself to relax and remain alert. He opened his connections with his first mate and the siren fully and let his hard-won sense of calm spread to them.

"She is coming. I sense her just on the edge of my perception," he thought to them. *"I want to give her the impression her spells are working."*

They mentally acknowledged the plan.

He opened his eyes and saw a ghostly-looking figure approach the fire from the other side. As it grew closer, he saw it was Juma.

She wore a simple sleeveless white shift and a white cloth wound around her hair. He saw ceremonial markings similar to the ones she'd worn when she'd cursed him on her face and bare arms. The darkness of her skin beneath all that white lent to the specter-like impression. It made the drawings and headdress seem to float in the night air.

He noticed Juma kept the fire between them. *"She is afraid of you,"* Belle informed him silently. *"I detect five different spells of protection."*

"Good; I have a nasty surprise in store for her," he replied.

Aloud, he said, "I have returned, Juma. It is time to finish this."

"I knew you would return, pirate. I have not forgiven you for the murder of my David. For that, you will die tonight."

He interrupted her. "Oh, one of us will die tonight, witch; of that, I have no doubt."

She paused just long enough to let him know his words had shaken her. She laughed harshly; but he recognized it as bravado rather than confidence.

"You dare to threaten me? You hold no power here. This is my domain, vampire. I have played you and used you to my own purposes. Do you know why the other Sisters call you the One?"

He refused to rise to the bait. His silence didn't deter Juma.

"The One brings change. He shifts the balance of power from many to one. I know you are the One, because I chose you to fulfill that role. Now, you have collected magic from all the other Sisters and brought it here to me. Once you are dead, I will take it and become even more powerful than the Elder!" Her voice took on a maniacal tone.

"Are we supposed to take that seriously?" Belladonna asked silently.

"She seems to. She stole the power she has now, if I was told correctly. I don't think she understands the consequences of that or of what she thinks I'm going to let her do," Vik replied. *"For the most part, her claim she chose me to be the One is a lie, and she is trying to take advantage of the situation. Right now, she is trying to intimidate me."*

Unaware of their mental conversation, Juma continued to gloat. "You are a fool, Viktor Brandewyne. You have now given me two tools to ensure your death. Knowing my power over the dead, did you honestly think you could use your vampire against me?"

"No; I brought him along to protect him from you," he told her the simple truth.

She cackled.

"Vik, she's sending a lot of power my way," Jim let him know.

"Play along as if she controls you. I feel it too. The Elder's Stone is trying to burn a hole through my shirt, but I don't want to reveal it too soon. If she tries to make you do something which will harm you just pantomime. With the fire between us, she won't be able to tell it's not real."

"Aye, Cap'n."

Jim dropped to one knee. "As you command, mistress."

"Hold the siren. I do not want her to interfere," she ordered.

He grasped Belle from behind and pinned her arms to her sides. She made a show of struggling but didn't put real effort into it.

"Come forward, slave," Juma said and motioned curtly to someone behind her.

A crouching, naked figure crept forward. Despite the awkward position the female had to maintain to achieve the crab-like crawl, she moved with inhuman grace. A wealth of black ringlets obscured most of her face. Skin once a rich golden brown now shone pale cream with a hint of gold.

"Hello, pet."

"Pet?!" Belladonna's shock and ire were not feigned.

The female turned feral eyes up to her sire. She snarled and bared her fangs. A low growl escaped her throat. A quick dart of her gaze, too fast for human eyes to notice, let Viktor know the hostility was not directed at him.

"I see you recognize your first Childe," Juma said. "You may stand, slave."

The nude vampire rose from her crouched position. Her body remained just as pleasing to look at as Viktor remembered it. She reached up and pushed her hair back from her face. He groaned in appreciation.

"He's mine!" Belle snarled. "You stay away from him!"

The vampire ignored her.

"Now, it is time for you to die, Viktor Brandewyne. Slave, if you wish for your freedom, you will kill this one responsible for your slavery," Juma decreed.

Viktor met his Childe's gaze. She gave him a sly smile and approached him slowly. Her gait proved very seductive and brought back memories of his time with her when they'd both been human.

In the time it took him to surface from those memories, she reached him. He vaguely heard Belladonna's pleas and curses for him to defend himself. He reached out and pulled the vampire to him.

She reached up and wrapped her arms around his neck. "*Mon Capitan*, why did you leave me here to suffer?"

"It was not my intention, Carmella. I did not understand what I had done to you. Do what you must; but do it quickly." He leaned down and kissed her.

Belladonna shrieked her rage, jealousy, and grief.

Mamaan Juma reveled in triumphant glee. Thanks to the pirate's vampire progeny, she would soon escape the Elder's prophecy. What's more, she would gain the powers of all the true Sisters of Power.

What started as vengeance now turned into the perfect opportunity.

She watched as her slave embraced the man she had cursed. Even better than outright killing him, it looked as if Carmella would turn her sire to a true vampire. Juma had to admit she hadn't considered the possibility of placing the One fully in her sway, only of eliminating him.

She blinked when sparks from the fire got too close to her face. Carmella no longer embraced Brandewyne; she had vanished, and he stood smirking at Juma. She felt a sudden burning sensation in her throat then lightheadedness.

She could not feel her body.

Her sight faded.

Everything faded.

Carmella eased Viktor's dagger from its sheath at his nape while she kissed him. She'd almost forgotten how skilled he was. Her body ached to have him in her. Juma never permitted her to bed anybody. The witch treated her little better than an animal.

She pulled back from the kiss and smiled at him. He returned the smile.

His smile then transformed to a smirk; and he cast his gaze toward the witch.

As directed, she acted quickly.

Belladonna played her part enthusiastically; her jealousy and rage only partly feigned. At the unspoken cue from Viktor, she shrieked. Embedded in the supposed expression of rage sounded a simple, two-note weather spell. A tiny whirlwind swirled a shower of sparks from the fire toward Juma's face.

Belle wished Viktor would permit her to blow the entire blaze onto the witch; but such was not his plan.

Carmella took advantage of the momentary distraction to move unseen behind her tormentor. She used her sire's blade to remove Juma's head.

The witch's body collapsed forward into the bonfire and writhed and twitched.

The stench of burning cloth and the aroma of roasting meat soon filled the air.

A shockwave of energy burst from the burning body and nearly knocked the vampires and siren off their feet.

Viktor strode over to Carmella and took the witch's head from her. He looked at it with a frown and cast it in the fire on top of the body.

"You can let go of me now." Belle wriggled in Jim's arms trying to get loose.

"But you feel so nice," the first mate replied with an impish grin.

"Jim, take Belle with you back to the ship."

"Aye, Cap'n; you want me to keep her occupied?"

"No. I've already lost one first mate to an angry siren; I don't want to lose another."

"If you think I am going to leave you alone here with her —."

He held up a hand to stop Belle's tirade. "That is exactly what you are going to do, pet. I'll need her help gathering the ashes; and I have to decide what to do with her."

Belle opened her mouth to say something; he cut her off. "This is not a subject where I need your advice. Jim; now."

The other vampire launched into the night sky with the protesting siren. Viktor knew she wouldn't give Jim too much trouble once they were high enough.

Still, he sent a comforting thought to her. *"Thank you for your help, Belle. I do appreciate it."*

"You're welcome. Get rid of her."

He cut off the connection.

"Carmella, pet, I need to talk with you."

"Oh, but *mon Capitan*, there are so many much more interesting things you could do with your tongue."

He looked her over and smiled. "I am sorely aware of that, pet; but there are important matters we need to discuss. Have you fed tonight?"

She shook her head; a feral light returned to her eyes. "The bitch starved me for the past month in anticipation of your arrival."

He pulled out a large flask and handed it to her. "This should hold you over until I can arrange a proper feed."

"What is it?" She opened the flask even as she asked.

"Blood mixed with brandy; the alcohol preserves the blood during long voyages. It also stretches out the supply," he replied.

She didn't hesitate to drain the flask. She handed the empty flask back to him and licked her lips. "That was an interesting flavor change."

"I've grown fond of it." He placed the flask back in its carrier. "My senses are still a bit clouded from Juma's residual magic. Have you made any vampires?"

"I didn't know I could. I wonder if that was why she never allowed me near humans. I always thought it was just to protect her followers."

"Very probably; I've been told that creating a vampire gives you more power, but I also know it is unwise and frowned upon by most of the older vampires to overpopulate."

"You've met other vampires?"

"A few; some not much older than you; others positively ancient." He questioned her about something she'd just told him. "Am I to understand you've never had human blood? What have you fed on?"

Carmella made a face. "Mostly, she gave me goat or pig blood. Pig tastes better. If she was particularly pleased with me, she'd let me drink a calf. A few times I've caught rats and drained them."

"Rats?"

She nodded. "There were times she would starve me for several months and not let me die for the day. She would force me to crouch in a small crate in the sunlight.

Depending on the time of day, I would get horrible blistering burns from the light between the slats."

Impulsively, he reached up and cupped her face. "Oh pet, I am so sorry I was not permitted to come back for you sooner."

She placed her hand over his and leaned into the contact. "Why are you so warm?"

"I'm not dead, pet. I'm cursed. I think Juma hoped you would drink me."

He saw her eyes begin to glow at the thought. Celie warned him long ago not to taste vampire blood or let another taste his. He'd come perilously close to fully losing his humanity to Lady Carpathia. He would not risk it to his Childe now.

"Don't even think about it, Carmella."

"What?"

"Drinking from me; I will also warn you against trying to drink from Belladonna. If she doesn't rip you apart for it, her blood will end your existence instantly. Sirens are toxic to vampires."

The shock and anger on her face told him she'd been unaware of that danger.

"Juma tried to compel me to kill you and your first mate then kill the female. She meant to destroy us all."

"Aye, she very likely did. She was a vindictive bitch," he agreed. He sighed. "I take it your self-control is good. Can I trust you not to attack my crew?"

"My self-control has had to be good. I will not feed on your crew."

"Can you fly?"

"I do not know. Until I saw your first mate do so, I did not consider the possibility," she answered with a shrug.

He looked up at the sky then back at the fire. "It appears she has been fully consumed. Hold this bag open, and I'll put her ashes in it." He handed a blue cloth bag to her.

Obediently, she held it open as he scooped up handfuls of ashes and embers alike. He remained careful to not let the embers touch her flesh. Some instinct told him it would be bad if they did. Amazingly, the outside of the bag, when she handed it back to him, felt cool. The embers had no effect on it.

"It will be dawn soon; there isn't time to try to teach you to fly." Without further warning, he grasped her about the waist and launched into the sky.

Tamara. A. Lowery

Chapter 24

A searing wave of anger crashed into Viktor moments after he alit on deck and set Carmella on her feet.

Belladonna stormed over to him. "Why is she here?"

Unruffled since he'd expected this reaction, he said, "To leave her here alone would be irresponsible."

"You should have killed her."

Carmella met the siren's glare with one of her own.

Viktor stepped between them. "Enough! She has done nothing to merit it."

"It is because of her you are cursed!" Belle stood as close as possible to him without touching.

He gazed down at her, his voice pleasantly calm, a sure sign of his anger. "And I killed her for it. She helped me destroy Juma. For that she deserves my aide and protection, not my enmity." He turned so he could see both of them. "I will have peace between you on this ship. Is that understood?" He put power into his words.

Both women shivered. Belle glared at him but nodded. Carmella crouched down and rolled fear-filled eyes up at him like a beaten dog.

He frowned; even the siren gave her a puzzled look. Viktor reached his hand down to her. "I am not Juma, pet.

I will not torment or terrorize you, nor do I bear you any malice. You are mine, and I take care of what is mine."

"He does," Belle affirmed. "The only times I've seen him treat anyone brutally have been when they deserved it, or the rare occasion when his control has been compromised." The last she said too low for any of the crew to hear.

Carmella took his hand and stood, looking at the two of them with something akin to awe.

"You are his wife, no?"

Belle blinked and shook her head. "No; he is my mate. I denied the fact to myself for a long time; but I was forced to admit it not so long ago."

Viktor raised an eyebrow, surprised by the siren's words. "After I get Carmella situated, I would like to speak with you alone, Belle."

She nodded.

He turned his attention back to Carmella. "First, I need to clothe you. The lads are already starting to drool; and you are not safe for them right now." He held up a hand to forestall any argument. "You haven't fed yet. I don't count that flask as a proper feed."

"Belle, have you any objections to sharing a meal with Carmella?"

The siren blinked in surprise. "Not really; only a fool turns down free food from a trusted source. How many from the larder did you intend to give her?"

"For now, just one; she has never tasted human blood. I want to see how she reacts first."

"She drinks blood, too?" Carmella sked.

"I like the taste of it, but I'm a meat-eater," Belladonna clarified. "I often consume Viktor's victims after he's finished with them. Otherwise, the ship would be overrun with vampires."

"Oh."

"Jim, escort Carmella to Mr. Grimm's cabin and make sure the porthole is covered."

"Aye, Cap'n." The first mate gave a half-bow and offered his arm.

She took it and asked, "Who is Mr. Grimm?"

"Someone who is no longer with us, my lovely. Now we best hurry; sun'll be up soon."

She needed no further prompting.

"Belle, tomorrow night I intend to make arrangements for her somewhere safe. We'll talk later. For now, pick out something healthy from the larder hold." He leaned down to kiss her; she let him but refused to put any passion into it. He sighed as he watched her head below. Something told him the siren would take out her frustration on him.

Later that afternoon, Belladonna knocked at Viktor's door.

"Enter."

She opened the door, entered the cabin, and shut it behind her. He sat behind his table making a log entry.

"A moment please, Belle." He finished his pen stroke, sprinkled sand on the fresh writing, wiped the quill clean on a small scrap of cloth, and placed the stopper in the inkwell. Once he brushed the sand off the page, he closed the logbook and carried it to the shelf where he kept it and a few other books.

Finally, he turned back to her. To anyone who saw him, he appeared calm, almost bored. Belle knew him too well. Her presence made him apprehensive. She had a feeling she knew why.

"I owe you an apology, Viktor." She fought not to laugh at his startled reaction. She was trying to make peace; she didn't need to antagonize him.

"For —?" he prompted.

"I let my jealousy over Carmella rule me. I remember you'd mentioned her when you first talked with me about your curse. For some reason, it never entered my mind that she would be vampire. I guess I just assumed you had prevented her rebirth. You rarely mentioned her again."

"Truth be told, I rarely thought of her, especially after you warned me Jeorge could use Melanie to spy on me. I knew Carmella had turned, but I never felt her try to delve further than my surface thought." He sighed and smiled ruefully. "I admit I didn't actively try to block her often."

Belle felt alarm; but, considering recent events, realized it was pointless. "Did you want Juma to know what you were doing?"

"I did. Oh, I was selective about what I let Carmella see; but she didn't pry as much as I would have expected. For an untrained vampire she has a remarkable amount of self-control in some respects. She resisted Juma's control."

"Or perhaps Juma's sway over vampires wasn't as strong as over the truly dead," Belle countered. "Why did you want her to know what you did?"

He smiled a little. "I wanted her to fear me. Each encounter with a Sister of Power made me more formidable. Also, if I'd openly blocked Carmella, Juma would've interpreted it to mean I feared her."

"I see; apparently your strategy worked. The bitch reeked of fear." She walked to the bed, sat down, and crossed her arms. "I sincerely hope you aren't planning on bedding Carmella any time soon; this isn't jealousy talking, either. My concern for you is genuine."

"You have my attention."

"She's had her first taste of human blood, and she liked it; got drunk, actually. She's definitely your daughter, too. She fucked her meal silly before she tore his throat out."

"Literally, I assume?"

Belle nodded and continued, "I don't think she meant to do that. She just bit him at first; but she lost control after that initial taste. I don't want you to risk getting bitten because she couldn't control herself. You're too close to being free of your curse."

He strode to her and caressed her face. "Believe it or not, pet; that thought had occurred to me. I don't know how many feedings she'll need to gain that control. Juma had been starving her in anticipation of my arrival."

"Well, now I want to kill her again."

He chuckled and gave her shoulder a light shove; this resulted in her falling back on the bed.

"I can think of much better uses for our time and energy, pet." He leered down at her.

She grinned back up at him.

The next night, while the *Incubus* still lay at anchor, Viktor reached out to his other daughter. *"Melanie, I need to speak with Jeorge."*

"I will see if he will receive me," she replied.

A short time later, she let him know she was in contact with her master. Viktor rejected the idea of possessing his Childe to communicate directly. The experience could be draining, and he still had to deal with Carmella. He would just deal with the delay of Melanie acting as relay.

"Greetings, Jeorge; I have a problem I wondered if you might be willing to help me with."

"Captain Brandewyne, it is always a pleasure. Direct as ever, I see. What is your problem?"

"I have recently liberated my first Childe from the witch who cursed me. She has been severely mistreated by her former mistress and, until last night, had never had human blood. I believe she was also kept in forced celibacy until then. She was a highly skilled whore before I turned her."

"Are you saying she has had no training?"

"He seems upset about this," Melanie interjected.

"To my knowledge, my first mate and I are the only vampires she's ever met," Viktor replied. *"Belladonna monitored her feeding and disposed of the remains. The woman has been starved of any blood, even animal, for at least a month. She still showed enough self-control to thoroughly fuck her victim first."*

He waited for Melanie to relay that information.

Jeorge didn't keep him waiting long. *"Impressive; what would you like me to do?"*

"Would you be willing to take Carmella in and train her?"

"I can; I am curious as to why you don't tend to her training yourself, though."

Viktor sighed. He realized he would have to reveal something about himself he'd rather not. *"My time is running short. The witch who cursed me is dead, but the curse is still on me. Once I get Carmella situated, I sail to Savannah to have that taken care of. To be honest, I do not know what the breaking of this curse will do to the vampires I have made. I want Carmella and Melanie somewhere they will be safe but also not pose a threat."*

"I see."

Jeorge paused for a moment; Viktor held his silence to allow the ancient vampire time to reach a decision.

Finally, a reply came. *"Bring her to me. We will discuss the situation and my terms when you arrive. Now, I must hunt."*

"Thank you, Jeorge; Melanie."

Carmella caught her sire's scent wafting in under the cabin door, she quickly arranged herself on the bed. She'd enjoyed the human, but her Hunger eventually overrode other needs.

"Come in," she said when the cursory rap came at the door.

He entered the cabin, looked at her and smiled, but it held a note of sadness or perhaps regret. He did not cross the room.

"You aren't dressed, pet," Viktor said.

She frowned. "I don't understand. Does being a vampire make having sex impossible for a man?"

"Hardly," he said with a quick bark of laughter. "But it is not safe for you and me to be together that way at the present. Now please, pet, put something on; my control is not what it should be right now."

She gave him a sultry laugh. "I don't mind a little danger, *mon Capitan*."

The sudden chill in his voice terrified her. "I do not take unnecessary risks, Carmella. Put. Your. Clothes. On."

Quicker than a human eye could follow; she donned the dress he'd given her. She took just enough care to not tear the fabric. She didn't want to make him any angrier.

She jumped a little to see him standing very close to her now. It hadn't occurred to her he could move just as quickly as she could. She cast her eyes down and stood perfectly still.

His hand on her cheek felt feverishly warm; his touch was gentle. She closed her eyes involuntarily and leaned into the caress.

"I am not angry at you, Carmella. As I said, it is not safe for us to be together as lovers. I don't want to hurt you, nor do I want to risk being bitten by you."

She looked up at him in confusion. "You made me a vampire; how could my bite harm you?"

His smile made her heart melt. She wondered if she honestly loved him, or if all those years of Juma's cruelty conditioned her to cherish even the smallest sign of kindness.

"You are truly a vampire, pet; I am cursed, and my curse may be broken. If you bite me, there is the chance you could turn me. I would fully become a vampire, complete with all of the weaknesses I currently do not have." He lifted her chin and held her gaze, yet she felt no compulsion from him. "Carmella, I am truly sorry for what I did to you. Death, true death would have been kinder than leaving you to Juma's torments. Please tell me honestly, if you knew there was a possibility to be free of your Hunger, would you take it?"

She considered the question carefully. "My Hunger has been a source of torment for me. She used it against me at every turn. You have been free; how has it been for you?"

The look on his face told her he hadn't expected the question. Just as she hadn't; he didn't answer right away.

Finally, he spoke. "The Hunger is a dangerous addiction. I revel in the way I feel when I gorge myself on human blood. That is a danger; especially to young, inexperienced vampires. It can draw attention of the wrong sort if left unchecked. I don't like things which make me lose control of myself. Sometimes I think only my survival instincts from my years as a human and a pirate — and occasionally sheer luck, have kept me ahead of the hunters."

"I think I understand what you mean about how human blood makes you feel. Last night was amazing; almost better than being with a man after so many years," she said, relishing the memory.

His grin told her he understood completely. "I am afraid I can't afford to give you another victim all to yourself, but I do have a good store of rum mixed with blood. You will not go hungry on this voyage. As for your other need, I have a cadre of vampires on my crew. They rarely get to go ashore. Would you have any objection to servicing them? You and they are safe for each other."

She blinked at him. "How many of them are there?"

"Counting Mr. Rigger, eight. Don't worry, pet; you can set the terms of what order and how long each can spend with you."

"And if I do not wish to service any of them?"

"That choice is yours, pet. I will not force you to. They berth in one of the hold compartments. You have the use of this cabin for the duration of the voyage."

She tilted her head and studied him. Something about him seemed — she wasn't quite sure how to put it; not softer, but more — human? He'd been so confident, arrogant, and selfish when she'd first encountered him. Oh, he'd enjoyed pleasing her, but she knew he'd only used her for his own means. Now, he was trying to do something for her.

"Why are you being so kind?"

Although she hadn't intended them to, she saw her words had hurt him. She placed a hand on his arm and gave him a look of concern.

"I failed you, pet."

She shook her head. "No, I know you wouldn't have knowingly left me in that situation. I kept her cruelty from you whenever I reached out to you or you to me. I knew she wanted to kill you. If you'd known what she put me through, you would have come back before you were ready to face her. I've felt your power grow over the years; and I've drawn on it to resist and survive her."

Without warning, he embraced her and kissed her. His warmth flooded through her like wildfire.

When he released her from the kiss, she smiled up at him. "You have made me hungry for more than blood. I will see your Mr. Rigger; from there, we will see."

He hugged her again. "I'll send him in with a bottle. You'll need to feed."

"Thank you." She stopped him as he began to open the door. "Where are we bound for?"

"New Orleans; I have a friend there who can take you in and give you the training you need. His name is Jeorge. I have another Childe there with him named Melanie. They will help you."

With that, he left the cabin.

Tamara. A. Lowery

Chapter 25

Much as he would've liked to remain in Tortuga and wrest some valid information from the locals about Brandee's whereabouts, Critchfield had other duties to attend to. He'd managed to convince the Admiralty to leave him on pirate hunting duty rather than ordering him to fight the Colonist rebels' pathetic excuse for a fleet. He'd argued that pirates often turned into blockade runners if the greater profit lay there; and the Navy's battle strategies would best be served if he were allowed to hunt the southern waters for them.

When concern about rumors of a dreadnaught flying colonial colors had been raised, he'd reminded them of Brandewyne's possession of the erstwhile *HMS War God*, renamed *Incubus* by the pirate. This prompted the Admiralty to assign three fast sloops to Critchfield's *HMS Quicksilver* in addition to the two frigates already in his escort. He was given *carte blanche* to find the *Incubus* and retake her or sink her; but he still had to do patrols in search of other pirates and blockade runners.

With no idea what tack Brandee took when he left Tortuga, Critchfield opted to sail towards New Providence. The area often proved a good hunting ground.

Halfway to New Providence, the lookout spotted what appeared to be a derelict adrift. The tattered remains of the

Union Jack fluttered from her mizzen. Critchfield dispatched two longboats, each with five marines aboard, to investigate.

The sergeant noticed the buzz of flies the moment he and his squad boarded the *HMS Trent*. He saw only a few, but the sound which came from the cargo hatch hinted at millions of the insects.

He had a feeling he knew what they would find below. Still, he ordered a couple of his marines to open the hatch while the other two stood ready with muskets.

"It's not battened, Sergeant."

"Noted; open it."

They threw the hatch back on its hinges and took a step back. The flies grew louder, a few flying out the open hatch, but nothing moved below, nor was much visible beyond the square of sunlight on the deck of the hold. The smell of rot wafted up to them.

"Right," said the sergeant, "this has the marks of a fever ship. Tie scarves around your faces, men. No sense in risking sickness."

As soon as his men complied, they started down the ladder to the hold. The sergeant went down last. The second squad boarded as he started down; they headed aft to investigate the cabins.

Beyond the square of sunlight, an unnatural gloom filled the hold. It didn't take long to realize all the gun ports were shuttered. This struck the men as very odd.

"Oesterling, go open a couple of those ports. Let's get some light in here."

"Aye, Sergeant."

The man stumbled a bit on something underfoot hidden by the shadows. "Careful with your footing. There are things on the deck," he warned his companions.

He reached one of the gun ports, undid the latch, and pulled the rope and pulley system to raise the shutter. Diffused light streamed in; the port faced away from the sun.

A whispered sound of movement came from the other side of the hold.

"Rats?" one of the men asked.

"That sounded much larger than rats," the sergeant countered, "something big enough to kill them." He pointed at the obstacles, now visible all over the deck, which Oesterling had stumbled on. Dead rats, their throats torn out, several beheaded, scattered the deck.

"I don't like this, Sergeant Bowen," Oesterling said after examining a couple of the carcasses. "I don't see any blood on the vermin or on the deck."

"Aye, that is odd," another marine commented. "Why would they scrub the decks but leave the carcasses to rot?"

"Be careful. Garrison, make your way to that side and open another gun port."

"Aye, Sergeant."

Garrison eased his way into the lingering gloom and shadows, kicking the rat bodies out of his way as he went. He had to go on the other side of the cannon to reach the latch for the shutter.

He undid the latch and reached for the pull rope.

With a surprised grunt, he dropped to the deck, hidden by the gun.

"Garrison?"

A strangled gurgle could be heard, and his fingertips grasped at the air just visible above the barrel of the gun. They disappeared, and wet, sucking, slurping sounds reached the men's ears.

Sergeant Bowen caught Oesterling's eye and motioned for him to quietly investigate. The man eased over with his bayonet at the ready. The other two marines moved wide to cover him from either side.

"Oh God!" Terror laced Oesterling's voice.

His companions fired their weapons past him at whatever lay on the deck hidden by the cannon.

A gurgling scream, both human and not, rent the air.

A man-sized blur darted past Oesterling and struck the other two marines so hard the sergeant heard their spines snap.

The two men lay on the deck gasping and moaning. Oesterling stood with his back arched and head pulled back to draw his neck taut.

The darting blur now stood still, holding the struggling man in this position as if it took no effort at all. The dingy remains of a captain's coat and Navy uniform adorned the creature. It may have been a man once. Bowen saw little to mark it as human anymore. Blood drenched the lower half of a ghastly pale face. The mouth hung open in a grimace to reveal long sharp teeth like those of an animal. The eyes shone with an unnatural light.

"Sergeant Bowen, I was just about to dine; won't you join me?" The creature addressed him.

He shook his head, unable to look away from the horror before him, but unwilling to approach it, either. He raised his musket.

The creature's eyes glowed brighter, and it assumed the expression of a stern scowl. "Sergeant, I am Captain Vernon Kendridge of His Majesty's Royal Navy. I order you to lower your weapon and come here at once!"

He almost obeyed; the compulsion to do so was so strong. "No sir; you have attacked royal marines. I do not recognize your authority. You will release my man; or I will fire."

Sergeant Bowen, get out of there man!" came a call from the deck above. "He's a madman!"

The thing calling itself Kendridge grinned again. "He's right; I am quite mad — and Hungry."

It opened its mouth wide and bit deep into Oesterling's throat where it met his shoulder. It ripped a gaping, spurting wound and fed greedily at the crimson flood.

Bowen heard a scream. He realized it came from his own throat. He fired his musket. The marines on the deck above fired theirs as well.

Mini balls pierced the creature and Oesterling. The marine's body went limp in death. The creature dropped it and lunged for Bowen.

Just as quickly, it retreated to the shadows and beat at the flames which erupted when it entered the sunlight.

Bowen wasted no time clambering back up the ladder. He looked at the other sergeant and his squad. "What about Crowe and Plotkin? They're still down there. That — thing broke their backs."

"Then they're dead already, most likely. We've got the logbooks. Let's get back to the Commodore and make our report."

The moment he learned Kendridge had encountered Brandee some months back, Critchfield took a personal interest in the reports. Normally, investigations of derelict ships were handled by the lower ranks.

To an ordinary man, the log entries made by Captain Kendridge did seem like the ravings of a madman. He wrote of an empty ship; maddening hunger; food he could not eat because it tasted like ashes; wine he could not keep down; trying to eat rats raw after the food rotted only to discover the blood revived him; starving again after the rats were depleted; and an extreme intolerance for daylight.

To Critchfield, these entries merely validated what Mr. Westin had told him about vampires. They also confirmed the rumors of what Brandee had become.

He glanced out the windows of his cabin and reached a decision. Already, the westering sun neared the horizon.

He headed for the helm.

"Mr. Hastings."

"Aye, sir?" the deck officer replied.

"Have the remains of the away party put in quarantine and order a de-lousing. I have reason to suspect that derelict is a plague ship. Their report mentioned a multitude of dead rats. No one else is to approach it. I want it burned to the waterline, not scuttled. I don't want to risk any of the rat corpses floating up and passing infection along."

"Aye, Commodore; what about the men still on the thing? Shouldn't we send a boat for them?"

Critchfield knew his eyes held fury, but he kept his tone even, if curt. "They are murdered, Mr. Hastings. There is a madman aboard her. I will not risk bringing him aboard any of our vessels and spreading his sickness or madness. It would be far more humane to burn him with the ship. Chances are, he's dead. Both sergeants confirmed they shot him."

"Very well, sir; I'll get a detail on it right away."

Critchfield held up a hand. "Make sure to use flaming shot to do so. As I stated before, I want no one else to board her."

Hastings nodded his understanding.

Critchfield spent that evening pouring over the later log entries for the *HMS Trent*. The fact Brandee deliberately left Kendridge adrift without proper sustenance struck him as vile cruelty, ignorance, or retribution.

He did learn something about vampires which Westin hadn't informed him of. While a vampire could subsist on the blood of lower creatures, human blood was required to preserve and nourish reasoning intellect. Kendridge's log entries after encountering a small merchant ship became much more lucid, even if he'd stopped dating the entries.

I finally feel a little like myself again. For the first time in more nights than I can count, I can think clearly again.

Sadly, I know this reprieve from Hunger and madness will be all too brief.

A small merchant sloop came across my vessel this evening. I say merchant; in truth, they were scavengers. Having exhausted the population of rats aboard some time ago, I called out to them in my weakened condition when they boarded. Two came to investigate, pistols drawn. When they found me, one of the unlucky bastards shot me. Until that moment, I'd barely been able to move. Before I realized what I was about, I had the man's throat torn out with my teeth. The pure ecstasy of his blood pumping into my mouth and down my throat was, quite frankly, orgasmic. Not even bedding my wife had I ever felt such pleasure and satisfaction.

His companion stood paralyzed with fright. I had presence of mind enough not to gorge on the man right away. I didn't want to let the other one escape. I left my first victim on the deck and broke the legs and arms of the other man. It took him a full minute to start screaming. This brought two more over to investigate and lend aid.

I immobilized them as well, but no more would come. I could hear five more heartbeats aboard the other vessel and decided to take the ship.

Unfortunately, some unseen barrier kept me from crossing over to it. My efforts to do so proved enough to frighten the remaining scavengers away without attempting to retrieve their comrades.

I find myself trapped aboard this floating prison, perhaps until it runs aground. At least I have a food source for some time.

Critchfield rubbed his eyes and poured a glass of port before he continued reading.

It appears my condition is contagious. I finished draining my first victim on his second night aboard. On the third night, he woke with the same elongated, sharp teeth and Hunger which is mine. Thankfully, he seemed bound to obey my will, and I was able to prevent him from attacking the other prisoners. I ordered him to man the helm and sleep on deck; then I took the precaution of battening the hatches from below, as well as latching all the gun ports and the windows in my cabin.

My will almost relented the following morning. I felt him die, and it shredded my soul with pain and sorrow; but I could not afford to share my food with him. I have decided to ration myself with the remaining three men.

The last entry in the log had to have been made several days later, in Critchfield's opinion.

I fear the madness will take me again, if it hasn't already. Brandewyne appeared in a vision to me. He told me the currents had brought me to populated waters. He knew I'd depleted the blood available to me and sacrificed the vampires I had made.

Vampires; at least I have a name for what I've become. He gave me that. He also told me if I bled my victims with a blade instead of feeding on them directly, they wouldn't rise as new vampires. If I didn't have a blade, I should rip their hearts out or wring their heads off. He said I had the strength required to do that now.

Why he saw fit to help me, I do not know; but I am grateful for it. Hopefully, I will encounter another vessel before my Hunger drives me mad.

Critchfield closed the logbook, folded his hands under his chin, and contemplated his strategy for dealing with Brandee when or if he ever caught up to the pirate.

After determining the eastern waters were quiet, the commodore ordered his small armada westward toward the Gulf of Mexico via the Florida Strait.

Just after they cleared the Strait and approached Cuban waters, the lookout spotted sails.

Within a few hours, the *Quicksilver* approached the other vessel enough to make out its name through the spyglass: *Incubus*.

Chapter 26

"Bugger."

Jon-Jon shot a worried look at his Captain. Viktor ignored him and mulled the situation over. The timing was less than desirable. His control over his Hunger was tenuous at best. He really couldn't afford any extra delay.

"Cap'n, we can outrun 'em," Jon-Jon said. "Hasn't been that long since we careened, and the barnacles weren't that bad then."

He shook his head. "No, Mr. Jon; that bastard has built a small armada now. He won't stop coming. It's time I put a stop to this."

"Pet, I'm going to need your help."

He felt a sense of irritation from her; but she came to the helm just the same.

"You know we don't have time for this," she said low enough to not be overheard. "It's bad enough we're taking her to New Orleans instead of heading straight back to Savannah."

He shot a warning glare at her. She raised her hands in surrender. "Fine; I understand your reasons for making it a priority. I'll leave it alone. What do you need me to do?"

"I want this done with as quickly as possible. I can't call on the cadre right now. It won't be dark for at least another hour, and I don't want to wait for that. Can you prevent the faster ships from flanking us?"

The siren looked at the smaller vessels which gained on them. "Yes; I'll make sure the currents keep them grouped close together."

"Thank you, pet."

Over the next half hour, he had the helmsman bring them about to give the approaching Navy ships his broadside and ordered all the gun ports open on that side.

He took some satisfaction in watching the crew of the three foremost ships scramble to keep from colliding as the currents forced them together. It amused him even further to read the increasingly agitated signals between them and the *Quicksilver*. It seemed their inability to flank the *Incubus* had Commodore Critchfield quite vexed.

"The front three are almost in range, Cap'n," Jon-Jon informed him. "Shall I signal the gun crews?"

"No; I don't want to waste shot or powder on them. Lazarus, come forth."

The black cat emerged from beneath the wheelbase where he'd been napping. He yawned and stretched then gazed up at Viktor expectantly.

"Now is not the time to be lazy, Jim. I need you to scout the interior of the center ship in that grouping."

Obediently, Lazarus transformed into a raven and flew to his indicated target. It didn't take him long to relay the information to his Captain.

"Blimey! Wha's a raven doin' a'th'way out 'ere?" one of the deckhands aboard the *HMS Gauntlet* wondered. "Ain't nachrel, I tell ye."

"Quite you! Attend your tasks!" one of the officers barked. "We're about to enter battle."

The raven in question dove at the deck and dissolved into a black vapor which seeped through the deck boards out of sight.

"Lord save us; tha's an ill omen," the sailor muttered under his breath.

Even the officers who saw this exchanged worried glances among themselves. They'd watched the phantom bird come from the pirate ship they pursued. A bare murmur of, "witchcraft," could be heard circulating among the sailors and the gun crews.

"Belay that bilge! Attend your posts!" the first officer ordered.

Everyone aboard heard a whistling sound followed by a splintering sound and some impact on the bow near the waterline.

A moment later, flames, shrapnel, and screams filled the air.

"What are you planning?" Belle asked.

Viktor knew the question referred to his request for a harpoon, some thin line, and three grenades.

"Lazarus just confirmed where the forward magazine is on the center ship. I plan to destroy all three from there," he replied. "Can you force them any closer together?"

She nodded and sang a couple of notes. He felt the winds shift slightly and saw the outer boats drift so close to the center one to nearly foul their rigging together. He quickly lashed the grenades to the harpoon and lit their twined fuses with a cannon match. He took careful aim and launched the harpoon with inhuman strength.

The projectile whistled through the air with deadly precision. The steel head struck the timbers of the center ship just above the waterline with enough force to pierce the hull and another bulkhead.

It embedded in a powder keg in the ship's forward magazine. Moments later, the grenade fuses burned down to their charges.

The crew of the *Incubus, HMS Quicksilver,* and the two remaining Navy escort ships watched as the *HMS Gauntlet* erupted in a ball of flame and splintered wood. The two ships flanking it caught fire and took damage from the explosion. It didn't take long for the fires to reach their powder magazines as well.

Debris, burning, sinking wreckage, and bodies of the dead and dying littered the surface of the sea between the two dreadnaughts.

"Feel free to feast, pet."

"Later," she said. "This isn't over yet. The sharks won't be able to eat all of them."

"True; I seriously doubt this will stop the commodore. He still has two escorts." He turned and smiled grimly at the siren. "I'm feeling cold-blooded, pet. Is sea ice within your abilities?"

She blinked at him. "I've never tried it. Give me a moment." She closed her eyes. He sensed her search her memories for how sea ice felt and how dense it was.

Once she was satisfied with the spell, she opened her eyes and began to sing.

The air grew noticeably cooler. The wind which previously filled the *Quicksilver's* sails dissipated as if it had never been. The color of the water began to change. It grew paler, greener, and more opaque.

Before Viktor's eyes, solid chunks of ice formed just a couple of fathoms off the side. He watched the chunks bob and drift then gradually merge into a solid sheet.

The ice flow spread toward the Navy vessels at an ever-increasing rate, yet it never made a single move toward the *Incubus*. Within a few minutes, the ice surrounded the three British ships and locked them in place.

Belladonna looked at him for further instruction.

"You can have the escorts, pet; I'm going to go have a word with the commodore." He launched into flight.

As he flew to the ice bound *Quicksilver*, he saw the ice grind and crush the hulls of the remaining escort ships. By the time he landed, the ice around the damaged vessels melted enough to allow them to sink.

He chuckled and turned to face the white-faced sailors pointing weapons at him. He broke into a feral grin and watched them take a step back at the sight of his fangs.

"Where is Commodore Critchfield?"

Critchfield felt no surprise that Brandewyne knew his name. He'd made no secret of the fact he hunted the pirate.

Having read Kendridge's accounts, he also knew what he was dealing with, somewhat. It did surprise him the creature could move about freely in daylight, however. He wondered if there were other facets of vampirism he defied. Westin hadn't mentioned anything about vampires being able to fly.

He approached Brandewyne with caution, careful not to make eye contact.

"I am Commodore Critchfield; I take it you are Viktor Brandewyne."

"I am. You have much to answer for, Commodore. I have decided it is time to end this game."

"A bold and, dare I say, arrogant statement coming from a known and notorious pirate. You do seem to live up to your reputation." He watched to see how Brandewyne reacted. Other Navy officers might underestimate him simply because of his criminality. Critchfield had no intention of making that mistake. Pirates generally did not enjoy such long careers without being extremely resourceful and clever.

"That is why it is my reputation. You've built quite a name for yourself, as well."

Critchfield didn't rise to the bait. Brandewyne struck him as a man who enjoyed dealing out humiliation to the overly confident.

"For the moment, we seem to be at an impasse," he said. "You've destroyed my modest armada. You also stand here on my ship; alone and surrounded by some of the finest marksmen of the Royal Navy. Shall we retire to my cabin and discuss our terms?"

The pirate smirked at him. "I am a reasonable man; besides, this should be interesting. Shall we bring these lads with us, or do you have the balls to speak with me alone?"

He chose his next words with caution. Part of Westin's instructions on the nature of and rules governing vampires was that one could be bound to certain behavior by certain phrases. He realized these rules may not apply to the vampire before him; the man already defied several others.

"Your reputation marks you as a man of your word; something admittedly odd for a brigand. Do you give your word to remain peaceable and inflict no harm while in my cabin?"

The pirate revealed his unnerving grin again, as if the question amused him.

"Very well; I give you my word I will not harm you, Commodore, while alone with you in your cabin."

Knowing it was probably the best he would get from the man; he nodded and waved him to follow. He felt a rush of wind, and the man vanished from sight.

He frowned at the fearful muttering this brought about. "Belay that talk! Back to your posts!"

He shook his head and turned back toward his cabin.

The arrogant bastard lounged behind his desk, in his chair, as if he owned the place.

The fact Brandewyne knew the way to his cabin came as no surprise; the *Incubus* and the *Quicksilver* were nearly identical in design. The speed with which the pirate got there impressed him, however. To be told about vampire abilities was one thing; to witness them in action was quite another. It hardened his resolve on the tack to take with the pirate.

First though, he needed to establish his territory.

"You presume much, sir." He stared pointedly at his chair, careful to avoid direct eye contact.

In response, Brandewyne leaned back and propped his feet on the desk. "It is a comfortable chair, Commodore, almost as comfortable as mine." In a flash, the man stood, moved to the other side of the desk, and waved a hand toward the now vacant chair. "Still, I came here to put a stop to a nuisance which is costing me precious time. Baiting you, while entertaining, is counterproductive to my purpose."

Slowly and deliberately, Critchfield took his seat. He did his best to keep an eye on Brandewyne's location without looking at the man's eyes. It chafed at his pride to even appear fearful, but he didn't want to lose any more control of the situation.

The pirate frowned, leaned forward across the desk, and tried deliberately to catch his gaze. This forced him to openly look away. He barely repressed a shudder when he heard the distinct sound of sniffing.

Brandewyne's voice came from entirely too close by. "Are you a coward Commodore that you will not look me in the eye?"

The barb stung, and he felt heat rise in his face. "I am neither a coward nor a fool, Brandee; I have been warned of what you've become and have educated myself on the strengths and weaknesses of such creatures."

"Vampires, you mean."

"Aye, vampires." He turned back to look the pirate square in the chest. He only hoped the fighting trick would give him enough warning of any potential moves to evade an attack from the creature.

Brandewyne stood back and seated himself in one of the chairs facing the desk. His voice sounded calm and reasonable. "I know you picked young Mr. Westin's brain about vampires before you cruelly set him adrift. Tell me, was that because he learned of your involvement with Lady Carpathia?"

"Is that what he told you?"

"Some of it, but I catch the faintest trace of her scent upon you. Funny thing about a powerful vampire's scent; no amount of washing seems to scrub it away, even years after an encounter. I know you've bedded her; I also know she never fed on you."

The last statement startled him enough to almost look Brandewyne in the face. "How would you know that? My encounter with the Lady was long enough ago for any scars to have faded."

"You carry a trace of her scent; but her power does not ride you. It did ride Mr. Turlington. She'd fed on him often enough to possess his body and communicate through it."

"Westin never mentioned that ability."

"I doubt he ever encountered it."

"Was his connection with the Lady why you murdered my officer?"

The pirate laughed. "She tried to use him to enslave me, but he did not die by my hand. I travel with a siren, and she is very territorial. To her credit, she did everything within her power to limit or block my interactions with Thia."

Some disbelief must have shown on his face; Brandewyne added, "You accept the existence of vampires. You've even seen a small portion of what I am capable of. Why would you doubt other supernatural or mythical creatures exist?"

"You have me there. I suppose I will have to accept the reality of such beings." He sighed. "You mentioned something about your opinion that I have much to answer for. I am curious as to what crimes a known pirate, thief, rapist, and murderer would accuse me of."

Brandewyne sat back and crossed his legs with an air of smugness. "I freely admit the crimes you just accused me of. Not only have I committed them I have every intention of doing so again as my moods and opportunities present. We shall see if you do the same. We've already mentioned your unwarranted marooning of Britt Westin."

Critchfield interrupted him. "Why do you even care what happened to him?"

"He is brother to my first mate, Jim Rigger, and brother-in-law to my chief navigator."

"Rigger; I remember that madwoman, Miss Brumble mentioning you'd sent word back to old Tobias you'd taken his sons in revenge for his ill-treatment of a man by that name."

"That is correct."

"I know she found you in Tortuga; but she and her husband eluded me, and no one in port was very forthcoming about either them or you. I take it by your statement that one of her brothers still lives. Does the other one, as well?"

"I killed Thomas the same day I took his ship. Both he and Zachary serve me."

"You made him as you are?" This confirmed his suspicions gleaned from Kendridge's log that the vampire could convert others, and the Navy man hadn't been an anomaly.

Brandewyne waggled his hand. "In a manner of speaking; I did make him a vampire but not as I am. If you paid attention to Westin's tutorial, I am unique among vampires."

"You refer to your ability to endure sunlight."

"Among other things." At this, Brandewyne reached into his shirt and pulled out an elaborate gold cross encrusted in large, fine clarity emeralds. "I have no difficulty bearing the touch of holy or blessed objects; an immunity I have yet to witness in any other vampire."

Critchfield stared hard at the jewelry. "I know that cross."

"You should," Brandewyne said with a laugh. "You paid to have it smuggled along with two caches of set, cut, and raw emeralds. I'm sure the Admiralty Courts would not be pleased to learn of that transaction." He held up his hand with a smile. "Of course, they'll not learn of it from me; for obvious reasons."

He laughed in turn. "You really think they would take a pirate's word over mine? Even with the Brumble boys to back up your story, the fact they serve on your crew casts doubt on their honesty."

"As I said, obvious reasons."

"So, are there any other crimes or sins I have purportedly committed?" Grudgingly, Critchfield admitted to himself Brandee had a charismatic air about him. The combination of this and the pirate's reputed ruthlessness explained the level of loyalty the man enjoyed.

"You made a grave error going to Savannah."

"Ah, you mean my visit to the old witch."

"Mother can take care of herself; and I pity anyone foolish enough to cross her. I know it is something I will never do."

He blinked in surprise. The dreaded Bloody Vik Brandee both respected and feared the old marsh witch; even as powerful a creature as he now was.

Brandewyne continued, "However, your visit frightened Madam Grimm to the point she gave birth too early. Mother Celie was barely able to save her and the twins."

"She was hiding them? She's even more powerful than she seemed. She proved to me she had no need to fear the stake."

"And then there is the matter of the injuries you dealt Maggie."

"Who?" Surely, he couldn't mean —

"The madam at the Black Flag; Maggie holds a special place for me. She was my first." The look the pirate gave him, while pleasant and calm, was far from friendly. "I realize she is a working woman; that is no excuse for anyone to abuse her."

He did not reply right away. While he didn't hold with killing a whore unless she'd committed a crime or in self-defense, he'd always considered them barely a step above slaves. "I do not consider what I did to her as abuse. No permanent damage was done to her, not even as much as childbirth would cause. A whore's job is to cater to her client's pleasures. I merely got what I'd paid for."

"A fair and honest answer; I just hope you paid her well; you cost her a few days' work." The pirate rubbed his hands together and gave him a predatory smile. "So, now we come to our current predicament: how do I stop your nuisance harrying of me while I'm trying to be about my business?"

Critchfield leaned forward with an equally sinister grin. "I have put some thought into the matter; and I believe I have a solution we can both find agreeable."

"This should be interesting." He heard the skepticism in the pirate's voice.

"I am prepared to have you removed from the lists and give you a letter of marque — on two conditions."

"Two conditions: I assume one is to swear fealty to King George and share my prizes with the Admiralty Court. What is the other?"

He risked a look at the vampire's face. For what he was about to ask, he needed to see his reaction. "I am not a young man anymore, although I am still in my prime. I love the sea too much to ever take a wife; nor do I wish to retire. I want what you have: the strength, the speed, no more fear of growing old."

He became fascinated with the soft green light which emanated from the vampire's eyes.

"I think we can work out an agreement," he heard Brandewyne say.

Tamara A. Lowery

Chapter 27

"Greetings my young friend," Jeorge said with a smile. "Did you bring your fledgling with you?"

"Carmella is still on the ship. I've restricted her to her cabin for now. She has had a good feed recently, but she hails from a small port. A city such as New Orleans might overwhelm her senses," Vik said as he shook the vampire's hand.

"Ah, you wanted to make sure she could be safely secured first so she could be trained and gradually introduced."

"Exactly; I'm glad you understand, Jeorge." He sighed and shook his head. "I probably shouldn't have let her have so much in one feeding; but it didn't feel right denying her what I invited the rest of my cadre to share. She's suffered far too much starvation and deprivation at the hands of Juma already."

"I sense a story, my friend. Please, sit and share it with me." The ancient vampire bounced with an excitement which belied his centuries but matched his teen-aged appearance.

Viktor really needed him to take Carmella in. He decided giving Jeorge some entertainment would sweeten the deal.

He started with the battle with Commodore Critchfield's small armada and went from there.

"It truly got interesting after he named his conditions for removing me from the lists and offering me a letter of marque."

"Conditions I'm sure you had no intention of honoring," Jeorge commented.

"Of course not; could you picture me swearing fealty to any king or queen?"

"No, not really."

"It was his second condition that caught my attention." He paused for dramatic effect. "He wanted me to turn him."

Jeorge rewarded him with a laugh. "After all that bragging about knowing what a vampire's strengths and weaknesses are; let me guess: he fears dying."

Vik shook his head. "No, he is a career Navy man and accepts the risks. He fears growing old and feeble. He loves the sea too much to leave it. I fully understand the sentiment. I no longer feel at home on land, and I enjoy being able to do everything I want to."

"So, what did you do? Did you grant his request?"

He shook his head slowly from side to side with a sinister smile. "He hasn't earned it. If for no other reason, he's earned my enmity for killing Kendridge without my permission." He knew from Jeorge's expression that he didn't have to explain the unique situation with Kendridge. He'd turned him as punishment; no one else had the right to release the wretch from that.

"First, I took advantage of the fact he'd finally made eye contact with me and took his will. I held him insensate with me for another hour or so; long enough for the sun to set. It was no easy task, either. His will is quite strong."

"Why to sunset? I know you have no difficulty functioning in full daylight."

"I called my cadre over to the *Quicksilver*. They couldn't safely leave the hold until then. I had Mr. Rigger bring Carmella, as well. The lads crossed the ice Belladonna so kindly conjured; Jim flew over with Carmella."

"I take it he is the only one of your vampires to achieve flight," Jeorge interjected. "Melanie has not reached that level of power yet."

"At that time, yes; Jim is my second Childe. Carmella is my first. I still do not know the full extent of her abilities, but she is not so strong you should have any problem managing her."

"Are you saying she can fly now?"

He nodded. "As I said, it was a very good feeding after years of near starvation."

"Please, continue with your narrative."

Viktor grinned at the memory. "I marched the Commodore out to the helm and lashed him to the wheel. I released him from my thrall and gave him a quick education on how a fledgling vampire is subject to the will of his or her sire. I then proceeded to inform him I would not turn him personally."

"At that point, I released my vampires to feast on his crew."

"And you say his ship is sister to yours? What is the compliment?" Jeorge asked.

"Five hundred men, give or take; those we didn't kill are currently crowding my larder hold. I made sure no viable corpses were left behind."

Jeorge raised an eyebrow at this. "You didn't leave any potential vampires at all?"

He shook his head. "No; but I left Critchfield with the impression I was going to. I told him I might turn one of the lads who served as powder monkeys or perhaps someone from the brig. I reiterated that a new vampire rises ravenous as to nearly be mindless until they've fed, which meant their victim's death would be very painful."

He chuckled and grinned at his host. "As a final touch, I sliced his shirt and coat off him, baring him to the waist; I used my favorite dagger to draw a few shallow cuts down his arms, chest, and back. They didn't cause any real damage; they just bled profusely."

"I had a little trouble keeping Carmella off him after that. The lads were used to following my orders without question when they were still human. Carmella was a talented whore before; she was used to manipulating men rather than following orders."

"My friend, most women excel in that area," Jeorge said with a laugh.

"Too true."

"I thank you for your tale. You make me feel young again with your adventures. That alone is payment enough for me to take your Childe under my protection. I already have a room for her. If you will call for her, we can get her situated."

Viktor nodded and contacted both Jim and Carmella mentally. *"Jeorge is ready to receive you now, pet. Jim, guide her directly here; no detours."*

"Aye, Cap'n," came Jim's reply.

All he got from Carmella was a sense of uncertainty. *"Don't worry, pet; he will not mistreat you. Melanie is of my bloodline and has been under his rule for a few years. She can help you adjust."*

"Merci, mon Capitan."

"Mr. Rigger is escorting her here," he told Jeorge. "She was nervous until I told her Melanie could help her adjust. I hope that is agreeable."

"But of course; I had planned to partner them. If you are successful in breaking your curse and they survive, they will be able to comfort each other through the pain of your loss." He shook his head with a rueful smile. "As I learned long ago, even if one wishes to be free of their sire, the transition is quite painful; both emotionally and physically."

"Thank you for understanding."

"Now tell me, while we wait; did you just leave the Commodore adrift and lashed to the wheel to starve and dread the coming night?"

Viktor waggled his hand. "Yes and no; I had Belladonna reinforce the ice floe which locked his ship in place with the crushed remains of his last two escort ships. She then redirected the currents around it to send it back toward Tortuga. The ice should be mostly melted by the time it reaches the island. If he starves, it is no less than he deserves. If he survives, his rescuers will think him mad. I took all of his logbooks and charts as well as those he took from Kendridge. The corpses left on board were beheaded and any fang marks carefully obliterated. I even wasted just enough blood to scatter over them to hide the fact they'd been drained."

"A clever and wise move, my friend; powerful we may be, but our survival depends on our ability to remain in the shadows as rumors and superstitions. To draw attention to our kind and confirm the fact of our existence is a sure path to destruction. Humans fear so many things and enough of them hunt down and eradicate what causes their fear as to make it a true threat."

"Indeed; as a pirate, I know that all too well," Vik agreed.

Both vampires stood as a human servant ushered Jim and Carmella into the room. Viktor did so to help put her more at ease. He suspected Jeorge's initial reasoning was similar; but he caught a fleeting and, to his experience, uncharacteristic gleam of lust in the older vampire's eyes.

He peered more closely at his two oldest Children and noticed his first mate seemed a bit fixated on Carmella, as well.

Her scent carried to him, and he understood why.

Even though Jim had led her flight directly from the ship to Jeorge's manse, she'd seen and sensed enough of the life which New Orleans teemed with to bring her to full arousal. She seemed to emanate an aura of raw sex not unlike the one Belladonna was capable of emitting.

"I see you have the potential to be devastating to the male population of my city, my dear," Jeorge said as he bowed over her hand.

Carmella smiled demurely. "*Merci, m'sieur*; I like men — in every way."

"Perhaps I shall test your skills later. I am Jeorge, and I shall be your master for as long as you remain within my territory."

She gave him a puzzled look, glanced at Viktor, and turned her attention back to the vampire before her.

Vik provided an answer to her unspoken question. "Jeorge was but a lad when his sire turned him; but he is older than this city by several centuries."

Her eyes grew wide as a wave of power washed over her. It emanated from the seeming teenager. Viktor suspected Jeorge did it to prove his age; but it had the added effect of quelling Carmella's allure somewhat.

"Ah, that is better my dear," Jeorge said and visibly relaxed. "It was difficult to think straight with your aura out of control like that. We shall teach you how to control and use it to our advantage, of course." His expression grew stern, and he sent out another, lesser wave of power. "However, it would be wise to never try to use it to manipulate me. I like to think of myself as a fair and just master; but make no mistake, I am master."

Carmella crouched into a fearful, groveling position. Jeorge moved over to her and placed a gentle hand on her shoulder. "You need not fear me, child; you have offered no offense. I merely wish you to understand there are consequences for trying to usurp my place. I give you my word I will never give you or any of my vampires reason to wish to unseat me."

She looked up at him, a hint of fear still in her eyes. Viktor closed off his emotions from her. Her fear bothered him on a deep level; and he didn't want to deal with it or the sense of guilt it brought. The loss of Hezekiah was still too raw. Carmella's fear was another reminder of his failings.

"I see there is much abuse I shall have to overcome," Jeorge said. "Misplaced fear hampers your chances of survival in the world. I shall go gently with you." He looked over at Viktor. "Given how strong she is, I would like to bond her to me before you leave, Captain Brandewyne."

"Of course," Vik said with a nod. "I believe it will help calm and reassure her, as well."

While Carmella still crouched on the floor, Jeorge undid his shirt cuff and rolled the sleeve up to his elbow. He bit into his own wrist and tore the fresh wound wide to allow better blood flow. The thick, nearly black liquid oozed from the open wound even as it visibly began to close.

He held his wrist in front of her face.

She wrinkled her nose at it. "Your blood is dead. I cannot eat that."

"You only have to taste it, pet," Viktor told her. "You will still have your bond with me, but you will also have a bond with Jeorge. If you are to stay here, you must do this."

"*Por qua?*"

Jeorge slipped one finger under her chin and directed her gaze to him. "You must do this to remain safe here. I realize you've been isolated from our kind, so I wouldn't expect you to merely accept my word on this. As a general rule, we are territorial creatures. Partaking of my blood will mark you as being under my protection. All the vampires in this city are of my line or have taken this blood oath to serve me. When they encounter a vampire without this mark, they are not pleasant to deal with and often deadly."

Without further hesitation, she put her lips to his wrist and tasted the blood. Her eyes widened, and she fed in earnest.

Viktor felt the rush of power which emanated from the rite and for a brief moment caught a glimpse into Jeorge's mind. He quickly strengthened his own mental shields before the older vampire could sense his mental presence.

He didn't worry about Jeorge spying on him; instead, he didn't want the older vampire to feel threatened. What he'd seen in that brief instant gave him much to think about.

After what seemed hours, though only a few scant seconds passed, Jeorge tapped her on the cheek. "That is enough, *Cherie*."

Obediently, Carmella released his wrist, licked her lips, and looked up at him with a hungry expression. He smiled and chuckled. "I shall have a few subjects brought up from the cellar. They will provide us a meal as well as allow me to assess your sexual skills before I sample the latter myself."

"Wouldn't you rather be pleasantly surprised, my master?" she asked.

"Tempting, very tempting," he replied. "However, I feel I've had enough surprises for one evening. Besides, watching and experiencing are entirely different things."

She nodded and stood, obviously more relaxed than when she'd entered the room."

Viktor placed a hand on Jim's shoulder. "No offence, Jeorge, but Jim and I need to return to our ship. I've urgent business to be about, and it grows more urgent by the day."

"Of course, my friend; I hope you find the freedom you seek."

"Thank you." Vik inclined his head; Jim followed suit.

Without another word, they turned and left.

Chapter 28

Two hours into the voyage from New Orleans to Savannah, Viktor sensed Belladonna's return. She'd stayed behind to dispose of the dead and ensure any wreckage from Critchfield's armada would not be found.

Her sexual aura told him she'd fed well; something he was glad of. His Hunger kept growing stronger. He hoped some sport with her would provide sufficient distraction. He didn't want to slaughter his crew.

He frowned when she reached his door; he also picked up a sense of worry from her. If she felt it that strongly, he knew he needed to address whatever caused it.

"No need to knock, Belle; come on in," he called out. "What is troubling you?" he asked after she closed the door behind her. He noticed she did not move far from the door into the cabin.

"What state is your Hunger in right now?"

He sighed. At least they both seemed to sense the problem. "It is growing stronger. Truth be told, I could do with some distraction — and a little boost from the winds and currents. I'd like to reach Savannah as quickly as possible."

"I was afraid of this. I understand why you felt the need to deliver Carmella to a safe haven; but it was a delay you could ill afford." Her sigh echoed his.

He leaned against the table and crossed his arms. "More than the delay has you bothered. Out with it."

"I just finished disposing of the carnage you and your vampires created. I know the difference between their kills and yours; a disproportionate number of the bodies were yours, Viktor." She leaned against the door with her hands behind her back, presumably to open it quickly if need be.

"I am aware, pet. I know I let myself lose control." He rubbed the bridge of his nose then shook his head. "I had hoped overindulging would tide me over until I could get back to Celie and get this curse dealt with."

She gave him a sardonic smile. "It only made your Hunger worse, didn't it?"

"Yes! Damn this; it's like an addiction."

"Viktor, it is an addiction. Unfortunately, it is also necessary for your survival." She sighed and stepped away from the door. "Ordinarily, I would say the feed you had would last you at least a month, but I can feel your curse twisting your Hunger."

"Aye, Celie warned me it would get worse until I started wasting away regardless of how much I fed. She also said she didn't know how long I had to gather what I needed to break the curse. Still, before this my worst episodes came when I got off course."

He shot her a worried look. "Do you really think going to New Orleans first was too much of a deviation from my quest?"

She studied him silently for a few moments. When she finally spoke, her words surprised him. "No, I don't. You made the right decision." She walked over to him and placed a hand on his arm. "Viktor, you are so close to completion. The worst thing you could do now is start second-guessing yourself. It's not like you; and it damn well won't help you."

Her concern made him smile. He cupped her face and leaned down to kiss her.

"Thank you, pet. I lost myself for a moment." He kissed her again, and she returned it with fervor.

"We are wearing entirely too much clothing," he murmured against her lips.

"Mmm, you did say you need a distraction."

The distraction worked for a while. Belladonna could hold her own with him in both magic and sex, an important factor in this situation.

A human lover wouldn't be able to keep his Hunger at bay. The siren's magic combining with his gave him more than enough to concentrate on.

Vampire and siren lay soaked in sweat, basking in the afterglow.

Finally, Viktor sighed and said, "If you think you can manage it, pet, now would be a good time to sing up a steering wind and current to speed us on our way."

She giggled. "I took the liberty of doing that before I came back aboard. I had a feeling I might be too preoccupied later."

He chuckled. "Naughty little fish I'm going to open some more windows, then. I could do with a breeze in here."

He stood and stretched. She groaned in appreciation at the sight. He smirked and strode over to the window casement. In short order, he had all of them open.

He closed his eyes and smiled as a tropical breeze flowed over his body and evaporated the sweat beaded there.

Finally, he turned his attention back to the siren. She remained in his bed, lounging seductively and giving him a decidedly heated gaze. He felt himself grow hard again, which brought a grin to her face.

"It seems you are as insatiable as I am this afternoon."

"I fed well the past two days. I need to burn off some of this energy."

He gave her a wicked chuckle. "That would be my pleasure, pet."

Hours later, well after sunset, they finally took another break.

"I think I'd like to have a swim, pet," he said. "I haven't had one in what seems like ages."

"I'll join you. I give my word I will not try to eat you this time," she added the assurance.

"Thank you for that, pet."

Without further word, he stepped into the open casements and dove into the sea behind the ship. The splash drew the attention of the aft lookout. He used his blood bond with his crew to find the pirate's mind and prevent him from raising the alarm.

Moments later, Belladonna dove out the window. She entered the water with barely a splash. Although her face and hands remained in their human guise when she surfaced, he spotted her dorsal and pectoral fins. Even if he hadn't, her movements in the water could only be achieved with her shark-like tail manifested.

This was the closest he'd been to her in the water since she'd bitten a chunk out of his shoulder and eternally bound herself to his will. He appreciated the fact she'd fed so well recently. While he knew she could easily devour as many men again, it gave her enough control to keep her predatory nature in check.

A stray thought sparked his curiosity. "Was the Commodore still alive when you finished clearing his ship?"

She took the abrupt change of subject in stride. "Yes, although his sanity may truly be in question by the time he's discovered."

"Oh?"

She showed him her true grin. "I ate a few of his officers in front of him — slowly. The scent of his horror added a pleasant spicy tang to the dead meat."

"You naughty fish; did he get sick?"

"A little; right after I pulled out a liver, took a nice chunk out of it, and licked his cheek." She smiled coquettishly. "To his credit, he neither lost consciousness nor control of his bladder."

"Hmph; they can't all be as entertaining as Harris."

"No, they can't," she said with a sigh. After a moment, she added, "I rerouted him to Nassau."

"Why?"

"Conservation of energy; getting you to Savannah takes priority. Maintaining a current to push the *Quicksilver* toward Tortuga and a counter current to push the *Incubus* through the Florida Strait would weaken both. Nassau is more in line with our course," she explained.

He pursed his lips and shook his head. He hadn't considered the problem and felt gratitude the siren kept his best interests in mind.

Now that he thought about it, his critical thinking did seem to be a bit off lately, ever since Juma's death, in fact. No, that wasn't right. He'd been out of sorts ever since Hezekiah Grimm's death.

The unbidden memory of that event brought a wave of grief, remorse, and anger.

"Viktor?"

Rather than answer her, he shot out of the water and flew back to the ship and his cabin.

He didn't bother shielding his thoughts from her when he sensed her worried probing. Instead, he let her feel the full blast of those emotions storming through him. They threatened to overwhelm him. He felt his self-control slipping away by the moment, which added fear and frustration to the emotional barrage.

In retrospect, returning to the ship may have been a bad idea. His senses seemed more heightened than usual. The fetid aroma of his unwashed crew mingled with the stench of the bilge and the pungent sweet/sour scent of the livestock kept for the galley's use. Every heartbeat on board pierced his eardrums; no two rhythms alike. The sheer cacophony threatened to drive him to distraction.

Almost subconsciously, he reached out through the blood bond he maintained with his crew. Within moments, every human heart aboard beat with the same rhythm, a single pounding pulse.

That took care of the maddening noise and triggered a maddening Hunger in its place.

Belladonna landed on the open window casement just in time to see Viktor sink his fangs into the second mate's forearm. Jon-Jon did not cry out. In fact, he seemed completely unaware of his surroundings or circumstances.

The moment her legs formed, she ran to the jewelry casket Viktor kept his emerald cross in. Finding it locked, she extended a single talon and picked the simple mechanism.

Once she had the glittering gold and green object in hand, she sent a mental shout at her master.

Viktor looked up, blood dripping from his mouth and Jon-Jon's wrist. The vampire seemed dazed. The human looked far too pale already for Belle's liking.

She knew the opening wouldn't last long. With blinding speed, she slipped the chain holding the cross over the vampire's head and darted back to the window. She wanted to be able to escape quickly if he turned on her.

He snarled and clutched the cross. For a moment, she feared he would rip it off. She felt him hold her in place with his will. A split second later he was on her.

She couldn't even extend her talons to defend herself.

To her surprise, he kissed her tenderly. She saw sanity return to his eyes when he pulled back from the kiss and released his mental hold on her.

"Thank you, Belle."

Jon-Jon dropped to the deck unconscious and interrupted the moment. Belle slipped past Viktor and knelt by the prone man. She wrung some seawater out of her hair into the puncture marks on his wrist and sang a single note.

The wounds sealed instantly. His breathing remained labored, though.

"You almost killed him, Viktor. He will survive; but we'll be lucky if he's recovered enough to function by the time we reach Savannah."

He remained silent. She saw a haunted look in his eyes as he gazed at the second mate.

"Viktor?"

"I am losing my battle, Belle. All I could think about was feeding. Nothing and no one else mattered." He caressed the cross as a note of frustration bordering on fear entered his voice. "I feel this draining even now. I really wish someone other than Jon-Jon had been closer."

"The ship can function without him for a while," she told him.

He shook his head. "My Hunger is out of control. This is the only thing keeping it in check right now. All I smell is blood; all I hear are heartbeats." He moved forward and grasped her shoulders with lightning speed. "I need your help, Belle; you have to trap me in here until we reach Savannah — for the crew's sake."

Now she understood why he'd said he wished someone other than Jon-Jon had been his victim. Very few among the mates could command the crew efficiently. With Hezekiah dead and Jim only able to fulfill that duty at night, he needed Mr. Jon's aid.

"I think I may have a solution which doesn't involve binding us to your cabin." She hoped what she had in mind would work.

He furrowed his brow. "You don't sound entirely confident."

"It is a gamble," she admitted. "You know how my instinct to attack takes over when I am in my true form."

"I do."

"You also know I can and have consciously kept control of myself rather than give in to my predatory nature." He nodded, and she continued, "It took me at least a century to gain that control."

"I don't see how that is helpful, pet. We need to get Mr. Jon out of here before I fully exhaust this thing and finish him off."

"Viktor, you don't have enough control left to safely let anyone else in here." With a growl of frustration, she said, "The explanation is taking too long. Best I just do it and hope for the best."

She fully lowered all of her mental defenses and blasted his open, as well.

Hunger; maddening, all-consuming Hunger. His gut wrenched with it to the point he wanted the crumple into a ball and scream.

She felt its full impact; the sheer torment of it. Without further hesitation, she fully immersed her psyche into his.

He sensed her presence, her total surrender. It distracted him from his Hunger even as that entity threatened to fully possess her. She was about to sacrifice herself to save him, without any reservation. He could not, would not, let that happen.

They had to feed. The Hunger insisted on it. They could smell the blood and the living flesh of the human.

"No! We cannot! We need him alive. We both know the Hunger lies to us. It can never be truly sated. It would not stop at one man. It would compel us to devour the entire crew. We must be Master, not it. The Hunger must serve us, not rule us."

Together they fought off the Hunger until they had it back in its figurative cage.

Gently and carefully, they withdrew back into themselves.

"Thank you for your help, pet." He looked over at the siren and immediately recognized the fire of his Hunger shining in her eyes. "Belladonna?"

"I never realized how bad this was for you, Viktor." Her voice sounded hoarse with the stress of holding the beast at bay. "How you haven't slaughtered the entire crew long ago is beyond me."

"This is the worst it has ever been." He reached out a hand and lightly touched her arm. She snarled, and their connection strengthened. "Perhaps we should keep this connection open for now. I've a feeling it will take both of us to fully control it until we can get to Mother Celie."

She took a deep breath and nodded. "I think you are right."

Tamara. A. Lowery

Chapter 29

It took four more days to reach Savannah. Belle insisted she could get them there faster; but Viktor refused to allow her to overtax her weather magic. He knew she needed all her concentration to help keep his Hunger in check.

They had an opportunity to take a prize just north of St. Augustine. As much as he would've appreciated the extra blood stock, Viktor opted to stay on course. He only admitted to the siren his fear he wouldn't be able to stop feeding if he took fresh kills. She concurred.

He paid a price for the decision, however.

Even though he made liberal use of his bloody brandy stock to the point of nearly depleting his supply, his body began to waste away.

The visible deterioration by the hour unnerved much of the crew. Even Belladonna grew haggard and tired looking because of her efforts to help him control his Hunger.

By the time they reached the mouth of the Savannah River, Viktor looked like a man who'd starved for months; cheeks sunken, skin stretched taut over his skeletal frame, hands and feet long and claw-like. In his eyes shone the barely contained madness.

Luckily, Jon-Jon recovered enough to bring the ship into port. Viktor and Belle took one of the launches back down the river to Skidaway Island. The river's flow helped speed them to Mother Celie's.

Viktor simply did not have the energy to walk there or fly. He had just enough control and self-awareness left to realize if he fed now, he wouldn't stop until every soul in Savannah was dead.

Celie hid her alarm at how her foster son looked when he and the siren arrived at her tabby hut. She had known the curse was growing stronger; she'd seen it in her fire. Still, she hadn't expected the sheer deterioration.

In fact, it puzzled her. With Juma dead, the curse should have stabilized rather than accelerated.

"Took you long enough to get here, boy," she said by way of greeting. "Do you have everything I sent you to get?"

"I do." He slipped the chain with the silver vial over his head and started to hand it to her; he stopped short with a frustrated expression. "Mr. Jon isn't here."

Celie frowned then realized his supposed dilemma. She smiled gently. "Viktor, my magic is already in there. You don't need a magical null to transfer it to me. The magicks were given to you. *You* must give it to me. I cannot take it."

He blinked at her. "It has been so long, I forgot."

She held out her hand, and he placed the vial in it. She closed her hand and cocked her head toward the shack. "Come on in, both of you."

They followed her into the shack. She pointed to a couple of stools at the table with her walking stick and said, "Sit."

She laid the silver vial on one end of the table and headed to her special cupboard. Some agitation in Viktor's movements told her she'd best hurry this along. He grew even gaunter by the minute. She noticed the near exhaustion of the siren and surmised Belladonna was lending energy to him to help him cope. Celie knew well Viktor didn't possess the strength or control to draw from the siren on his own in his present condition.

"Did you bring Juma's ashes?"

He looked at her for a few moments as if he didn't comprehend the question. Belladonna touched his arm cautiously. He snarled at her; then recognition hit.

"Juma's ashes; Juma's ashes; oh, aye, I have them here." He reached inside his shirt and pulled out the blue bag he'd placed the necromancer's remains in. He handed it to Celie.

Alarm and understanding dawned on her as she examined the bag. The drawstring at the top had come untied, and the bag had opened slightly. Now she knew why he had reached the state he was in.

She quickly tugged on the drawstring to snug the bag fully shut and placed it on the table next to the vial. Viktor sat a little straighter, and the madness of his Hunger dimmed in his eyes. He seemed to breathe a little easier, as well.

"How long have you carried this with you?"

"With the exception of when Belle and I were sporting to try to keep my mind off my Hunger, I've carried it in my shirt since before arriving in New Orleans to drop off Carmella."

She nodded. "That was nearly two weeks. The knot has come undone, and you were exposed to Juma's magic concentrated. No wonder you've suffered so much."

She sighed. What came next had to be Viktor's decision alone. As much as she would like to, she could not influence him. She had manipulated him enough already; something she knew he would be angry about if he discovered it. Still, she wondered if he would be angry with her or with himself.

"You're stalling, Mother. What is bothering you?" he asked.

She narrowed her eyes at him and almost wished she hadn't sealed Juma's ashes. She'd forgotten how observant Viktor was when he was fully alert. He just raised an eyebrow at her.

"Never could get much by you, boy. You won't like what I have to say."

His slight "humph" of a chuckle and wry smile gave her pause.

"Then let me say it for you, Celie. You have been manipulating me for years; since I was a boy, if I don't miss my guess. You raised me; you know my nature. If you wanted me to do something you would either point out how I could profit from it or expressly forbid me to do it."

She saw the siren watch him as if he'd grown a second head. Celie sat and placed her stick in front of her to prop her hands on. She nodded. "Continue."

"You have even lied to me about this curse."

Belladonna straightened and gazed back and forth between the two of them.

"I did," Celie admitted.

"Wait," Belle interjected and stared pointedly at Viktor. "You aren't angry about this. Are you feeling well?"

Celie couldn't keep the faint smile from her lips. The siren voiced the same concerns she had. Celie knew the pirate better than any other living being.

"Obviously, I do not feel well. I have suspected Mother's machinations for some time now. The difference is I trust her to act in my best interest. She knew how stubborn I could be and acted accordingly, as any good mother would." He turned his attention back to Celie. "I did not fully discover the lie until you sealed that bag; and it was more of a half-truth than an outright lie. You told me the only way to break the curse was to gather magic from all the Sisters and bring it to you. I believe killing Juma was the true key; yet even that wasn't the full cure."

Celie smiled. "Almost right, boy; what I thought to be a lie very nearly turned into the truth. I told you the curse would eventually kill you; and it almost did, as your current state shows. Juma's death put an end to her influence on the curse, or it should have. The blue bag was imbued with the ability to contain her magic; but it would have helped to make sure it was securely shut. Carrying it on your person only amplified her malice. Make no mistake, though; you are still cursed. You are still vampire."

"And the magicks you had me collect?" A slightly peeved tone entered his voice. It let her know he was beginning to recover.

"Necessary to my purposes; you think my Sisters were the only ones in need of restoration? I told you the truth I would need all their magic to help you."

She stood and hobbled back over to her special cabinet. From this she retrieved a simple wooden bowl and carried it back to the table. She reached over and snagged the bag with Juma's ashes and opened it.

"What are you doing? Do you want to kill him?" Belladonna exclaimed.

"Peace, pet; I am safe," Viktor reassured the siren.

Celie nodded at her with a faint smile. She poured the contents of the bag into the bowl and waited for the ash cloud to settle. Not a single speck fell outside the bowl or remained in the bag.

Next, she flipped the catch of the silver vial open with her thumb and poured the contents over the ashes.

"Come here, boy."

He rose and cautiously approached her and the bowl full of magic.

"Take the Elder's Stone and stir this for me."

"Won't that neutralize the magic?" he asked.

She shook her head. "Not in this case; just trust me."

He shrugged and slipped the chain holding the milky crystal over his head. It glowed softly as he poked it into the bowl of damp ashes and began to stir. He seemed mesmerized by the stone's reaction to the magical concoction.

Celie nodded to herself and took advantage of her foster son's distraction to disrobe. She noted the siren silently watched everything closely.

"Huhn," she heard Viktor grunt. As he stirred, the Elder's Stone gradually absorbed the contents of the bowl.

By the time he finished, the bowl stood empty, and he held a glowing crystalline dagger in his hand.

"Viktor, take that and stab me in the heart with it."

He looked at the woman who'd raised him and felt his heart clench at her words.

"No."

She scowled at him, but he refused to give in to old habits.

"Boy, you mind me."

"I can't; I won't."

He knew she didn't remember Grimm or how raw that loss still was to him. She couldn't realize how much her words tormented him. The thought of losing her too was too much.

"Viktor, it is the only way to lift your curse."

He shook his head. "Celie, you are the only mother I have ever known. I just can't do it. I cannot kill you. I couldn't bear it. I would rather the curse take me than have you die by my hand. Besides, my Hunger has all but abandoned me since you took the bag of ashes from me."

Celie shook her head in turn. "The choice must be yours but know this: if you do not plunge that crystal shard into my heart soon, your Hunger will return with a vengeance. You will kill me anyway, with no hope of redemption." She fixed him with a stern stare. "You know how it can take you; you know this is true."

He wanted to put on a strong face; but he could never lie to Celie. She always saw through him like no one else ever could. He felt the hot sting of tears and tasted the bitter salt. Impulsively, he embraced her.

"I love you, Mother," he murmured into her hair with a choked voice.

He quickly plunged the crystal blade home and screamed his agony.

He gently lowered Celie's lifeless body to the floor and turned away, unable to stand the sight of his crime. Through his tears he saw Belladonna looking at him with an expression of awe and horror. It took him a few moments to realize she looked past him rather than at him.

He opened himself to her and found she had not shielded herself from him. Nor did she hold any condemnation for his actions. The source of her fear lay behind him.

Almost against his will, he turned back to Celie's body. He immediately shielded his eyes. It glowed as brightly as the Elder's Stone in the presence of the Sisters' powers.

Once his eyes adjusted to the radiance, he watched as the wrinkles and sags he'd known all his life began to smooth out and fill in. As it took on a youthful appearance, her skin grew translucent. He saw the blood flow through her veins and found it one of the most mesmerizingly beautiful sights imaginable.

Oddly, it did not stir his Hunger. Only when he realized that fact did he become aware that her heart beat again.

Play of the light drew his attention to her hair. He'd half expected it to darken, as Gloribeau's had when she'd transformed. Instead, it took on a crystalline appearance. Her glow prismed through her hair and cast rainbows about the interior of the little tabby shack.

He heard a voice in his head. *"Remove the dagger."*

He knelt beside her and placed a hand on her shoulder. With his other hand he grasped the hilt of the crystal dagger. He gave one quick pull.

In his hand he held the Elder's Stone, returned to its original form.

Tamara A. Lowery

Chapter 30

Celie opened her eyes and smiled at him. She reached up and brushed the tears from his face. He grinned like an idiot.

"You did well, son; I'm proud of you." Her voice sounded different to him, but he figured that was due to her growing younger.

He helped her stand.

Once on her feet, Viktor felt a tremendous power emanate from her. Before his eyes, a silky sheath wove itself and covered her nudity. Finally, her magical glow abated.

The shack seemed to grow dark; then his eyes adjusted once again.

"Much better," she said. "I know that had to be painful to both of you."

Belladonna finally found her voice. "All-Mother?"

"Yes, child; I told you he is both a dealer of death and a giver of life."

"I remember," Belle replied. "How is this possible?"

Celie laughed. "Have a seat, and I will try to explain in a way you'll both understand."

They obediently took seats at the table and awaited her explanation. Viktor felt light-headed bordering on euphoria. He did his best to concentrate on her words.

"I have become the embodiment of the Heart of Hell's Breath Island. I'm sure you realized, siren, the Elder's Stone is a shard of the form you first saw me in. All of the Sisters of Power carry aspects of my power."

Belle leaned forward in interest. "So, it was the medium through which they were transferred to you. Does that mean they would have been transferred to anyone he would have stabbed with that dagger?"

Celie shook her head. "No, although I'm sure some of my Sisters thought it would. It could only work on Gloribeau or me. Remember, we are twins. We are also the only ones of the Sisters to be truly born of Hell's Breath. We are the only two who can bear this mantle."

"Why didn't Glory try to convince me to return to her instead of you, then?" Viktor asked. "Hell, all she would have had to offer was another night in her bed."

Belle glared at him; but Celie just chuckled.

"She knew that, boy. She also warned you of the danger to both of you were she to take you as a lover again. No, Gloribeau has already borne this mantle. She has no desire to take it on again. Even I no longer had a desire for it; but I knew it would soon become necessary for one of us to."

The siren cocked her head to the side. "Forgive me, All-Mother; why would she not want your power again? For that matter, why did she give it up? Or was it taken from her?"

Celie reached over and patted her hand.

Belle quickly pulled her hand to her chest and rubbed it as if it ached. Her eyes grew wide and wild. She shuddered a little.

"No forgiveness is necessary, child," Celie said. "As that little taste should tell you, it is not an easy burden to bear, even for someone capable of it. Glory bore it well, but it drew the attention of those who would seek to take or manipulate the magic for their own nefarious purposes."

"Tulimanchulo," Viktor stated. "Zeke said the demon was her last lover before me. He stole part of her magic."

Celie nodded. "Yes, but he reached her after she'd been diminished. Several others had sought her out already. They fell to her might; but a few attacks threatened to overwhelm her. Zeke decided to intervene. He summoned her to Hell's Breath and performed a ritual which reduced her to only one aspect of the magic. A messenger was chosen to distribute the other aspects among six other women with natural talent or the potential for it."

"Dorada, Rosalia, Venoma, Clarissa, Circe, and Juma," Viktor supplied.

She shook her head. "No, you are only partially correct. Juma was the messenger. She was supposed to bring the necromancy to me; I had the greatest natural talent for it. Instead, she stole what should have been mine and kept it for herself."

She let him ponder on that information for a time. He seemed to grow pale; but she quickly realized it was not in response to her words.

"Viktor, did you hear me?"

He nodded then slumped to the floor.

"Viktor!" Belladonna cried. She looked up at Celie with fear in her eyes. "Help him! He's dying! I can't hear or sense him anymore."

Celie knelt beside her foster son. She gently stroked the hair from his face and called his name again. He managed to open his eyes; she saw they'd begun to glaze and lose focus.

"Pry his mouth open carefully; he cannot survive your blood in this state," she instructed the siren.

Belle obeyed with a questioning look.

Faster than the siren could react, Celie grasped her wrist and applied pressure in just the right spot to trigger the extension of one of her talons. Celie then drew her own wrist across the razor-sharp point and let the blood dribble into Viktor's mouth.

He felt so cold and distant. All he wanted to do was sleep. Vaguely, he knew Mother Celie was telling him something important; but he just couldn't find the strength or energy to concentrate on it. He felt so tired; couldn't he just rest?

He felt/heard a stinging in his head. He knew Belladonna was worried about him nearly to the point of panic. He wanted to soothe her fear; it just seemed like so much effort, though.

A warm hand touched his face. A familiar voice called his name with gentle power.

He opened his eyes but only saw blurry shadows with no color to them. Couldn't they just let him sleep? He was so tired. He'd done what he had to do. Now he just wanted to sleep; to rest.

Life and awareness flooded his being even as the sweetest nectar filled his mouth. As much as he wanted to savor it; he felt the desperate need to swallow. He closed his mouth and felt the warm fluid dribble on his lips. He licked them, and his sight returned fully.

He saw Mother Celie crouched over him, her wrist sliced and bleeding on his face. His eyes grew wide with alarm. Faster than he thought possible, he moved to stand in the doorway. He wiped her blood from his face with the back of his hand.

She stood and waved her other hand over the wrist wound. It sealed, and the remaining blood there vanished. She fixed him with a stern gaze.

"Finish that. It is a gift not lightly given."

Only then did he realize his Hunger had not stirred at the taste of her blood. Obediently, he licked his hand clean. It tasted just as sweet as before and nothing like human blood. Perhaps that explained his dormant Hunger.

Celie nodded her approval. "You no longer need to return to Hell's Breath to be freed from your curse."

"How do you explain my speed and heightened senses?" If his curse was gone, why did he still have his vampire abilities? He could even sense all the vampires he'd created.

She laughed at him. "The curse was that your Hunger would control and destroy you. Boy, you already made your curse into a gift. You used it to your advantage and your powers grew and still grow. Now you fully control them rather than are controlled by them. You can even appear fully human if you want to."

At her words, he felt his fangs transform into normal canine teeth. He probed them with his tongue and found the sensation — odd.

"I'd gotten used to them, truth be told," he said.

"Then manifest them again," she stated simply.

"You mean I can change the appearance of my teeth like Belle does?" He liked the sound of that.

She nodded. "Your Hunger no longer rules you, either; although I would advise feeding on human blood at least once a month to keep your senses sharp and your powers at full strength — unless you wish to become fully human again."

He smirked. "I know that tone, Mother. You believe that would be a poor choice. I know it would mean a return of my mortality. Why do you counsel against it as well?"

"You have other challenges ahead of you, Viktor; ones in which your current abilities will serve you well, perhaps to the point of being crucial to your survival."

He pinched the bridge of his nose. "Of course; because the Sisters weren't challenge enough."

"They were especially difficult because they feared you would succeed, and I would once again have a body," the All-Mother spoke through Celie. He picked up on the very subtle difference in their voices. He doubted a human could.

She continued, "A few were foolish enough to think they could contain me in my entirety; but the others feared the loss of their magic once I ascended again."

"That explains much. Can you tell me what these new challenges will be or where they will come from?"

"You must summon Hell's Breath Island and speak with Zeke."

He frowned in frustration. "The Elder's Stone no longer works in that respect. It has been months since I've set foot on the island; and I have tried to summon it to no avail."

"The island did not answer because you did not truly need its help at that time. Await the full moon. The Stone will guide you on your course."

Tamara. A. Lowery

Chapter 31

Three nights after the *Incubus* left Savannah behind, the moon reached her full stage.

Viktor stood at the railing and looked out across the glassy sea. When the wind died earlier that day, he'd ordered the sea anchor set. A part of him still doubted, despite Celie's reassurances. Hell's Breath hadn't answered or appeared the last time he'd tried this.

As the moon peaked in its celestial path, the milky crystal at his throat grew warm. He pulled it out of his shirt by its silver chain and saw its soft, pulsing glow. Hope began to fill him. He slipped the chain over his head and secured it to the end of a heaving line. Satisfied the knot was secured, he lowered the crystal to the water.

A single, bright pulse of light emanated from the Elder's Stone as it touched the water's surface. The light illuminated the ripples as they spread and bounced off the ship's hull.

Toward the horizon, a thick fog bank formed. Within moments, it surrounded the ship. Even with his heightened senses, Viktor could see nothing around him.

He pulled the rope up and retrieved the Elder's Stone. As he placed the chain back over his head, he felt the surface he stood on grow steady. He knew he was no longer on his ship.

Patiently, he waited for the fog to clear. It did so more slowly than he expected, which puzzled him.

Finally, he saw a faint red glow through the thinning fog. He moved toward it cautiously yet confidently.

After what felt like an hour or more, he reached the hollow which housed Zeke's fire. He didn't see the old man; but this didn't trouble him. He picked out a rock and sat down.

The fire danced and swayed with a soothing, crackling sound. He wondered if Zeke had thrown some sort of herb into the blaze. It carried a heady, sweet scent which bordered on cloying. Figures seemed to move about in the flames. They looked familiar, but he couldn't seem to place them.

"Welcome back, boy."

Viktor was startled and looked to see Zeke sitting across the fire from him. "How long have you been there?" He still had enough wits about him to know a great amount of time had passed while he'd been mesmerized by the flames.

The old man chuckled. "I've been busy elsewhere on the island; so only a few minutes. Did you learn anything from the fire?"

He shook his head. "Not really; I think I recognized some of the people and places it showed me. Seemed pretty vague, though. I couldn't make any sense of it. What did you put in it to make it do that?"

Zeke peered at him with a cryptic smile. "I didn't put anything into the fire. A magic within you called to it."

He tilted his head at the old man. "It's never done that before."

"You didn't have this magic before."

"Celie's blood; is that why?"

Zeke nodded. "You catch on quick, boy. That's good. In time and with practice you'll master this new ability."

The old man poked at the fire for a bit, while Viktor mulled over the unexpected bonus.

Finally, he asked the old wizard, "What am I supposed to do now? I've completed my business with the Sisters, as far as I know. Celie has become the All-Mother, as Belle calls her. She sent me here to see you; but she didn't say why."

Zeke nodded. "Already knew all that; I also know bein' done with those biddies ain't the only reason you don't know what to do next."

"No; I tried to summon Hell's Breath a while back, to no avail. I lost Grimm." He sighed. "I can't even let his family know what happened to him; no one seems to know what happened to them. Even Celie has no memory of them or of Grimm sailing with me these past few years."

The look the old man gave him was impossible to read. He remained silent so long Viktor almost fell under the fire's spell again.

"I had a foreshadowing of what would happen the last time you visited. Celie did, too; she knew your impatience would win out and you would use too much moly for the final dose. She'd cast a spell on it to ensure that happened."

"Why would she want that?"

Zeke looked at him sideways and shook his head. "Don't tell me I was wrong about you bein' quick to catch on, boy. You need a first mate, and she wanted to make sure you had one." He scratched his head and spat in the dirt beside the fire. "I am puzzled about Celie not remembering, though. I have my suspicions about whom or what is responsible for it, mind you."

Viktor arched an eyebrow at him. "You care to enlighten me?"

The old man cackled. "No; best she does that herself. Do you still have the Elder's Stone?"

Vik blinked at the sudden change of subject. He thought about pressing the issue of Celie's memory; but he doubted Zeke would be any more forthcoming. Instead, he answered the question.

"I do; I'm surprised you asked. How do you think I summoned the island?"

"You did that with the power you gained from Celie. The Stone just let you know it was time. She knew you needed that little boost of faith, or you wouldn't believe it possible."

"Are you saying I can summon Hell's Breath at will now? I thought you told me the island has a mind of her own."

"I am. I did. She does," Zeke confirmed. "What you're forgetting, boy, is the All-Mother's blood flows in your veins now. She is the Heart of Hell's Breath Island. She recognizes you as her favored child; and she will always answer your call." He gave Viktor a stern look. "Do not abuse this privilege."

He nodded and said solemnly, "I give you, and her, my word I will not."

The ground tremored just enough to make the flames quiver and tiny pebbles dance around briefly. He took it as the island bearing witness to his vow.

"Good; now that business is out of the way," Zeke said. "The time of your need of the Elder's Stone is almost at an end. The challenge ahead of you now requires a different kind of magic."

Viktor thought of a point he felt he should bring up. "What if these new challenges bring me back into dealings with the Sisters?"

"They have no power over you. Gloribeau is the only one who presents any kind of real danger, and she's already warned you about that."

"The All-Mother's blood again?"

Zeke merely nodded. He stood and motioned for Viktor to do so, as well.

"You need to go inland. Search for a stone with an inset to receive the crystal; you'll know it when you see it. A guide is waiting for you." As he spoke, the sky grew light.

"It's almost dawn. Did we really spend all night here?" Vik asked.

"We did. For what you have to do now, you'll need the daylight. The moon is too tricky with the light. Now scoot, boy; I have other business to attend to."

Fog rolled in and obscured the fire and the hollow which housed it as Viktor climbed the landward side. He glanced across what seemed a pond of vapor to see his ship anchored just offshore. He turned and crossed the lip of the hollow to descend to a narrow, rocky valley.

"Of course," he muttered. "Tell me to find one specific stone then present me with an entire valley full of them."

A slight breeze ruffled his hair. It carried the scent of green, growing things and came from across the low ridge which formed the other side of the valley. He also heard a soft buzzing hum.

His curiosity peaked. He didn't see the promised guide in the stone valley; so he decided to investigate over the ridge.

It took longer to climb than he anticipated, partly because he kept scanning the stones he passed, looking for the inset to hold the Elder's Stone. When he reached the crest of the ridge, the scene before him amazed him.

A wide meadow of wildflowers spread out before him. Whitewashed bee hives dotted it sporadically; the source of the hum he'd heard. He'd never seen so many kinds of flowers in one place, not even in Dorada's domain. The combined aromas this close to their source proved quite heady. He even smelled the richness of the honey in the hives. It made his mouth water.

Beyond the bee meadow sat a small stone cottage with a slate roof. A tidy vegetable garden grew beside it, and a clear stream glinted in the early sunlight as it wound its way between the meadow and the cottage. Yet another meadow, this one surrounded by a low stone wall, spread from the cottage to a woodland on the other side. Sheep and goats wandered about in it.

In the yard of the cottage, a tall blond man played with two small children. A petite, dark-haired woman came out bearing a tray with cups and ewer.

Viktor's heart clenched, and unshed tears stung his eyes. A sad smile gently curved his lips.

He turned away and faced the valley of stones.

Tamara. A. Lowery

Chapter 32

Zeke stood there and barred his way. "You're going the wrong way, boy. Go on down there and be sociable."

Viktor shook his head. "No; even from here I can see Hezekiah is at peace. He's more than earned it. My presence would just be a disturbance and an intrusion. I will leave him be."

The old man smiled at him and laid a warm hand on his shoulder. "That is the most selfless thing you've ever uttered; and I know you mean every word of it. Still, you need to go down to him."

He sighed and looked at Zeke. He saw understanding there; but he also saw the old wizard felt this was something important; something which needed to be done.

"Very well; but only to say goodbye and to give Brianna my apologies." He ignored the sharp, knowing look Zeke gave him.

Hezekiah Grimm smiled at the small treasures his twin children brought him. Celeste clutched a handful of clover blossoms, and Henry held out a shiny pebble from the stream for inspection.

He took the flowers and began to braid them into a small crown for his daughter. "That's quite a pretty gem, son. Would you like Papa to make a little chest to keep it and the other treasures in?"

"Uh-huh! Tank-oo, Papa!" the boy said with an enthusiastic nod.

"Come here, little love," he called his daughter closer. He placed the flower crown on her head and cupped her cheek. "No princess ever had finer jewels. Go show your mother."

The child beamed at him and turned to find her mother. She stopped and pointed across the stream to the flower meadow. "Pwettie man!"

Hezekiah looked where she pointed and felt his mouth grow dry and all the blood leave his face. For a moment, he thought he might black out. "Captain? Vik?"

He swore the apparition nodded at him. It had to be an apparition. Hell's Breath could do some strange things.

"Mama! Mama! Lookit th' pwettie man!" he heard his daughter chirp.

"What are you going on abou…," Brianna's question ended in a gasp.

Just as Hezekiah heard his children shriek for their mother in alarm, the apparition vanished. A blast of wind buffeted him as he turned in his wife's direction.

Viktor Brandewyne stood holding the drink tray in one hand and supporting Brianna with his other arm, a look of dismay and concern on his features.

While Celeste looked back and forth between her mother and the "pwettie man" with confused tears in her eyes, Henry's face turned scarlet with the toddler's rage. He threw his shiny pebble at this stranger who held his mother and screamed, "My mama! Let go!"

Viktor glanced down at the child with a bemused smile. "Ow."

Faster than he realized he could still move, Hezekiah sped over and scooped up his son. "Easy there, little man; the Captain isn't going to hurt your mama," he soothed the boy.

"Thank you, Hezekiah; but if you could please take this tray? I'm about to drop it," Viktor said.

He set the boy down and took the tray from his friend's hand.

Viktor scooped Brianna up into a more comfortable position. "I didn't mean to frighten her like that. Damn, she hardly weighs anything." He carried her over to the nearby bench and sat with her in his lap.

Hezekiah reached to take her from him, but stopped at the pleading look Viktor gave him.

"Just a few moments more, Hezekiah. I just need to prove to myself she is real; all of this is real."

"I could say the same about you, Vik. I never thought I'd see you again. That you're here now is mind-boggling." He wanted so badly to touch his friend to prove to himself his eyes, mind, or the island weren't playing tricks on him for some perverse reason.

At about that moment, Brianna regained consciousness. Upon seeing whose arms held her, she let loose with a string of curses in several languages. Hezekiah could only follow a few of the curses; they came so quickly; some of them were in tongues he was unfamiliar with. Still, the general gist seemed to be berating the Captain for putting them through such emotional trauma.

His heart nearly stopped when she slapped Viktor hard enough to leave a hand mark on his face.

He saw the vampire's eyes flash with emerald fire and knew he could never reach his wife in time to save her.

Relief washed over him as Viktor kissed her firmly and passionately. He then chuckled at himself for feeling relief over the fact his best friend was holding and kissing his wife. He definitely preferred it to the alternatives.

Finally, Vik pulled back from the kiss. Brianna wore a dazed expression and remained silent. Vik got a wicked gleam in his eye, and Hezekiah felt it time to intervene.

He moved over to the bench and lifted his wife from his Captain's arms, still chuckling. After a few moments she realized he had her and buried her face in his shoulder, a crimson blush stealing across her features.

The children followed him back to his stool but seemed to take comfort from his laughter and remained quiet.

"*Mon Dieu*! I never realized! Oh, Hezekiah, I didn't —."

He stopped her with a gentle finger on her lips. "I should have warned you, Love. The Captain has only two, no, three responses to a woman slapping him like that: kiss them, strike back, or feed. I am grateful he went with the one he did."

She glanced over at Viktor who continued to wear a wickedly smug smile.

Even though he knew his senses weren't as acute as the vampire's, Hezekiah caught the change in her scent. She'd had a taste and was curious. He gave his friend a grimace.

"Thank you so much, Vik. Now I have my work cut out for me tonight if I'm going to make her forget that kiss."

"You're welcome, Hezekiah; always glad to be of service."

They both laughed as Brianna hid her face in her hands. She began to laugh, as well.

"Scoundrels, the both of you!"

"You wouldn't have us any other way, Love; and you know it," Hezekiah said and hugged her.

She looked up at him. "I understand now why you said you wouldn't fault me if he were to ever seduce me." She glanced over at Viktor almost wistfully. "He would be very hard to resist."

The vampire stood and gave a flourishing bow. "I assure you, Madam Grimm, I would never enter your bed — without invitation. Wouldn't want to ruin you for your husband." He grinned, and Hezekiah noticed the absence of fangs. "Of course, when the day comes that he's too old to perform, I'll be more than happy to step in."

"Imp!" Brie laughed at his flirting.

"You've broken your curse, Vik?" Hezekiah asked.

"My Hunger no longer rules me. I am still vampire, though." Before his eyes, Viktor extended and retracted his fangs. "Thought it best not to alarm the little ones."

"Speaking of little ones," Brianna said and got out of her husband's lap, "it is time for these to have their snack and nap."

"I not s'eepy, Mama," the boy protested.

"You say that now." She gently guided him toward the cottage door. "You too, Celeste."

The girl walked over to Viktor and held up her arms. "Up!"

Brianna shook her head. "You might as well. She's a stubborn thing."

Viktor smirked and lifted the child to his hip. A brief look of stunned surprise crossed his face. Hezekiah caught it; Brianna had her back to them, busy with their son.

Vik shot him a look which told him they would discuss it in private.

Hezekiah picked up the forgotten drink tray and carried it in behind them.

Once the children were settled, Brianna served a round of drinks.

"Mmm, what is this? I'd guess it has honey in it?" Vik asked. It tasted both sweet and potent.

"Aye," Hezekiah confirmed. "It's mead. I remembered my father's recipe for it and taught it to Brie. She's proven a better brewer than I am."

He inclined his head to his hostess. "This is excellent, Madam Grimm; your husband keeps giving me incentives to break my word and steal you away from him."

She gripped her cup a little tighter, yet he still caught the slight tremble. It let him know he probably could have her if he put the effort into it. She fought it; but he saw it was a struggle to do so.

He knew he never would. He loved them both and respected them both too much to do that to their relationship.

"Hezekiah, do you know how you came to be here? I think I may already know how or at least why your family was brought here."

Brianna's smile wilted, and a touch of fear or discomfort tainted her scent. Vik noticed and said, "I do not mean to distress you, Madam Grimm."

She frowned outright and replied, "Why do you keep calling me that? You know my name."

He gave a half-smile at her irritability and used his most seductive tone. "I do so to remind myself of whose wife you are, pet; but if you would prefer I be more — intimate, I will willingly accommodate you."

She laughed nervously and scooted a little closer to her husband. She also changed the subject back to his question. "It does make me uncomfortable to talk about Hezekiah's arrival; still, you have a right to know, Captain Brandewyne. I thought I'd lost him."

"So did I," Vik murmured just loud enough for his friend to hear.

Hezekiah put a comforting arm around Brianna's shoulders and squeezed. "We all did. When I hit the water after that bastard tossed me, I thought I was dead. At first, everything hurt like fire. I couldn't move; I couldn't breathe. Then the pain stopped. I couldn't feel or hear anything. Just before my sight faded, I remember regretting not being able to see Brianna or the children again. She appeared above me; then I woke up in bed here."

"You weren't easy to put in the bed either," Brianna said. "I found him soaked to the skin and bleeding, lying in the bee meadow. His eyes stared at nothing; he would not answer me; nor was he breathing. I must have sobbed and screamed over him for an hour or more. I still don't know how the twins didn't hear me and wake."

She hugged herself and continued, "All of a sudden, he coughed and drew in a deep breath. The bleeding, which had stopped, started again for a few minutes and turned his shirt crimson. When I opened his shirt, I saw five close-spaced wounds. They closed before my eyes, and the bleeding stopped for good. I ran back to the cottage and got a blanket. I had to roll him over onto it to drag him back to the cottage. From there, it was a matter of getting him inside and onto the bed. Thankfully, the bed is low."

Vik grinned at her. "You are an amazing woman, Madam Grimm. I envy Hezekiah; for you are a fine prize indeed."

Once again, Hezekiah hugged his wife to him; this time in a proprietary manner rather than a comforting one. "You said, when you were holding Brie, you needed to prove to yourself she and all this was real. Why?"

"When Belle couldn't find your body, we assumed the dragon ate it before I killed him. After I finished up with Circe, I returned to Savannah to deliver the bad news and make provisions for your family." He looked at his friends and knew the hollow, haunting sorrow of that time showed in his eyes. "It was as if you had all been erased. No one remembered Brianna, the twins, or the fact you sailed with me these past few years as first mate. Well not entirely no one," he added on reflection. "Cord McVarish, the current head-banger at the Flag remembered overhearing Harris tell Commodore Critchfield about us delivering a pregnant girl to Celie's."

"Celie couldn't tell you anything? There were only a handful of people in Savannah who even knew about them," Hezekiah interjected.

Vik shook his head. "The extra tabby hut was gone without a trace, and she had no idea what I was talking about. Last she remembered of you was when we parted ways over your opium use. Maggie was sick and comatose; the priest who performed and recorded your wedding and the children's christening died in a rectory fire which destroyed those records, as well. I even went to Charleston on the possibility old Worthing had learned of Brianna's presence and somehow managed to spirit her away."

He sighed. "The crew all remembered, at least. It wasn't until I finally dealt with the Brumble girl that I encountered anyone else who remembered you were my first mate."

Brianna held one hand over her mouth to muffle a sob and placed her other on his hand. Unshed tears welled in her eyes. Hezekiah wiped them away with his thumb and kissed her cheek.

"We know we were properly wed and the children baptized, Love. We don't need some piece of paper to prove it," he said.

She shook her head. "It's not that; just the fact we were so thoroughly removed. Why?"

Viktor gently pulled his hand from under hers and patted hers lightly. "I believe the island did it to protect you all, but specifically to protect your daughter."

She knit her brows. "I know this place is magical, but it is just an island. You talk of it as if it were alive."

He grinned. "She is. Hell's Breath Island is one of the forms of the All-Mother."

"The All-Mother? Is that some pagan god?"

He shrugged. "That I could not tell you, even though some of her blood and power flows through my veins now."

Hezekiah raised a finger, opened his mouth, and closed it again. "I'll get back to that later. Does this have anything to do with the shocked look you got when you picked Celeste up to carry her inside?"

Vik nodded. "Aye; she is born of the island."

Both of them looked at him in confusion. He smiled and said, "I know the twins were born at Celie's. Some powerful magic is connected to your daughter, though. Remember Celie said she had to fight to keep the twins and Brianna alive? Celie and Gloribeau are also twins and are born of the island. I think she used part of her own life-force to save the children."

"So, what does this mean for Celeste?" Brianna asked.

"She is heir to the mantle of the All-Mother. Glory wore it in ancient times. Because of others like Tulimanchulo, she had to relinquish the magic, and it passed to the women who became the Sisters of Power. Now Celie is the embodiment of the All-Mother. If any reason arises which would cause her to relinquish the title, your daughter stands next in line."

Hezekiah tilted his head. "Are you saying Celeste is a Sister of Power?"

Vik took another sip of his mead and mulled the question. After a while, he shrugged and replied, "I'm not sure. I think she has the potential, though. Zeke might be able to tell you more."

He looked at his friends and asked the question which bothered him most. "I know why I felt shocked on finding you here. Why did my arrival cause such a commotion? You knew I came to the island on occasion."

"We thought you were dead, Captain," Brianna blurted. Hezekiah winced at his wife's bluntness.

"What? Why?" Viktor found the answer only confused him more.

Hezekiah stood and nodded toward the door. "It will be easier to show you than try to explain it, Vik. You can tell me how things played out with the dragon and Circe on the walk there."

"I need to tidy things up," Brianna declared, excusing herself from the excursion.

Hezekiah gave her a sympathetic look and led Vik out of the cottage. They headed toward the tree line beyond the livestock meadow.

"She seemed uncomfortable again. I never meant to cause such distress to you and yours, Hezekiah."

"I think she took your supposed death harder than I did, probably for my sake. You and I have always known and accepted that a violent death is always a high probability for a pirate."

"Aye; that it is."

They walked along in silence for a few minutes before Hezekiah broke it again. "So, the dragon; what happened there?"

"Bastard was bloody hard to kill; I know that much. All our shots just bounced off him. We tried to go for his eyes, but he swatted the cannon balls away like pebbles. I flew up to attack him; managed to take one eye. Most I could do after that was poke between his scales. Stung him, but didn't do any real damage; so, I did something incredibly stupid."

He saw Hezekiah grin at that last statement. "They never see something like that coming, do they?"

"No; I had both my sword and yours with me, and I figured if I couldn't kill him from the outside, I'd do it from the inside."

"What?!"

"Flew down the bastard's gullet and cut his head off from the inside out. Even that wasn't easy; he healed almost as fast as I do. It almost cost me my legs, too."

"How so?"

"His body began to shrink to human proportions soon after his head separated. I barely managed to cut my way out before it could pinch me in half. As it was, my legs and hips were crushed. Thankfully, Belle was able to get all the bones in their proper places before I could heal. I still don't know how I survived being covered in siren's blood."

"Damn, Vik!"

"Indeed."

They stopped walking. "We're here," Hezekiah announced.

Viktor found himself standing in the middle of a small cemetery. All the stones, save one, held inscriptions too old to make out, even with his preternatural sight. In the midst of these stood a black granite marker polished to a mirror-like finish. He saw no markings on it.

"Huhn; those weren't here before," his friend said, looking at something on the other side of the stone.

Vik walked to look at that side. The name carved in the stone stopped him in his tracks: Viktor Brandewyne.

Just below the name, a cluster of irises bloomed; at least he thought that was what they were. He'd never seen blood red irises before, not even in Dorada's realm.

A strong compulsion to touch them took him; he knelt to do so. The petals felt velvety soft between his fingertips. A heady fragrance reached his nose.

In the next moment, the petals darkened from red to a purple deep enough to pass for black. The blooms soon turned to ash; and the stems and leaves became dried husks which blew away on the slight breeze.

The polished stone lost its luster and faded as if aging decades before their eyes. The name remained the same, but a weathered date appeared below it now: 1619-1641.

"What do ye think it means, Vik?"

He looked up to see fearful awe on his friend's face. He knew a wry half-grin showed on his.

"I think it means this is the stone, and you are the guide Zeke spoke of to me."

Hezekiah frowned, confusion in his eyes. "What exactly did he say?"

Vik slipped the Elder's Stone and its chain over his head and removed the milky crystal from the silver chain. "He said my need for this was almost at an end. I was to find a stone with a recess to receive this, and a guide waited for me."

He held the crystal's length horizontally and compared it to the carved mark between the dates on the grave marker.

Hezekiah tilted his head and remarked, "Damn if they aren't the same shape and size. The mark has even been notched out for the stone's setting."

"Indeed." Vik placed the milky crystal into the niche to find it fit perfectly. It glowed only briefly, no brighter than a quarter moon. When it faded again, the grave marker bore no inscription and returned to its polished sheen. The Elder's Stone glinted white in the glossy black granite.

Raw earth seemed to boil up in front of the marker. Eventually, a small chest pushed to the surface.

Viktor touched the hasp, and the box sprang open. Inside, nested in red velvet, lay a glossy black cross. It appeared to be carved from a single piece of obsidian. Silver wire filigree laced around it and ended in a loop for a chain. Set in the center, a large clear crystal glittered in the evening light.

He reached in to pick it up and hissed as the edge of the volcanic glass cut a thin slit in the pad of his thumb. A single drop of blood oozed from the slice before it healed shut.

Viktor watched, entranced, as the blood beaded and followed the path traced by the silver filigree. When it reached the crystal, the faceted gem absorbed it and turned ruby red.

"That is the different magic Zeke told you would be needed for the challenges you will soon face," a female voice spoke from behind them.

Tamara. A. Lowery

Epilogue

Viktor turned to see Celie standing at the edge of the cemetery. He blinked to hide his surprise.

"I didn't hear you approach, Mother."

"Mother? Vik, are you saying that is old Mother Celie?" Hezekiah blurted.

She nodded and smiled. "Hello, Hezekiah Grimm. You knew me as Mother Celie; I now wear the mantle of the All-Mother. I am the embodiment of Hell's Breath Island."

She turned her attention to her foster son. "You are the One-Who-Will-Bring-Change; the true Viktor Brandewyne."

"I read the inscription; I know there was one before me thought to be the One. I didn't realize he bore the same name."

She waved her hand over the graves surrounding the black monument. The inscriptions became legible as the years of weathering faded away. Every stone bore the name, Viktor Brandewyne. The dates ranged back millennia.

"There have been scores before you. Each had some potential to fulfill the task of restoring me to a physical body. None ever made it past more than three of the Sisters before they met defeat."

"Which three?"

"It depended on what order they found them," she replied.

"Huhn," he grunted. "At least I understand why some of them refused to believe I was the One, now."

Hezekiah interrupted. "Forgive me, Celie; Vik said my daughter was 'born of the island.' Does that mean she'll become a Sister of Power?"

She shook her head. "No, she is going to be more powerful than any of them when the time comes. The time of the Sisters is finally coming to an end. Already their powers have started to wane; it was borrowed power, after all. Only Gloribeau will retain her full strength."

"If my suspicions are correct, their powers started to weaken before I was born," Vik said.

"Yes; that is why I took the gambles with you I did. I didn't train you to the job from your youth; I let you choose your own path with the occasional nudge, of course."

He smirked. He recognized now what he'd missed as a boy. All she'd had to do to keep him on the course she'd chosen for him was to expressly forbid him to do something. She knew his inherent rebellious nature and encouraged it without seeming to.

"I did more than that, Viktor," she said as if she'd heard his thoughts; she probably had, for all he knew. "I arranged for your initial encounter with Juma."

This news genuinely surprised him. He leaned back against the black granite marker and crossed his arms. "Do tell, Mother."

Zeke seemed to materialize from nowhere. "I helped her. I sent the sea witch to sing up the storm you sailed into." He held up his hand to forestall any interruption.

"She didn't know why I wanted her to, so don't go fussin' at th' girl."

"I wasn't going to," Vik said. "I'm just curious why you both wanted me to cross Juma's path — and at that time."

"To give you the tool you would need to succeed, and the edge you will need to fulfill your ultimate purpose," Celie replied.

"The curse?"

"The transformation; the curse part of it only provided incentive and motivation for you to complete your tasks. I reasoned the powers you've gained would agree with your nature. You are not the first vampire to be created the way you were, although Juma had no hand in making the other one."

"Who did?" Hezekiah asked.

"I did," she replied.

Vik noticed she looked embarrassed about it. He began to suspect where the conversation would eventually lead. He pushed away from the stone and took a step closer to her.

"Something went wrong, didn't it? What do I need to know about this vampire; and what do you need me to do once I find him or her?"

Relief crossed her features. "You always were quick to catch on, boy. I like that about you. However, this is a conversation best held indoors. Even on Hell's Breath, some things should not be spoken of openly."

"Celie?" Brianna blinked and peered at her as the group entered the cottage.

Vik and Hezekiah looked at each other surprised the woman recognized Mother Celie despite the drastic change to her appearance.

"Yes, child; I have become the All-Mother now."

Brianna smiled and embraced her. Celie whispered something to her, and she pulled back nodding, laughing, and crying all at the same time.

"Oh yes! Very much so! *Merci; merci*!" She hugged her again.

"The children will remain asleep until I have done this for you. No sound we make will disturb them," Celie proclaimed. "For now, we have important matters to discuss."

Viktor noticed Zeke remained reverently silent. The old wizard shot an adoring glance at Celie when he thought no one was looking. He wondered what the exact nature of their relationship had been or was. Zeke had always called Celie Mother; and she'd called Zeke Uncle; but Vik didn't know if those were just honorifics or true reflections of their connection.

If Celie noticed the looks, she didn't let on.

"Millennia ago, not long after Gloribeau was forced to relinquish the mantle of the All-Mother, but before the Sisters were ordained, I saw the need would arise," Celie spoke. "I already knew what powers were to be distributed, and I helped Zeke decide on the candidates to become Sisters. Juma was chosen to be the trusted courier to deliver each power one at a time."

Zeke spoke up. "My decision to strip Gloribeau of the powers for her own safety dictated that the courier not be permitted to transport more than one at a time. The magicks had to remain divided. Celie and I both saw they would be reunited at some time, and she would take up the mantle of All-Mother."

"I was to be the last to receive my portion; necromancy, because I already had a talent for it from birth," Celie resumed. "I knew how all the other powers worked. Gloribeau and I, being twins, had a deep connection then; it has faded over the last few centuries. I determined to recruit a champion to quest for the powers so I could unite them and claim my place."

She paused and lowered her gaze to the table with a heavy sigh. Zeke reached over and gave her arm a comforting squeeze. She smiled and looked directly at Viktor.

"Being young and foolishly impatient, I made the first vampire. He was much like you in cleverness and intelligence. I did not fully understand the nature of what I had created or what he was capable of."

He narrowed his eyes, trying to come to terms with Celie's admission of a mistake. Belladonna sent him a reminder of his similar admission to Carmella. He cringed mentally; he'd forgotten she was listening in, and mildly surprised Zeke hadn't blocked her.

"I have been guilty of the same with Carmella."

She gave him a grateful smile for his understanding. "I know the siren reminded you of that; but thank you for being mature enough to admit it."

"Why did you make the vampire specifically?"

"I wanted to make sure he would have the ability to face and survive all the Sisters. Unfortunately, another attribute he shared with you was his appetite for women. Before long, he turned one of his lovers."

"Granted, I'd expected something like that to happen," she continued. "I didn't expect the extreme difference in nature between my creation and his, though. There had never been a vampire made by another vampire before."

Viktor stroked his beard and said, "So, in essence, she was the first true vampire. She had the same limitations all vampires but your original and I have; correct?"

"Viktor, at this time you are the only vampire with little or no limitations or weaknesses. His new Childe had to obey him, of course; but he kept her as a lover and did not keep up his control in a moment of passion. She bit and infected him. The change came about gradually over about a month; but he eventually became as all other vampires are now."

"He did not like that he found himself under her command because of this, and he destroyed her before she could fully realize the power had shifted. He also blamed me for his predicament."

"He intercepted Juma," Zeke interjected. "She had already delivered powers to the other Sisters. He used his ability to influence in order to convince her to keep the necromancy for herself rather than deliver it to Celie and make her more powerful. In his spite, he wanted to make sure she never gained all the powers of the Sisters to become the All-Mother."

"But you cured me; surely you could've cured him," Vik said.

She shook her head. "I could have before his Childe turned him, but not without possessing all the powers of the All-Mother. Once his body died and he became true vampire, he went beyond my ability to lift the curse. The best I could do was to give him his transformative ability, much like the one you and Jim possess.”

“I did that in an effort to win him back to my cause,” she continued. “I thought if I gave him a means to once again move about in daylight, he would relent and seek out the other Sisters.”

“He proved me wrong.”

“So he just decided to remain bloody uncooperative?” Hezekiah asked.

“Worse,” Zeke said. “Over the millennia, he arranged for the weakening of at least two of the Sisters. He recruited the demon which seduced Gloribeau and stole a good portion of her magic; more recently, he arranged for Venoma to cross paths with that slave trading magician. Dorada, Clarissa, Circe, and Rosalia were all responsible for their own weakening.”

Viktor posed another question. “Were any of my predecessors made vampire?”

“No; once I saw how it turned out with the first one, I determined the risks seemed too high. Part of me believes my reluctance led to their failures. By the time you arrived, I’d lost the skill to do it; hence arranging for you to cross paths with Juma, whose power had grown as mine had diminished.”

She turned her gaze directly at him, and he became lost in its depths. He saw and understood much he knew she would never say. He was the only one she’d raised from infancy; all the others had been chosen as older boys or young men. She’d believed the All-Mother had sent his mother to her as a last, desperate hope of regaining a corporeal form. She’d carefully observed his development and guided it to make him the man he'd become. She'd almost sacrificed her last chance and not set him on an intercept course with Juma, not out of fear of unleashing another monster upon the world but out of love for him. In that, Zeke intervened at Hell's Breath's behest.

He also saw what she wanted him to do.

"What is his name; and how do I find him?"

Hezekiah and Brianna both scowled with shocked concern.

"Vik, you can't mean you want to hunt this creature down."

"Oh, I do, Mr. Grimm. He is enemy to the All-Mother, to me," he fixed his friend with a chilling stare and added, "and to you and your family."

"What?" Brianna exclaimed. "Why? We have never even encountered him."

Hezekiah grasped the gravity of the situation quickly. "He's the one who sent that vampire bitch we bottled up."

"Aye." Vik looked at Celie and Zeke for confirmation. "Celie made him, and they shared some faint connection. If I'm not off course, he always sent out hunters every time you sent out a champion, didn't he?"

She nodded. "He did. Occasionally they found and destroyed my Viktor before he could even locate one Sister. He did not come after you until I set you to find the Sisters. He saw my love for you and my reluctance to set you on this course as a sign of admitted defeat. I saw his rage and his dispatch of his eldest surviving Childe to hunt you down and destroy you. She was sent, because you were the only Viktor equipped with the means to truly stand a chance of being successful."

"He is vindictive beyond reason. He knows you defeated her somehow but did not kill her. When he learns how — and he will learn how — he will stop at nothing to wreak vengeance on those responsible for her defeat and imprisonment." She looked at Brianna. "If he does not kill Hezekiah before he learns he is the only one who can release his Childe from her imprisonment, he will go after you and the children to try to force her release. He will recognize Celeste as my heir and will seek to kill her or worse."

"Or worse?"

Hezekiah supplied the details. "He'll turn her vampire in an attempt to control the All-Mother."

Zeke nodded.

"That is why the island brought you here and blocked my memory of you," Celie said. "The Dragon cannot set foot here. Hell's Breath is my holy ground."

"The Dragon; so that is why Carpathia was called a Daughter of the Dragon," Vik said. "Is that his only name?"

"He has many names and changes them every century or so to avoid detection by human hunters." Her mouth quirked up in a sardonic smile. "That has been one of my gambits in our age-old battle. It vexes him to no end that I set the first hunters after his kind and taught them the weaknesses of vampires. To be hunted by your own prey can be a troubling thing."

Viktor chuckled. "Aye; pirate hunters have learned that the hard way when they've encountered me. I take it you do not know what name he uses now."

"No; he does not personally say his names very often, especially if he suspects I am listening or watching. He made that mistake only once and learned quickly from it."

She placed a hand on Viktor's and gave him an apologetic look. "Had I been able to get word to you at the time, I could have advised you to learn from the captain of Carpathia's ship where his orders came from."

Zeke looked down at the table for a moment, which drew everyone's attention. When he looked up, he said, "The Dragon will send other hunters, but she was his best. He will want to investigate her disappearance personally. You must prepare yourself for him. To do so, you will need to study vampire lore and hunting techniques. I believe you know where the closest resources are for that."

Vik nodded.

"New Orleans."

Fin

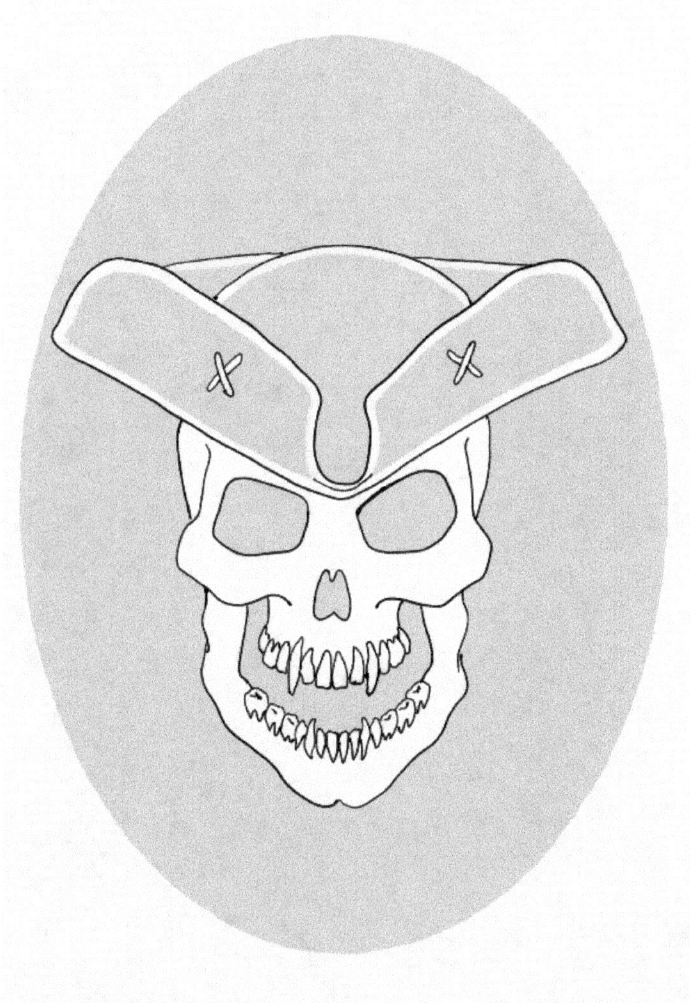

Tamara. A. Lowery

Here Be Spoilers

Blood Curse

After being shipwrecked by a British Navy ship and a killer hurricane, Bloody Vik Brandee and the survivors of his crew make shore in the fishing village of Terra Beau on the north coast of Hispañola. While waiting for a suitable ship to steal, he kills a local boy over a tavern wench, incurring the wrath of *Mamaan* Juma.

Juma sends her zombies to fetch the pirate. She curses him to become a living vampire. The tavern wench, Carmella, becomes his first victim.

Vik returns to his home port, Savannah, and learns from his foster mother Celie, aka the Thunderbolt Witch, just what has happened to him and how to break the curse before it destroys him. While there, Jim Rigger, his first mate, becomes his second victim. Celie resurrects Jim as a black cat which can take the form of a raven.

Celie sets Vik to find the seven Sisters of Power and sends him to Hell's Breath Island to Uncle Zeke, an ancient wizard of sorts. Zeke sends the siren/sea witch Belladonna with him to locate the Sisters using her visions.

She pinpoints *Madre* Dorada on the Isle of Youth. En route, Vik learns an old friend, Hezekiah Grimm aka the Grimm Reaper, has been taken by pirate hunters in

Havana. He detours to rescue Grimm despite warnings from Zeke and Belladonna not to stray from his course.

Manages to find and rescue Grimm but arrives at the Isle of Youth only to find Dorada fled. With the aid of Paella, a local girl, he manages to track the Sister down and brokers a deal with her: one of her golden tears in exchange for an opal pendant called the Mermaid's Tear.

After some misunderstanding of what the Tear actually is, he finds it, helps Dorada regain her magic, and makes the exchange.

Demon Bayou

Viktor tracks the next Sister, Granny Glory, to the bayous north of New Orleans. When he finds her, she sets him to capture the demon Tulimanchulo, who possesses the body of a white alligator. He finds and captures the beast with a magic cast-net but is wounded in the process.

Glory slaughters the demon gator, collects its blood in a cauldron, and has Viktor remove all its teeth. She throws them in the blood and pulls them out as a necklace. Viktor must take it to Zeke. She warns him not to wear it at any time. She then has him toss her into the boiling blood. The hag emerges as a beautiful woman.

On Hell's Breath, Zeke burns the alligator teeth, releasing the demon's spirit. He fishes out a coal from his fire and puts it in a conch shell for Vik to return it to Glory with instructions no one else is to touch it and not to let it extinguish.

Vik returns to New Orleans and discovers a storm has altered the paths through the bayous.

While waiting for a guide back to Glory, he encounters true vampires for the first time. He ends up tangled in the local vampire politics because of attacks on two of his favorite brothels, one by agents of the Church, and the other by vampires curious about him. To get out of this predicament, he must kidnap the daughter of the Lord Mayor and make her vampire. This gives Jeorge, king of the local vampires, a means to spy on him.

On his final return to Glory, Belladonna begins to grow weak as the Sister's black water magic wars with the siren's salt water magic. She falls unconscious into the swamp but does not change into her true form. Vik must remove the coal and place it in his mouth to protect it before he can dive in after Belladonna. He knows she'll drown if she remains in human form. When he surfaces with her, the boat with his other companions is no longer in the area. He climbs out onto a hammock of land and Glory appears to him. He passes the coal to her via a kiss, returning the powers the demon stole from her ages earlier. She adds her spit to the golden tear of Dorada in the silver vial Vik carries for that purpose.

He returns Belladonna to the sea and sacrifices several of his crew to her appetite to restore her. He then abducts a couple of unwary sailors from port to swap for Grimm and Jon-Jon, rescuing them from Glory's amorous clutches, as he's learned she now has the nature of a succubus.

Silent Fathoms

The search for the third Sister, *Tia* Rosalia, takes Viktor to Mexico. He lands on the Gulf coast and must travel over the central mountains to the Pacific coast to reach her. She first tries to deceive and enslave him. Her spell manages to control his crewmen traveling with him, but his power proves stronger at the cost of one pirate's life. The Elder's Stone proves to her he is the One, and she gives him the quest of procuring Devil's Hoof, a key ingredient in her spells. She deliberately doesn't tell him where to look or what it actually is.

He follows rumors of a cave in the mountains where the Devil is said to live. Instead, he finds an old *brujo* (male witch) who was once Rosalia's lover. He tells him Devil's Hoof is an extremely hot pepper said to cause hallucinations with its spiciness. The pirates return to the ship. Navigator Zach Brumble tells Vik about such a pepper his father once dabbled in trading found in the northern part of the Bay of Bengal.

When he tries to contact Belladonna to sing up favorable winds to speed the voyage halfway around the world, he cannot reach her or even sense her presence. Unbeknownst to him, Zeke and Hell's Breath Island have sent her to hunt down the mermaid Alyssa, whom Viktor impregnated while seeking for the Mermaid's Tear. He'd also fed on the creature, and she began to turn while still alive. Belle must kill the mermaid but return the child to the island and Zeke's care. To prevent Viktor's interference, Zeke blocks them from any mental contact until her task is done.

The siren is finally able to rejoin Viktor as the ship is caught in the doldrums near the middle of the Indian Ocean. They make their way to a Bengali village near the Sundarbans, a salt swamp jungle. After warnings from a local elder not to anger the jungle goddess, Bonobibi, or the tiger god, Daskin Rey, they enter the swamps to find the pepper (known locally as the naga pepper). They must also harvest honey to safely transport the peppers in. One of their guides harvests more honey than they need, hoping to profit enough to laze away the wet season. This leads to an encounter with the local deities and the man's death.

With Devil's Hoof acquired, Viktor opts to cross the Pacific directly to Rosalia's home port.

Once back in Mexico, she tries her best to enslave him using fresh ingredients for her spell. He proves his power is stronger than hers, and she begrudgingly agrees to give him the portion of her magic he requires for his quest to break his curse.

After he returns to his ship, Hell's Breath manifests. Zeke introduces him to his son by Alyssa and orders him to get the child off the island. When the island vanishes again, Viktor finds the ship has been transported back to the Caribbean.

Black Venom

Viktor and his crew find themselves deposited close to Havana by the disappearance of Hell's Breath Island. Grateful for not having to sail around South America, they make for New Orleans. He must find a home and guardian for his merchild son, Robert, and wants to see if Gloribeau will take the boy on.

Glory agrees in exchange for Viktor in her bed for one night. The sheer magnitude of magic released by their climax alerts Jeorge, king of the New Orlean vampires, to the child's presence. He also becomes aware of Viktor's increasing powers, growing far faster than those of a truly undead vampire.

Jeorge "summons" Viktor to join him in a hunt. Because he needs to arrange protection of his son from the vampires, he agrees. They attend a reception at the Lord Mayor's for the new governor. Jeorge uses it as a fishing expedition to learn more about the boy and to put the new governor in his pocket.

Samantha Brumble and Captain Bainbridge arrive at the Islas de los Roques and encounter *Madre* Dorada. They learn that the lead which led them there is nearly three years old but gain valuable information about the nature of what Viktor now is and who sails with him.

After dealing with a small British blockade of the entrance to Lake Pontchartrain, Viktor heads for the Florida Strait. Belladonna rejoins the ship there and is given a victim to induce one of her visions to locate the next Sister of Power. *Mere* Venoma Noir directs a psychic attack back at the siren, revealing her power over all things venomous, even over Belladonna.

Jeorge's curiosity gets the better of him, and he sends a couple of his vampires to investigate Viktor's son. Gloribeau's dealing with this invasion of her bayou costs him both his minions and convinces him to leave it alone.

As the pirates near Venoma's territory, she uses her power to attack through the siren. Only the Elder's Stone and Viktor's blood can override the sister's magic. After landfall, she actively tries to kill him and the crew remaining aboard the *Incubus* with hordes of venomous creatures. Once he succeeds in reaching her, she relents and instructs him to retrieve an amulet imbued with her power which was stolen by a notorious slave trader,

Quentin LaForte. They make for the west coast of Africa to search for him.

Commodore Critchfield encounters Lady Carpathia and Captain Wormsloe when they return Commander Turlington to the *HMS Quicksilver*. He has a dalliance with the vampire, never realizing what she truly is. They exchange information about Viktor, and she directs him to sail to Amherst in search of a vampire expert and hunter.

Venoma warns LaForte in a dream that Viktor is hunting him. He doesn't trust the old witch, but makes plans to protect himself nonetheless, especially since she alerted him to the possibility of using Belladonna against Viktor.

Close to the Azores, Viktor pirates a pirate which just took a packet ship. In a bid to thwart Viktor getting ransom for a promised bride taken prisoner, the other pirate kills the woman he believes to be her. The victim was actually the handmaid who'd changed places with her. The true bride, Brianna Belmont, stabs the pirate at the same time Viktor does. Grimm claims her as his share of the spoils and lets her know her intended husband was actually a pimp who specialized in well-bred virgins.

Samantha and Bainbridge arrive in Havana looking for fresher news of Viktor and Grimm. At the Crescent Inn, Luz passes a message to Sam from her brother Zach to abandon the hunt for her own safety. They learned the likely next port Viktor went to was New Orleans.

Lady Carpathia and Captain Wormsloe follow an old lead to the slaver, Delacroix. She learns about Samantha's hunt but nothing else of value. She kills the slaver and a priest looking to buy some new altar boys. The remaining children there, she takes for blood stock.

Viktor gets a lead on LaForte in Tenerife which sends him to Abidjan. They arrive in port and find the man in the process of exchanging a trader's hobbles for his own on a young female slave. She gets loose and provides enough distraction for LaForte to use his black magic to teleport away. They take the woman back to the *Incubus*.

Viktor learns she is called Nahila, and she is LaForte's daughter. She agrees to lead him to the slaver in exchange for her freedom. She leads them to a nearby river. As Viktor takes a small group upriver, LaForte teleports back to his shore camp. He uses the power of Venoma's amulet to ensnare Belladonna and sends her to kill the crew still on the ship.

Grimm's portion of the Elder's magic frees her from the spell. They stage the ship for the slaver and his crew. Viktor gets word from the siren and flies back to the ship. LaForte falls for the trap. Nahila is brought back and kept captive for her part in helping her father try to trap Viktor.

Viktor nearly kills Grimm for keeping the Elder's magic a secret. Brianna's intervention saves the 1st mate.

They learn Nahila serves as a familiar for her father's black magic when the ship is mired midway across the Atlantic in a mass of jellyfish. Viktor has her drugged, and Belladonna creates a current to clear the obstacle and speed them back to South America.

Venoma requires Viktor and LaForte to fight to the death. Only the slaver's death can release the amulet's magic back to her. When Viktor is victorious, but the magic doesn't return, they tell her Nahila holds part of it.

She makes the dead man's blood flow onto the slave and turns her into a scorpion. She gives Viktor a drop of the venom as her portion of magic.

The scorpion stings itself, turns back into Nahila, and dies, leaving Venoma forever magically crippled. For good measure and a bit of payback, Belladonna calls a lightning bolt and fuses the sand around Venoma's feet into glass, trapping the witch.

Hell's Dodo

The revelation that Brianna Bemont is pregnant with twins by Hezekiah Grimm temporarily interrupts Viktor's quest. The *Incubus* travels to Savannah to deliver her to Mother Celie's care. Grimm officially marries her and swears faithfulness to her alone. Celie pulls Viktor aside and warns him the unborn children carry part of the Elder's magic due to Grimm's connection with the old wizard. If he ever breaks his vow, the children will die, and that portion of magic will be forever lost to the world, possibly destroying it in the process.

Viktor tries to release Grimm from his service and the crew, but the first mate won't hear of it. As they clear Tybee Island, heading back to sea, they encounter and take the *Georgia Belle* and her captain, Chadwick Harris. One of the prisoners manages to shoot Viktor in the neck, rendering him mute temporarily. He gives the man to Belladonna to torture and eventually eat.

The vision she has as a result confuses her with its vagueness. After describing it to Viktor and his officers, Zach Brumble realizes she's seen the kitchen at a tavern in Salem, Massachusetts, called The Dragon and the Dodo.

Commodore Critchfield finds Britt Westin in Amherst and proceeds to learn as much as he can about vampire hunting. During the voyage back across the Atlantic to Caribbean waters, the younger man tells him of his quest to hunt down Lady Carpathia and exact revenge for the murder of his family. Britt remembers his father accidentally killing his mother over believed unfaithfulness and abandoning his little brother, Jim. However, he thinks these were false memories implanted by the vampire who later turned his father.

Viktor and crew make use of a newly acquired Colonial Navy flag to get into Salem's harbor. They learn the Sister fled months earlier by turning into a bird and flying away. Instead, they find an excellent cook in Nathan Trundle, the owner of the tavern who uses a trick she taught him to addict customers to his egg pies: add a drop of blood to the custard before cooking it.

Samantha Brumble and Captain Bainbridge arrive in New Orleans looking for news of Viktor Brandewyne. The revelation of her last name, but not her true gender, lands them in custody of the *gendarmerie*. The Lord Mayor has them released when he sees she is not male and learns her brother Thomas is innocent of the kidnap of his daughter, Melanie. Later, Jeorge has one of his vampires abduct Sam and questions her about why she seeks Viktor. He erases the memory of his interaction with her and returns her to her ship.

Back in the Caribbean, Viktor and crew take a Brumble & Sons convoy. In the process, they acquire an old salt by the name of Leland Stoud who once sailed with Billy Black, Viktor's former mentor.

In Cartagena, Viktor encounters Lady Carpathia for the first time. He finds himself unusually attracted to her, much to Belladonna's consternation. The siren warns him this is the vampire sent to hunt him. During the encounter, however, he leaves a few drops of his blood on Carpathia's blade. Neither vampire thinks much of it at the time.

Britt Westin inadvertently discovers his bunk mate aboard the *HMS Quicksilver*, Commander Turlington has been bitten by Carpathia. He tries to warn Commodore Critchfield. Not long after, Britt is cudgeled and set adrift. Critchfield has the information he needed from him and sees him as a liability now.

Having no luck on finding Auntie Clarissa, Viktor sacrifices two crewmen to the siren for a clear vision. She returns to the ship just in time to keep him from killing Grimm when the vampire's Hunger takes control. The truly blessed emerald cross brings Viktor back to his senses, but Belle has to seal herself in the cabin with him to protect Grimm and the crew before the power drains from the cross.

She directs Grimm to make a course to Tierra del Fuego, south of the Magellan Strait. Days later, Viktor and Belle both wake from the sleep spell she used to dampen his Hunger.

The *Shining Star* came across Britt Westin adrift in a small boat. Sam is struck by his close resemblance to the dream man who ravaged her and left her severely weakened. She nurses him back to health. They bond over their hatred of Commodore Critchfield and compare notes in their respective hunts for Carpathia and Brandewyne.

Viktor reaches the previously uncharted Tierra del Fuego. He, Grimm, and Zach Brumble go ashore to seek Clarissa, while Belladonna goes hunting and takes a leopard seal as prey. The pirates find the Sister. She names three different prices she'll accept in exchange for the portion of her magic Viktor needs. The first two, he recognizes as traps. He has no choice but to agree to the third: the eggs of a dodo and a dragon, and a drop of blood from the Daughter of the Dragon. She then turns into a hummingbird and flies away.

Not knowing what a dodo is but remembering Jeorge's extensive library of ancient texts, Viktor decides to make for New Orleans. It takes much of Belle's weather magic to race the ship north ahead of the southern hemisphere's winter and sea ice.

During the voyage, Stoud tells of once bedding the siren when he was a young man. Jon-Jon refuses to believe until Belladonna confirms it and reveals she is a few millennia older than she looks. The old salt regales the crew with tales of encountering a kraken and even of the existence of dragons. This last draws Viktor's attention, and he finds out he needs to hunt that egg in the islands between Asia and Australia.

Lack of ships to pirate forces Viktor to put in at Port-of-Spain, Trinidad to hunt. He again encounters Carpathia. They hunt together, then she has him as a guest in one of the local vampire kiss' safehouses. During their tryst, he spots her tattoo of a dragon twined around a scythe and learns she is the leader of the Daughters of the Dragon. When she dies for the day, he steals some of her blood and places it in the vial Clarissa provided him. He returns to the ship and sets sail for New Orleans.

Carpathia pursues the next night aboard the *Lorelei*. Belladonna becalms her ship and delays the pursuit to the point that many of the crew fall prey to the vampiress before the wind returns. Still, she knows where he's headed.

Critchfield arrives in Savannah and heads to the Black Flag looking for news of Brandewyne. A drunken Chadwick Harris gripes about his treatment by Brandewyne. Maggie, now owner of the Flag, bars him from her establishment and has him abducted and shipped from Savannah to protect him from both the Navy and Viktor. Critchfield has Turlington take Harris' ship, the *Georgia Belle*, to act as bait for the pirate-turned-vampire, since Viktor seems to bear Harris some grudge.

Critchfield seeks out the Thunderbolt Witch to verify rumors of the pirates delivering a pregnant girl, supposedly the reaper's bride. Celie keeps Brianna hidden. She proves to the Navy man he has no power to truly threaten or harm her. After he leaves, Brianna goes into premature labor from the stress.

Viktor learns from Jeorge only what a dodo is and where it was discovered. The vampire king of New Orleans does not try to prolong the visit this time, catching Carpathia's scent on the pirate.

En route from New Orleans to Savannah, the *Incubus* encounters the *Quicksilver.* When sent to spy on the Navy man, Lazarus finds himself instead transported to Mother Celie. She shows him the twins and sends him back to Viktor with the message to avoid Savannah until he finishes with Clarissa. Having escaped the pursuer in a fog of Belle's making, Viktor takes the advice and sets course for Africa.

Carpathia arrives in New Orleans and proceeds to make Jeorge's unlife miserable. When she learns Viktor delivered his merman son into the old swamp witch's keeping, she sends men in to find the child. Gloribeau uses her succubus powers to deal with them but leaves one man alive to carry her warning back.

Carpathia finds dried blood on one of her blades from her first encounter with Viktor months earlier. She consumes it and forms a bond with him instantly but tries to hide her presence. He picks up on it and gets Belladonna to help him distract the vampiress. The build-up of pure power from his and Belle's passion proves enough to force Carpathia to vomit up the blood and break the bond.

In Mauritius, Viktor learns from a local teacher and historian, Jean Beaujolais, that the dodo has been extinct for over a century. He continues to the East Indies to try to acquire a dragon egg. The encounter with a Komodo dragon costs one crewman a leg. The siren, well fed from a mermaid hunt, uses her healing magic to regrow it.

Hell's Breath Island intercepts them on their trip back to Clarissa. Viktor is grateful for the encounter after learning that dodos still exist on the travelling island. Zeke agrees to give him an egg in exchange for the vial of Carpathia's blood. The old man then reveals that the siren is branded by the Daughters of the Dragon and that, as a siren, she is the daughter of a sea dragon. Her blood will fulfill the Sister's requirement.

Viktor completes his journey to Clarissa. She uses the ingredients to make a pie, which she then consumes. She transforms into a bird and lays an egg. This, she breaks and crushes into the vial with the magical tokens from the other Sisters of Power. Too late, she realizes her plan to gain control over Viktor with the blood in the pie has actually enslaved her to the source of the blood. Zeke knew what a disaster it would've been to give control of one of the Sisters to the second oldest vampire in the world. Belladonna has no desire or need to control her.

As a parting gift, Viktor leaves Nathan Trundle with Clarissa, since she acquired some of the siren's sexual appetite, and the cook was prone to seasickness.

The Daedalus Enigma

Viktor and crew spot the *Georgia Belle* near Sapelo Island and give chase, thinking to have some fun at Chadwick Harris' expense. He soon realizes his favorite target no longer sails the ship. Instead, the pirate captures Joseph Turlington, who'd been set to catch the pirate by Commodore Critchfield. Viktor takes Turlington to his cabin, where Lady Carpathia takes possession of her pet's body and ensnares Viktor.

Belladonna kills the human and uses her blood to prevent him from rising as a vampire of Carpathia's line. She initiates a passionate round of lovemaking with Viktor in an effort to free him from the Daughter of the Dragon's trap. During this, he feeds on the siren and almost dies from it. Her toxic blood frees him from Carpathia's power, though.

They make port in Savannah. Grimm goes to Mother Celie's to reunite with his wife, Brianna, and to meet their twin offspring. Viktor heads to the Black Flag tavern and brothel to learn from Maggie what really happened to Harris and what events had happened in his absence.

When Viktor goes to Celie's, Lazarus and Belladonna join the assemblage. The siren tells him of a vision about the next Sister of Power he has to deal with. She is located somewhere in the Aegean region of the Mediterranean. He gives Grimm the option to remain with his family. The first mate chooses to remain part of the crew. They engage in a subterfuge to get the twins christened without revealing Grimm's family is staying with Celie. They then sail north to hide their true destination across the Atlantic from any possible British spies.

On the crossing, Belladonna reveals she would be in danger of being claimed by a male siren as mate if she returns to the Mediterranean. Viktor gives her a couple of men as sacrifice for a clearer vision of where to hunt the Sister. This results in learning he must deal with Circe, the witch from Homer's *Odyssey,* who can turn men into animals. Belle insists on staying with him to aid in passing the navigational hazards surrounding the witch's island.

The siren guides them through a reef, a watery maze of rocks, a series of whirlpools, and a fog-shrouded ship graveyard to get to Circe's island. Only Viktor, Grimm, and Belladonna go ashore. Lazarus remains undetected in his raven form.

Circe tries to get them to eat something, but they politely refuse. She does confirm she is the same Circe who dealt with Odysseus. She tries to seduce first Viktor, then Grimm with no success. The power Zeke the Elder shared with Grimm frightens her and convinces her to stop with her games. She directs Viktor to a labyrinth beyond her dwelling on the island. He is set to retrieve a puzzle box which lies at its center. Lazarus surreptitiously helps guide him through and avoid any traps.

He finds the box, but several portions are missing from the puzzle. He learns he must revisit the other Sisters of Power to retrieve the missing pieces, which the Elder disbursed among them.

After Viktor's departure, Circe summons Xandricus, the sea dragon/male siren. Other than the ship graveyard, all the island's outer defenses magically disappeared with Viktor's arrival. She wants the dragon to restore the enveloping fog. He agrees after discovering Belladonna has been there and will return. He plans to await her return and claim her as his mate.

Viktor decides to visit Venoma *Noir* first, thus getting the most unpleasant of the Sisters out of the way. She sends him into the depths of the cave she dwells in to find the portion of the puzzle box in her possession. He encounters Arachne, a giant spider-like creature that can take on human form. He ends up killing the creature and cutting a red crystal from its forehead, the puzzle piece he sought.

Next, he visits *Madre* Dorada. Paella now bears the title and power of the Sister, Carina having passed menopause thus unable to control or use the power. He meets his daughter, Viktoria Auna. Dorada agrees to give him her portion of the puzzle, a piece of moss agate, in exchange for siring a son on her. While he is fulfilling the price with great relish, carina tries to kill Viktoria and reclaim the power. Both Dorada's and the child's magic combine to call the golden vines and destroy Carina and heal Viktoria.

On his way to New Orleans and Gloribeau, Viktor and crew take a packet ship carrying Jean Beaujoulais. He decides to take the old tutor to New Orleans himself, knowing the man is in search of Jeorge's library. He also takes three young women being sent to escape the brewing war in the colonies and several bolts of valuable silk from his prey.

In New Orleans, he finds Carpathia in residence. She destroys two of Jeorge's vampires as punishment for him not informing her or her sire about Viktor's frequent visits to the port. When she threatens to use Melanie to track and control him, he proves he is more powerful than her by mentally holding her motionless and sending his Childe to the safety of his ship.

At Gloribeau's, he encounters his son, Robert, now a gangly youth. The boy should only be a toddler, but he is half merman. Glory's price for her portion of the puzzle is two-fold: deal with Carpathia and take Robert to find a mate among his own kind. Her powers are very similar to those of a succubus, and she is a danger to the young mer, who is rapidly approaching sexual maturity.

Belladonna tells him how to trap Carpathia. He manages to trick the vampire and captures her in a silver-lined bottle in her amorphous form, as she is one of a very limited number of vampires that can change forms. Gloribeau uses her magic to seal the bottle so that only Grimm, who corked it, can ever open it. Later, Robert is introduced to a pod of mermaids to mate and live his now adult life.

On the way to Tierra del Fuego and Clarissa, Lazarus spots and visits the *Shining Star,* hoping for the luck of taking his human form as Jim Rigger and having some sport with Samantha Brumble. Instead, he finds her with Britt Westin and learns they are long-lost brothers. He'd only been a small child when their father accidentally killed their mother then abandoned him, taking Britt away with him. Those painful memories had long ago been suppressed. While there as Lazarus the cat, he witnesses Sam and Britt marry. He bites his brother as the newlyweds sleep, ensuring he will never lose his family again.

By the time Viktor reaches Clarissa, his Hunger is trying to get out of control. He takes a crewman with him as a potential meal when he goes ashore. He attacks and almost bites the Sister when she shows herself. Her power brings him back to his senses. She does not have a piece of the puzzle for him, as she and Circe never got along. She sends Mr. Trundle back with Viktor in exchange for the man he had planned to drain.

Sailing north along the Pacific coast of south America, headed for Mexico and Rosalia, Viktor's Hunger gets back under control. Belladonna, however, seems to lose much of her power and eventually goes into a sort of coma. When Viktor forcibly revives her, she miscarries the child he unknowingly had sired on her.

Rosalia makes herself difficult to get to and places traps to hopefully enslave Viktor to her, she fears him that much. She agrees to give him her portion of the puzzle, a black opal, in exchange for his promise to never enter her territory again.

Viktor sails south, hoping to pass back through the Straits of Magellan before turning back north toward the Caribbean. He seeks to face *Mamaan* Juma to get the final puzzle piece. It quickly becomes clear they'll never make it before winter and sea ice close the passage, so he has the ship turn back north.

Hell's Breath Island intercepts the ship. Viktor, Belladonna, and Grimm start ashore, but the island separates them. Grimm is returned to the ship. Viktor is allowed to continue on to find Zeke. Belladonna is transported to a submerged cavern within the island and a crystalline entity known as the heart of Hell's Breath, an embodiment of the All-Mother. She explains something of Viktor's nature to the siren and gives her a contraceptive spell to preserve her magic in the future. She then sends the siren to rejoin Viktor.

Zeke tells Viktor he's not ready to face Juma yet and reminds him there is another Sister of Power he knows,

Mother Celie. The island transports them to just off the Bahamas. From there, Viktor sails on to Savannah.

Celie no longer possesses the final puzzle piece, a sardonyx ring with the carved face of the god Janus, but she knows who has it and roughly where they are. She directs Viktor to sail to western Ireland to seek out Darcy O'Malley, a descendant of Grace O'Malley the pirate queen. She also gives him a box of moly, a magical herb which will protect him from Circe's transformative powers and instructs him on the dosage and that he must finish all of it before returning to the witch's island.

During the crossing, Viktor grows to hate the headaches and temporary weakening of his powers associated with using the moly. Finally, he sees there is only about one dose left after doctoring his food. He decides to just finish it off and be done with it. He gets no headache this time but grows strangely detached. He accidentally cuts himself and doesn't immediately heal as he's used to. Lazarus appears and licks the blood off his arm, convulses, transforms into Jim, and promptly dies for the day. Viktor blacks out.

Belladonna and Grimm have a couple of hapless crewmen apply peppermint oil to revive Viktor. He attacks and feeds on the man chosen, calling Jim back to awareness to feed on the other sailor. His moly-rich blood gives Jim the ability to take and keep human form at will.

In Ireland, Viktor, Grimm, and Zach Brumble visit Harlowe, a smuggling contact known to young Brumble as well as a former fence the two pirates used to do business with. He informs them of the recent widowing of Darcy, and the political plotting of her suitor/kidnapper, Lord Brookston. Harlowe gives this information in exchange for Viktor taking about twenty young hotheaded Irishmen who want to go to the colonies to fight the

English off his hands. He'd contracted transport for them, but the captain had gotten conscripted by the Royal Navy. Having the lads still about would be bad for business if the Navy came calling.

The pirates go to the village Harlowe indicates. They make contact with one of the women who help smuggle messages in and out of the O'Malley keep. They then have a satisfying brush-up with a group of Brookston's thugs behind the village tavern. Viktor experiments and learns the moly has given him the ability to take the form of any creature he's ever eaten. He takes a small amount of blood and some hair from Darcy's dog, the message carrier, and takes on its form to get into the keep.

He flies Darcy out then helps her entrap Brookston into admitting to her husband's murder. This gains him the ring piece of the puzzle box. Assembled, it reveals a lock. He surmises Circe has the key.

Hell's Breath intercepts them again shortly before they reach Gibraltar. Zeke informs Belladonna she has earned a pardon and is no longer barred from entering the Mediterranean. He revokes Xandricus' claim to her. Of course, he points out that won't stop the sea dragon from trying anyway.

Near Circe's island, the sea dragon boards the ship and demands Belladonna come with him. Viktor challenges him. When Grimm moves to protect his captain, Xandricus stabs him with his talons and throws him overboard. Battle between the pirates and sea dragon ensues. Viktor eventually defeats him by flying down the dragon's maw and cutting his head off from the inside. He is nearly crushed in half as the corpse shrinks back to human proportions. Belladonna heals him.

Grimm's body cannot be found afterward.

When Viktor takes the puzzle box back to Circe, he learns of her collusion with the sea dragon and decides to torment her for her part in the loss of his first mate. She lies to him about having to wait until dawn to retrieve the keystone and key and offers him a bed and a meal. Knowing it for the trap it is meant to be, he accepts her hospitality.

Sensing her strong desire, he pretends to seduce her, working her up even more. She grows extremely agitated when he eats some of the pork she'd cooked. He knows of the transformative spell on the meat, but the moly protects him. He continues to eat until she cracks and begs him to stop. She tells him she can save him if he'll make love to her. He refuses. She finally admits she doesn't have to wait until dawn to get the keystone and key to open the box. When she leaves to retrieve it, he disrobes and deliberately turns into a hog, then a dog, a hog again, back to human and gets dressed again. He hides the box.

She arrives with the items and panics over the missing puzzle box. When she leaves to try to find it, he puts it back on the table and disrobes again. She returns and desperately opens the box, mixes the contents with her wine, and drinks the solution to restore her full power. Viktor picks that moment to transform back into a hog.

She tries to turn him human again. He resists her powers completely and turns into a dog, just to rub it in. Finally, he turns human when she tries to turn him back into a pig in her ire. He refuses to tell her how he escaped her spells.

Jim arrives with Jon-Jon to collect Circe's portion of magic. She transforms into a sow, and Jon-Jon gets a single drop of milk from her to add to the vial of the Sisters' combined magic. When she returns to human form, she begs Viktor to make love to her. He refuses and denies her the use of either of his companions. He lets her know he killed Xandricus and holds her partially responsible for Grimm's death. He reminds her that Grimm carried a portion of the Elder's magic and she may have to answer to the Elder for the loss. The pirates leave.

Tamara. A. Lowery

About the Author

Tamara A. Lowery, who once considered herself close to becoming a Crazy Cat Lady is now down to three cats. She lives with them and her husband in Tennessee and builds cars to pay the bills when not writing. She's been writing since the early 1980s but only published since 2011.

In addition to the Waves of Darkness series, she is the author of a steampunk episodic serial, The Adventures of Pigg & Woolfe.

She hopes to release a short story collection sometime in the near future, as well.

Website: talowery.wordpress.com

Facebook: facebook.com/Waves.of.Darkness

Instagram: Instagram.com/talowery_author

Plurk: plurk.com/Viksbelle

YouTube: youtube.com/user/Viksbelle

Waves of Darkness

Sisters of Power arc

Blood Curse

Demon Bayou

Silent Fathoms

Black Venom

Hell's Dodo

The Daedalus Enigma

Maelstrom of Fate *October 2024*

Daughters of the Dragon arc

Hunting the Dragon *2025*

The Adventures of Pigg & Woolfe

Season 1

The Girl Who Fell from the Sky (S.1 omnibus)

Episodes

A Chance Encounter

The Truce

In the Woolfe's Den

Chase the Lightning

Peril in the Philippines

Rendezvous in Hong Kong

Double Jeopardy

Chance and Fortune

The Italian Connection

Rescue at Sea

Ghost Riders in the Sky

Castle in the Clouds

Season 2

Turmoil in Tunilia (S.2 Omnibus)

Episodes

Airborne Alliance

Under the Mountain

Reversal of Fortune

Frustrations

Going Underground

Evade and Elude

Escape

Sanctuary

Message in a Bottle

Strange Bedfellows

Family Reunion

Berthing Assignments

Season 3

Pathway to Downfall (S.3 Omnibus)

Episodes

The Canary Has Flown

Truth and Consequences

Detective Work

Family Secrets

Organizing a Fox Hunt

Divided Forces Part I

Divided Forces Part II

Queen of the Nile

Foiled Again

Doom in Khartoum

Fly Me Away

The Fall of Tunilia

Season 4 *2024/2025*

(Publication dates subject to change)

Diamond of the Mind (S.4 Omnibus) *TBD*

Episodes

Aftermath

Laying Low

Regroup

The Cost of Salt

Across the Sea

The Forgotten Kingdom *December 2024*

Staying Afloat *February 2025*

Black Sea Resort *April 2025*

The Italian Connection Redux *June 2025*

Peace Talks *August 2025*

Forces Reunited *October 2025*

The Canary's Eye Conundrum *December 2025*

Season 5 *(TBD)*

Tamara. A. Lowery